GORDON KORMAN

Cover by Trevor Keen

Scholastic Canada Ltd.
Toronto New York London Auckland Sydney
Mexico City New Delhi Hong Kong Buenos Aires

Scholastic Canada Ltd.
604 King Street West, Toronto, Ontario M5V 1E1, Canada
Scholastic Inc.
557 Broadway, New York, NY 10012, USA
Scholastic Australia Pty Limited
PO Box 579, Gosford, NSW 2250, Australia
Scholastic New Zealand Limited
Private Bag 94407, Botany, Manukau 2163, New Zealand
Scholastic Children's Books
Euston House, 24 Eversholt Street, London NW1 1DB, UK

www.scholastic.ca

Library and Archives Canada Cataloguing in Publication
Title: Game on! / Gordon Korman ; cover art by Trevor Keen.
Other titles: Novels. Selections
Names: Korman, Gordon, author. | Container of (work): Korman, Gordon. Chicken doesn't skate. | Container of (work): Korman, Gordon. Toilet Paper Tigers.
Identifiers: Canadiana 20210239689 | ISBN 9781443182423 (softcover)
Subjects: LCGFT: Novels.
Classification: LCC PS8571.O78 A6 2021 | DDC jC813/.54—dc23

Photos ©: cover: Carolina Hanna/Shutterstock;
back cover: Snitovets/Dreamstime, Alhovik/Dreamstime.

7 6 5 4 3 2 1 Printed in Canada 114 21 22 23 24 25

GAME ON!
CONTENTS

The CHICKEN Doesn't SKATE

For Michelle

1

RANGERS UPDATE: CAPTAIN ADAM LURIE REPORTING

A science fair more important than hockey?

Give me a break! In this part of Minnesota, *nothing* is bigger than hockey. If the Moose People from Neptune invaded St. Martin during a big game, they'd encounter zero resistance. Everybody would be at the rink. Only the losers would be left to fight them off — a loser being anyone around here who doesn't skate.

Of course, I'm kind of biased since I'm pretty good at hockey. So good that I'm captain of the South Middle School Rangers, even though I'm only a seventh-grader. To be totally honest, I'm officially in sixth grade, but that's only because I flunked science last year. So I had to take it again in summer school and I kind of flunked that, too. In the summer, Rollerblade hockey is very big.

The bottom line is, I'm in all grade-seven classes except science, where I'm stuck with the little sixth-grade losers — a loser being anyone who can spend five seconds in that lab without going insane from boredom.

So my ears were receiving Mrs. Baggio raving about this year's science fair, but my mind was on the ice, stickhandling, stopping on a dime in a shower of snow, streaking down on a breakaway, he shoots, he—

"Does everybody have to enter the science fair?"

That was Zachary Gustafson. *Definite* loser. King of losers. Know why he was worried about doing a project? Because all that work might interfere with his writing schedule. Rumor has it the kid churns out dozens of screenplays and mails them off to these big-time film studios, who reject them because they stink. Not that I've read any, of course. I don't even want to think about such a boring thing in such a boring class. It's like boring squared!

"Naturally, everybody will be doing a project, Zachary," said the Bag. "But only one per grade will be entered in the fair."

Instantly, all eyes turned to Milo Neal. Milo is the reason why this dumb science fair is front page news in St. Martin. Check out the name: Milo *Neal*. His dad is Victor Neal, the famous astronomer. His TV show

The Universe and You is the top-rated program on the Science Channel.

Victor Neal is sort of St. Martin's claim to fame. He grew up right here. He and Milo's mom were high school sweethearts. The whole town followed his career. Man, when he won the Nobel Prize for charting all those galaxies, this place went apewire! We even threw him a parade. You'd have thought he'd won the Stanley Cup!

That parade had been Milo's first look at his parents' hometown. He must have been about nine. It was January — eighteen below — I've never seen anybody so cold in my life! I guess that's when it hit me. Professor and Mrs. Neal were native Minnesotans, but Milo had lived in Los Angeles all his life. To him, cold meant you had to wear socks. It must have been hard for him when, two years later, his folks got divorced and he and his mom left California and came back to St. Martin to live.

So that's why the son of the most famous scientist in the country was the center of attention in the lab that day. Not only was Milo expected to go to the science fair — he was expected to ace it.

"There are no restrictions," Mrs. Baggio went on, "except it has to be science" — she looked me straight in the eye — "which means it isn't going to be about hockey."

"What about ice?" I challenged. "That's pretty scientific."

"Very well, Adam, do ice," said the teacher. "But there had better not be any skates on it. Or pucks." She turned to the rest of the class. "Your topics must be approved by me by the end of the week."

Kelly Marie Ginsberg (loser) nudged my arm. "You're fixated on hockey."

Like that's a bad thing. "Yeah? So?"

"So a fixation could turn into an obsession," she insisted. "And that could turn into a psychosis."

I was going to give her another "Yeah? So?" but some of the gung-ho types started chiming in with their topics. Disgusted, I thought about my seventh-grade classes, where everybody played it cool.

"Bats," piped up Sheila Martel.

"Recycling," announced Kelly Marie.

"Dolphins."

"Solar energy."

A hush fell. Milo Neal had raised his hand.

"Yes, Milo?" The way the Bag almost whispered it, you'd have thought he was going to tell her where he hid the lost continent of Atlantis.

Milo pushed his Bertrand St. Rene glasses higher up on his nose. "My project will be entitled 'The Complete Life Cycle of a Link in the Food Chain.'"

Well, that must have been something good because Mrs. Baggio beamed like a lighthouse.

"That's so deep," breathed Kelly Marie. Ten to one she had no idea what he was talking about.

"Awesome!" added Zachary. Twenty to one for him.

I rolled my eyes. "Okay. I'll bite. What does it mean?"

The Bag was all over that. "Yes, Milo. What the class wants to know is the subject of your study. What link in the food chain?"

California Boy looked importantly around the classroom. "The chicken."

2

DOWNLOADED FROM THE FILES OF ZACHARY GUSTAFSON

TERROR IN THE SEWER

Scene 1

[INTERIOR SHOT: City sewer – night]

Dank, dirty, disgusting. Rats are everywhere. Out of the darkness come two figures running . . . MAX AND PAULINE, terrified.

PAULINE

(exhausted)

Oh, Max, I can't go on!

MAX

I think we've lost him!

Suddenly, a giant mutant three-eyed ALLIGATOR rises up with a bloodcurdling roar. Rats scurry in fear.

[CLOSE-UP: Rows of razor-sharp teeth, dripping with steaming toxic drool.]

PAULINE

Aaaaugh!

MAX

Aaaaugh!

The mighty jaws come crushing down on—

"Whoaa!!"

All of a sudden, someone yanked the cafeteria bench right out from under me. My notebook flew one way, my pen the other, and I was lifted up by the waistband of my underwear.

"Wedgie!!" It was a chorus of voices behind me.

"Aw, come on—" I protested.

All at once, my assailants released me. *Crash!* I went down hard amid scattered laughter and applause.

My spinning head cleared just in time to catch a glimpse of Adam Lurie and a few other muscleheads from the hockey team sneaking out past the food line, trading high fives.

I'd show those guys. When I was the hottest screenwriter in Hollywood, I'd have my agent cut a deal with all the theaters in Minnesota not to let them get in to see any of my hit movies. Then I'd call the pay phone in front of the Rivoli on Main Street — from poolside at my Beverly Hills mansion. When Adam answered, I'd say, "How's thirty below, butt-brain?" He'd recognize my voice from my acceptance speech at the Academy Awards. That's when I'd said, "And a special *in your face!* to the South Middle School Rangers in St. Martin!"

I got to my feet, picked up my stuff, and set the bench up again. You can't let idiots interfere with your art. Now, where was I? Oh, yeah. The sewer . . .

PAULINE

Kill it! Kill it!

A giant slimy forked tongue shoots out of the ALLIGATOR's jaws and wraps around MAX's neck.

MAX

Let go of me, you repulsive reptile!

He struggles madly but is slurped down like a meatball. The ALLIGATOR celebrates with a mighty belch.

I stopped and chewed on my pen. No, that wasn't it. Who was Pauline going to marry in the final scene if I killed off Max? I scratched out the last part.

MAX

Let go of me, you repulsive reptile!

As he struggles, MAX pulls out his Swiss Army knife and begins flipping utensils: the fork, the nail clippers, the toothpick, and . . . *a giant samurai sword*! He rears back and slices the ALLIGATOR's disgusting three-eyed head off. The eyes close, one at a time.

MAX and PAULINE are doused by a fountain of green alligator blood.

ROLL OPENING CREDITS

What a great beginning: The audience gets to watch the alligator bleed to death in the sewer while their popcorn is still warm and buttery. *That's* entertainment! This could be my big break.

Of course, it takes more than just talent to make it in the movie business. You've got to have luck; you've got to have timing; and most of all you've got to have connections.

You could be the best writer in the world, but if nobody ever reads your screenplay, they can't turn it into a blockbuster movie. But if you know a director, or a producer, or someone who does — if your aunt's cat's former owner is a good friend of the third cousin of Steven Spielberg's bowling coach, you're in. You've got connections.

Unfortunately, it was tough to develop connections when you were eleven years old and living two thousand miles and seventy Fahrenheit degrees away from Southern California—

Milo Neal walked into the cafeteria.

—unless the connections came to you! I'd been giving this a lot of thought. Milo's dad had connections coming out his ears! He was a big star on cable TV; his science books sold millions; and he was a famous rich guy living in L.A. He probably went to parties with all the actors and producers and directors. Victor Neal was the world's best connection! And he was right here under my nose!

Well, his son was, anyway. He lived in St. Martin with his mom. I know it looks bad — like I'd be friends with Milo just because of my career. But I actually liked Milo a lot — sort of. He was very serious, maybe even a little bit dull. Hard to get to know. To be totally honest, I only talked to the guy once and he ignored me. But we were going to be great friends. *I had to meet his father!*

And anyway, we had one thing in common. He was going to be a great scientist and I was going to be a great writer, so at least we were both going to be great. That part was definite.

"Hi, Milo. How's it going?"

Milo's eyebrows went up behind the Bertrand St. Rene glasses.

I refreshed his memory. "Zachary, from science class, remember?"

"Oh, yeah. Hi." He didn't know me. I could tell. That was because he never looked to the left or right in the lab.

Weird guy, my best friend. He was probably very focused. Or he had a stiff neck.

So by this time I was panicking because there was no conversation. Suddenly something went "Peep!" and there was this little yellow head peering out of his tooled-leather knapsack.

I rolled up my notebook and brandished it like a weapon. "Hold still! There's a giant bug on your bag."

"That's not a bug," Milo said quickly. He reached back and brought out a small baby chick. "This is the beginning of my science project," he explained.

"Are you going to dissect it?" I asked, intrigued.

Milo looked down his long, straight nose at me. I've got to develop a look like this for when I move to California. It really makes the other guy feel like worm guts.

"I'm going to document the complete life cycle of this hatchling," Milo said finally. "As a link in the food chain, it feeds and grows until *it* becomes food."

"Far out," I said, not really paying attention. Who was I to try to understand the science project of Victor Neal's son? I reached out to pat the hatchling on its fuzzy head. Zap! The little beast pecked me! I sucked on my finger where it was bleeding. "If you need anybody to wring its little neck," I couldn't help but mutter, "I'm your man."

"Oh, no," said Milo, deadpan. "The proper way to

slaughter a chicken is decapitation. But this one's not nearly old enough, of course."

What? Was that supposed to be a joke? Just in case, I laughed. It earned me another look down his nose. I was worm guts again. Then Milo headed down the hall, cradling this dumb bird in his arms.

"Hey! Wait up!" I called, slaloming my way through the crowded corridor. We got to the science lab at the same time.

Instantly, the whole class crowded around Milo, oohing and aahing at the baby chick. Lots of people petted it. It didn't bite any of them.

"He's so cute!" cooed Sheila Martel.

Milo, my soon-to-be best friend, awarded her the worm guts look. "This is a female, of course. A male would occupy an entirely different place in the food chain. You see—"

"What's her name?" interrupted Kelly Marie Ginsberg.

Milo looked mystified. "She doesn't have a name. She's a scientific experiment. You wouldn't name a test tube or a microscope."

"A test tube or a microscope doesn't have a beating heart," Kelly Marie retorted. "Now, what can we call her?"

"Give me a break!" Adam Lurie grumbled.

"How about Chickee?" This from Brendan Walters. He was on the hockey team, too — the goalie — but he wasn't a jerk like Adam and the others. Maybe because he was only in sixth grade.

Kelly Marie's face turned political. "Chickee is sexist."

"Not for a baby chick," I pointed out.

"She won't be a chick forever." Kelly Marie was definitely running the show by this time and, as usual, she had a lot to say. "Can you imagine calling her Chickee when she's a full-grown hen? I know. We'll call her Henrietta!"

"We don't need to call her anything," was Milo's opinion.

But everybody was kitchy-kooing that stupid bird, welcoming "Henrietta" to the lab.

"Hi, Mrs. Baggio," called Kelly Marie. "Meet Henrietta. She's in Milo's project."

"She *is* the project," Milo insisted.

"Look what I've got," the teacher announced grandly. She was holding a milk crate lined with a soft wool blanket. Milo was about to place that lousy bird inside it. But Kelly Marie threw herself in front of him.

"Gently!" she barked, scaring the bird more than Milo. "You're introducing a baby into its new home!"

Milo surrendered the chick and Kelly Marie set it lovingly into the softest folds of the blanket.

"Now, watch." Mrs. Baggio positioned a desk lamp over the box and switched it on.

I couldn't resist. "The chicken is going to do some heavy reading? What? *Egg Digest*?"

I wasn't even surprised when I got the worm guts look from Milo. "It's for the heat, not the light," he explained. "In nature, she would have her mother's body warmth, but we have to improvise. It's kind of like an incubator while the specimen is still a hatchling."

Adam groaned. "We have to buy our own hockey pads, but the school provides an incubator for your chicken if your dad's on TV."

Mrs. Baggio didn't like that. "Adam, that will do. Raising Henrietta will be an excellent learning opportunity for all of us. Milo has generously agreed to let everybody help."

I'd already helped. I gave blood. But for my best friend, bosom buddy, and lifelong chum, Milo — I grabbed the birdseed.

Fade to black . . .

3

RANGERS UPDATE: CAPTAIN ADAM LURIE REPORTING

That semester I was enrolled in seven classes — math, English, shop, history, gym, French, and chicken. Oh, it still said SCIENCE on the door to the lab, but Mrs. Baggio wasn't teaching anymore. Officially, we were using class time to develop our big projects. In reality, I and twenty-four sixth-grade losers were devoting our lives to a dumb bird named Henrietta.

Can you believe it? Milo put up a job board, and all those numbskulls were breaking their necks to sign up to change the blanket and refill the water dish and feed Henrietta the fine cracked grain she eats.

I don't get it. I mean, even losers have lives, right? I

couldn't take a deep breath without thinking about how the Rangers had lost our first three games this season. It was killing me! Yet these little sixth-graders had nothing on their minds beyond performing service to a tweety-bird.

It wasn't exactly fun, either. Chickens don't come toilet trained, so Henrietta went through about five blankets a day. She'd peep and kick and squeak and struggle when someone held her. And nine times out of ten, she got dropped. Before you knew it, she was scrambling across the floor with all twenty-five of us *and* the Bag crawling around on our hands and knees, trying to grab her. Not that we could hold on for very long anyway. I was the only one who could get a real handle on her, because my grip is well trained from taking face-offs in hockey.

"Adam! Not so hard! You'll squash her!" barked Kelly Marie.

"Actually," Milo put in mildly, "according to my research, a hatchling isn't as delicate—"

"How would you like it if a monster fifty times your size squeezed the stuffing out of you?" she stormed.

"That's perfect for my new screenplay!" exclaimed Zachary, rushing off to one of the experiment tables to make notes.

"Look," I told Kelly Marie, "this is Milo's project. If Milo tells me I'm crushing his tweety-bird, I'll stop, but—"

Whack! I can't describe how hard she kicked me — right across the left shin with her Doc Martens. *And in hockey season!*

I dropped the bird. Kelly Marie made a grab for it but came up empty. Brendan Walters made a flying goalie dive at the fuzzy yellow blur. Nothing.

Peeping like a digital watch, Henrietta hotfooted it across the room at Wayne Gretzky breakaway speed. If anybody had looked in the window at that moment, he'd have thought we were filming a comedy special for the Loser Channel: the whole class throwing themselves at Henrietta, Mrs. Baggio running around with the milk crate, and me, hopping up and down on one foot, yelling about how this injury would slow me down on the ice.

"Keep her away from the window," ordered Milo, still calm. "A draft can be fatal to a hatchling this age."

Well, that was all Kelly Marie had to hear. With a cry of purpose, she hurled herself halfway across the room, landing flat on her stomach between the chick and the window. Henrietta squawked and made a U-turn, scurrying under the table where Zachary still sat making notes. And there was only one thing that could tear Zachary away from his stupid movie — a chance to suck up to Milo Neal.

"Oh, don't worry, Milo. I'll get her." He ducked under the table and reached out an arm. "Come on, Henrietta. Here you go, girl — *OW!!*"

The bird chomped down on his finger. Zachary jumped up like he'd been fired from a rocket launcher.

WHAM! He smashed his head so hard against the underside of the table that everything on top went flying: his movie notes, a couple of pens, and an entire five-pound bag of fine cracked grain.

There was a blizzard of birdseed and half the kids started coughing and sneezing.

"My screenplay!" howled Zachary, hurling himself into the mess after his notes.

At that, he was a good two seconds behind Henrietta. She waded in with both little chicken feet and started chowing. That was when the Bag swooped down and hustled her back into the crate under the warming lightbulb.

"Experiment proceeding on schedule," murmured Milo, updating his project logbook.

Like he didn't notice all the mayhem that was going on around him, courtesy of his chicken.

Picture this five times a day. That was sixth-grade science class.

***

Our school didn't have a skating rink, so hockey practice was held at the arena in the Community Center.

The guys were a little nervous when I showed up limping, especially since Brendan Walters had an angry red scratch on his face from his big dive at Milo's chick.

"That must be one tough science class," observed Donald Vincent, who was always called DeeVee for his initials.

"Nah," I grumbled, tying my skates. "I was attacked by an animal rights activist."

Normally, hockey practice was my favorite thing in the world. But working out with this team was getting to be downright painful. We really, truly, honest-to-Pete stank. We were 0 and 3 — and that was only because you can't get negative numbers in hockey. Our last loss was to Hoffman Junior High in Minneapolis, and those slugs are a bunch of country club croquet players who haven't beaten a Ranger team since the seventies. We were hopeless.

Kelly Marie says I'm taking it so hard because I have an obsessed personality. Actually, she doesn't know the half of it! I've been up whole nights sifting through our roster for weak links. At dinner, I can't eat because I'm diagramming our power play in the mashed potatoes. I got to thinking about our problems while I was in the shower last night, and I got so involved that I stood there for forty minutes until the hot water ran out. I can still remember the scream from my dad, who showered after me. That spray must have been ice cold. After all that pondering and wracking my brain and freezing my dad, the question remained: What was wrong with us?

We had talent. Joey Sorrentino and I were the best

right wing/center combination in the state. That's when Joey was getting along with his girlfriend, Lynette.

When those two eighth-grade lovebirds were on the rocks, Joey skated on his ankles. Unfortunately for the team, the couple could break up, reunite, and break up again three times a week.

In goal we had Brendan Walters from science class. Normally, I'd hate the idea of a sixth-grader on the team. But Brendan's brother was the Wall, the greatest goalie in Ranger history. Why, last year when the Wall was an eighth-grader, we won the South Minnesota Middle School Championship.

Today, though, Brendan seemed kind of down. "I'd like to quit the team," he confessed. "I let in a lot of soft goals last game. You should look for somebody better."

I couldn't have been more shocked if he'd showed up dressed in a rabbit suit! "But you can't quit! You're the Wall!"

"My brother was the Wall," Brendan insisted. "I'm not my brother."

"But you can be! You *will* be!" I protested. "It's in the genes."

He just sighed and let in another easy shot.

Kapow!

Everybody ducked. Only one thing hit the boards that hard and that was DeeVee's slap shot. It ricocheted three times and still hurt when it hit Coach Crenshaw on the shoulder.

"Vincent, what do you think you're doing?"

DeeVee had a wide, open, slightly stupid face. "Just working on my slap shot, Coach."

"Now tell me something I *don't* know!" snapped the coach. "During passing drill, you were working on your slap shot. Stickhandling is next. What are you going to do? Work on your slap shot?"

DeeVee beamed. "Gee, Coach, could I?"

"*No!*" bawled Crenshaw.

I should say that the coach was a really nice guy, but he never quite knew what to do with DeeVee. The kid was a talented athlete with tons of potential, but he *would not* practice anything except that slap shot of his. His skating was mediocre, his stickhandling needed work, and the guy didn't have enough patience for checking. All he ever wanted to do was hang around the blue line, waiting to unload that cannon of a slap shot. Which would be fine if it ever went anywhere near the net. But aim wasn't one of DeeVee's strong points, either. He just concentrated on power, and he had plenty of that.

Yet every time DeeVee touched the puck, he was totally positive he was going to score. *And* totally bewildered when he didn't. The rest of us were just happy that he didn't *kill* anybody.

We had rock-solid defensemen — big and tough, even if they did take a few too many penalties. We had real blue-collar wingers who weren't afraid to go into the corners after the puck. We should have been winning.

"It'll come," Coach Crenshaw promised. "Just keep working hard and it'll come."

Yeah, but what year?

Still, we had to put our faith in the coach, and for a very good reason. At the end of the season, the South Minnesota champions always met the best junior high team in Winnipeg, Manitoba, in the biggest game of the year. Well, back in 1959, our Coach Crenshaw was the captain of the Ranger team that beat the Canadians. No one had defeated them before or since. So he knew how to be a winner.

Maybe he could teach it to us.

4

DOWNLOADED FROM THE FILES OF ZACHARY GUSTAFSON

PICNIC OF DEATH

Scene 17

[EXTERIOR SHOT: Pleasant pasture – day]

A troop of GIRL GUIDES with picnic baskets skips gaily across the meadow toward a babbling brook.

GUIDE LEADER

(pointing out birds chirping overhead)

There's a robin redbreast . . .

there's a yellow-bellied sapsucker . . .

LITTLE JUNIE

Oh, look! Butterflies!

LITTLE MAISIE

Look at that tree! What happened to it?

> [POINT-OF-VIEW SHOT: The top of the tree rests on a pile of sawdust around a stump. Something has squeezed the stuffing out of this mighty redwood . . . but what?]
>
> The field of golden grain begins to undulate.

GUIDE LEADER

It's just the wind, girls . . .

> With a terrible hiss of death, a fifty-foot-long two-headed black-scaled boa constrictor rises out of the wheat field.
>
> [CLOSE-UP: Spirals whirl within the snake's huge eyes . . . four hypnotizer beams transfix the girls. Two at a time, the twin hideous disgusting heads pick them up and swallow them whole. We see their bodies as lumps traveling all the way down fifty feet of snake.]

I leaned back from my computer, frowning. If there's a problem with my writing style it's that too many of my characters die. That's great for the action but sometimes there's nobody left to be in the rest of the movie. So I deleted the eating part and rewrote:

GUIDE LEADER

Quick, Little Maisie! The flamethrower!

My brow furrowed. There was a believability problem here. Everyone knows a flamethrower won't fit inside even the largest picnic basket. The Hollywood studio executives wouldn't go for it. So:

GUIDE LEADER

Quick, Little Maisie! The grenade!

> LITTLE MAISIE opens her picnic basket, careful not to crease the red-checkered cloth.
>
> [CLOSE-UP: As she opens the Saran Wrap, uncovering the grenade, the lace of her sleeve rides up, revealing her Special Forces tattoo.]

LITTLE MAISIE

(lobbing the grenade into a snake mouth)

Die, reptile scum!

BANG!

It wasn't the sound of the grenade. It was a toy block bouncing off my printer. I wheeled in my swivel chair. My fourteen-month-old baby brother, Dewey, was standing there with his angel face on. Only the halo was missing. Don't believe it. Doomsday Dewey could hardly walk, and he couldn't talk at all. But he had the destructive power of a kiloton of dynamite.

Still smiling innocently, Doomsday reared back and hurled another block, and this one was headed straight for the computer screen. With speed I didn't know I had, my arm shot out and knocked it down at the last second. Before I could recover, he launched another one. I barely got my foot in the way.

"Cut it out, Dewey—" That's when I saw he was towing his whole bag of blocks. "Mom! *Mom!*"

But it was too late. A barrage of toys was en route to my precious computer. All I could do was dance in front of it, snatching and deflecting, stopping those blocks any way I could, including with my face.

"Zachary, your room is a mess! Why are there blocks all over the floor?"

I pointed an accusing finger at my little brother. "It's Dewey, Mom! He's trying to bust my computer!"

She picked up Doomsday and scowled at me. "Do you honestly expect me to believe that this little baby attacked you and your computer with blocks?" The kid's arms hung limply at his sides. He looked like he couldn't *lift* a block, let alone throw like Greg Maddux.

"He's not a baby," I muttered. "He's a very short terrorist."

"You have an attitude problem," my mother accused. "Fighting with your brother, fighting at school—"

Huh? "I haven't been fighting at school!"

Her eyes narrowed. "Then how do you explain that bump on your head?"

"I was under the table, trying to catch a runaway chicken—"

She cut me off. "Now, *really*, Zachary. I know your imagination is important to your writing, but please don't use it on me."

She stormed out, with Doomsday smiling at me over her shoulder.

"And clean up those blocks!" That part came from halfway down the stairs.

I checked over my computer. There was a little scratch where the block hit the printer but everything else was okay. Still, it was pretty upsetting to think that my writing career almost got smashed. I mean, how could I sit down and describe a fifty-foot-long boa constrictor blowing to pieces, with charred intestines and hunks of snake flesh flying all over the Girl Guides, when I was in a bad mood?

Great. Four o'clock on a Friday afternoon and already my weekend was shot.

Then it came to me like a bolt out of the blue. How do you lift yourself up when your spirits are down? You hang out with friends! And who was a better friend of mine than my good buddy, Milo Neal?

To be honest, we weren't yet quite as close as I'd hoped we'd be. That's probably because Milo was so busy with The Chicken from the Black Lagoon. Actually, he didn't really know who I was, which presented a problem: How could he introduce me to his famous L.A.-connected father if he didn't remember my name?

That was all the more reason Milo and I needed some quality time together. I was knocking on his door in three minutes flat.

I recognized Mrs. Neal from her pictures in the paper when she moved back to town after the divorce.

"Hi," I greeted her. "I'm here to see Milo."

"Oh, Milo's still at school," she told me. "He's working late on his science project."

Even now that stupid chicken was messing me up.

Then she pitched me a fat one. "Are you a friend of Milo's?"

I gave it a home-run swing. "Oh, yeah!" I said quickly, "I'm Zachary, probably his best friend in the whole school." That might not have even been a lie. "We had plans to get together today, but I guess he got wrapped up in our project." Okay, that *was* a lie, but thanks to Mrs. Baggio, everybody in the class was sort of Milo's partner.

She looked worried. "Oh, dear. Maybe I should call the school."

"Oh, that's okay, Mrs. Neal. I'll just walk along and see if I can catch him on the way home."

I spotted Milo a couple of blocks from the school. He was stooped over to adjust the blanket in Henrietta's milk crate. I came up behind and awarded him a best-friend slap on the back.

"*Whoa!!*" Shocked, he snapped back up like an elastic and glared at me through Bertrand St. Rene glasses that were slightly askew. It was worm guts time again.

"I watched your dad's show last night," I babbled, trying to smooth things over. "Well, not exactly, because my family's too cheap to spring for the Science Channel, so it was scrambled. But I heard most of it and it sounded great."

Milo picked up Henrietta's milk crate and started walking toward his house. I trotted along beside him. "How come you're taking the chicken home?" I asked.

"A whole weekend is too long to leave the specimen on her own," he explained. "She needs fresh food and water at least twice a day."

I peeked under the blanket. A baleful eye and a loud squawk warned me away. "Very cute," I totally lied.

"A chicken is not cute," Milo explained patiently. "A chicken is a chicken. It is not a pet. It exists purely to occupy a space in the food chain."

I looked at my hands, which were dotted with peck marks from guess who. "I think my fingers must occupy the space directly below that."

Milo nodded grudgingly. "I know it looks like the specimen hates you, but she doesn't possess the brainpower to single you out."

We were at the Neals' front walk. Milo seemed pretty weirded out by the fact that I followed him onto the porch instead of leaving.

"Well, good-bye," he said hopefully.

Suddenly, the door was flung open and Milo's mother was beaming at us. "Zachary! I see you found him. Milo, why didn't you tell me your friend would be stopping by?" She was so psyched about me that it seemed pretty plain she'd been worrying about her son being lonely in his new town. You wouldn't believe the look on Milo's face when she hauled the two of us inside for these great chili nachos she'd whipped up.

I was thinking, I'm in! I mean, surely it was just a short step from nachos with Milo to Victor Neal setting up a meeting between me and the president of Universal Studios. I could almost see their special-effects department building my fifty-foot-long boa constrictor.

Then the doorbell rang, and in a few seconds Mrs. Neal was calling, "Milo, it's another one of your friends."

I glared at him accusingly. But poor Milo looked so dumbfounded that I instantly forgave him for betraying our friendship.

Into the kitchen burst none other than Kelly Marie. She breezed past us and knelt over the milk crate.

"There's my little Henrietta! Hello, sweetie!" She looked daggers at Milo. "What's the big idea of taking her out of the classroom without ever thinking that the people who love her might be worried?"

Milo spread his arms wide. "The specimen couldn't be left at school all weekend."

"That's it!" Kelly Marie snatched up the milk crate. "She's coming with me!"

Milo was completely mystified. "Why?"

"Because at your house she's nothing more than a specimen, but at my house she's a guest!"

I picked up Milo's line. "A chicken is not a guest. A chicken is a chicken."

She was ready for me. "Shut up, Zachary."

Milo looked worried. "Hmmm."

I frowned. That was the best Victor Neal's son could do? Hmmm? What about, "Get out of here, you big-mouthed pain in the butt, and get your own chicken, and don't come back until *your* dad stars in *his* own TV show!" Instead, he said, "I have to maintain constant contact with my experiment."

"Fine," agreed Kelly Marie. She grabbed the notepad on the kitchen counter and scribbled her name and phone number. "Call me anytime," she added, slapping the paper in front of Milo. And out she went, carrying the milk crate with her.

That really burned me up. Here I was, Milo's best friend. But all Kelly Marie had to do was waltz in here, crab around for three minutes, and presto, he had her phone number. Quickly, I tore off another sheet and wrote down my number.

Milo was giving me the worm guts treatment. He was going to throw it out. I knew it.

If he wasn't my best friend, I'd really hate that guy.

Fade to black . . .

5

EXPERIMENT NOTES: MILO NEAL
10/28

> Did you ever get the feeling that there's something going on and everybody knows about it except you? And that something, if you could just find out what it was, would unlock so many mysteries?

> Like why Mrs. Baggio has dropped everything so the whole class can participate in my simple science experiment. Everyone else is doing a proj. What's so special about a chicken?

> Or why that girl Kelly Marie bulldozed her way into my house and walked off with my subject. {It's hard to believe these Minnesotans can't seem to accept that this is a specimen, not their darling Henrietta. They wouldn't adopt a lab rat as a pet?!}

> And Zachary Gustafson. I can't guess what's driving him, but I know *he's* driving me crazy. My father has an expression: "He sticks to you like ugly on an ape." ZG = a human boomerang; no matter how many times you throw him away, he always comes back. Now my mother thinks he and I = best friends.

> Things were a lot simpler in California. {I miss my dad. But I know if I lived with him in Los Angeles, I'd miss my mom just as much. Of course, the weather would be better. This town = deep freeze.}

> I had misgivings about releasing my experiment to KMG. Sure enough, on Monday, subj. had undergone a 6% increase in body mass.

Even an idiot could spot the size difference. And one did.

"No way that's Henrietta!" ZG accused. "I'll bet she croaked on you and you're trying to cover it up by buying a new chicken!"

> But then subj. pecked his hand so hard it bled, which was better I.D. than a social security card. It was still her, all right. {How could a chicken know to hate one person and not another?/further study req'd. Although sometimes I think chomping a hunk out of ZG's hand would make me feel better, too.}

"You overfed her," I accused KMG. "She's fat."

> KMG responds to an undeniable truth by going on the offensive.

"My mom was late for her PTO meeting so she could drive me to the Farmers' Union to buy birdseed infant starter mash. I fed her *what* you said. I fed her *when* you said."

"But not *how much* I said," I retorted.

"She ate it, didn't she?" snapped KMG, eyes shooting sparks. "If Henrietta's growing, it's because she's thriving on love, which is more than she could do at your house. You don't even like her!"

I responded, for at least the tenth time, "There's nothing to like or dislike. This is a science project. Yours is on recycling. Do you 'like' old newspapers?"

KMG leaned into my face like a Marine drill sergeant. "Recycling old newspapers cleans up the environment, which makes the ecosystem a better place for living creatures like Henrietta! So yes, I *love* old newspapers!"

> Arguing with KMG = banging your head against the wall. It's noisy, painful, and pointless.

"You know what your problem is, Milo Neal?" she went on. "Too much brain and not enough heart. It may be good science but it's definitely not living."

"However the size increase happened," I sighed, "I think it's just about time to stop treating her like a hatchling."

"What are we supposed to treat her like?" growled Adam L. "The Homecoming Queen?"

"A pullet," I replied. "That's the next stage in the life

cycle. She remains a pullet until she becomes a full-fledged hen."

"What's so different about being a pullet?" asked Brendan Walters.

"Well, for starters," I replied, "she can't live in that old crate anymore. She needs space to move around."

I had noticed Mrs. Baggio quivering with excitement throughout all of this. Finally, her enthusiasm bubbled over the surface.

"I have such a wonderful surprise for everyone!" She threw open an equipment closet and there stood a bale of chicken wire and two bags of sawdust. "We're going to build a chicken coop!"

"Mrs. Baggio!" I said, shocked. "The specimen couldn't possibly survive the harsh winter outside!"

"Oh, not outside," Mrs. B assured me. "Right here in the lab. There's plenty of room. We'll just move these tables, stack those chairs in the corner — come on, people. Let's all get to work."

> I wonder if all new students get this kind of special treatment. Here I was, worrying about finding a bigger box, and the whole class, including the teacher, was building luxury accommodations for my experiment. {This definitely wouldn't happen in California. Maybe it = small-town hospitality/further study req'd.}

The coop took up the entire southeast corner of the

room. Mrs. B stapled four-foot-high chicken fencing to the south wall and strung it across to the east wall. That made a triangular enclosure, which we filled with sawdust. Yes, I helped. Nobody asked me to, but I felt it was only fair that I pitch in with my own science proj.

When I leaned over to fix some tangled wire, I distinctly heard AL mutter, "I got a week of detention for a gum wrapper on the art room floor. But forty pounds of sawdust is no problem if it's for Milo's chicken!"

> Can't he see it's not my fault? It's Mrs. B!

"Don't listen to him, Milo, pal," whispered ZG. "He's just bummed because his hockey team stinks. By the way, I forgot to thank you for having me over on Friday. What a great time that was! A real party!"

> A party? Sitting in the kitchen eating my mother's nachos?

"Look, Henrietta," warbled KMG. "Look at your lovely new home!" She lifted the specimen out of the milk crate and placed her inside the pen. The pullet darted around, exploring her new territory.

The whole class broke into applause.

"Take a bow, Milo!" crowed Mrs. B.

> I must have been bright red.

Somebody, probably AL, muttered the word, "conceited."

> People always say Californians are strange. They've obviously never been to St. Martin, Minnesota.

6

RANGERS UPDATE: CAPTAIN ADAM LURIE REPORTING

I never planned to get stuck with the chicken. It was partially my own fault — kind of like my punishment for fraternizing with a loser. Not just any loser, but the Grand Master High Exalted Lord of the Losers, screenwriting's answer to toe jam, Zachary Gustafson.

Okay, I was cracking on the guy. Who could resist? I was hanging out with Barbara Falconi after school on Friday, killing time before the Rangers game, when Zachary came along. To my amazement, he was lugging Henrietta in a Macy's bag with airholes.

So I yelled, "Run for your life, Henrietta! He's taking you to the river!"

"I am not!" The dweeb was really insulted. "For your information, my good friend Milo has entrusted me with his specimen."

I was bug-eyed. "All weekend?" I couldn't imagine the amount of nagging it must have taken to swing that one.

"Well, just for tonight," Zachary admitted. "But when Milo comes over and sees how happy she is, he'll let me keep her until Monday morning. I've got an old rabbit pen that's perfect for a chicken."

"Why can't Milo the Great look after his own tweety-bird?" I asked.

"He can," Superloser replied. "But half the class volunteered. Milo picked me because he and I are such good friends."

I was genuinely curious. "Why are you doing this? Everybody knows you hate that chicken, and it's pretty obvious the chicken hates you."

"That's all in the past," Zachary explained. "Henrietta and I are getting along just fine now. See?" The dweeb opened up the sack to show us how he was stroking Henrietta's feathers. With a squawk of outrage, the bird rose out of the bag and went for Zachary with a vengeance, claws slashing at his face. He jumped so fast that he let go of the handle. And Henrietta was on the loose, hop-scrambling along the faded terrazzo floor.

"Oh, no! *Oh, no!*" howled Zachary. He took off like

Wile E. Coyote after the Road Runner. Barbara and I were hot on his heels.

"Look out!" cried Barbara. She could see what I saw — the custodian's rolling mop pail directly in Superloser's path. All Zachary could see was Milo's chicken, his big chance to suck up, getting away.

He galloped down the hall, wailing like a banshee. His high-stepping foot came down with a splash right in the bucket. But amazingly, Zachary didn't fall. Instead, his momentum started the wheeled bucket rolling. He stood there, poised like a figure skater, his free leg held high, while the mop caddy picked up speed. He zoomed past the art room, past the drinking fountain, and past Henrietta.

CRASH!

Do I need to spell it out? No hallway goes on forever. I grabbed Henrietta, and Barbara ran over to Zachary, who was lying in a pool of dirty suds by the wall he'd just smashed into.

Eyes tightly shut, he felt around the wetness and whispered, "Is it blood?" Then, a little louder, "And more important — is it *chicken* blood?"

I had to laugh. "The chicken's alive and so are you." I reached out my free hand and hauled him to his feet. He looked a little unsteady.

"I think we should take him to the nurse's office," Barbara decided.

"Aw, he's okay." I turned to the victim. "Aren't you, Zack?"

Zachary replied, and I quote, "'Doomsday, stay away from my computer.'"

"Well, I'm taking him!" said Barbara firmly. And she started off toward the stairwell, leading the dazed Zachary.

I held up Henrietta, who was trying to wriggle her way out of my grasp. "But what am I supposed to do with the bird?"

She shrugged. "Find Milo and give her back."

"But I've got a *game* to get to! Coach wants us in the locker room in twenty minutes!"

She scowled at me. "Don't be so selfish. Who cares about hockey when somebody could be really hurt?"

I do! But the heavy doors thumped shut and I was alone in the hallway.

"Way to go, bird," I growled at Henrietta. "Thanks a lot."

It took forever to wrestle her back into the bag. Then I started running all over the school, looking for the great Milo. No Milo. No *anybody.* Most of the kids were probably over at the Community Center to get good seats for the game. It would be crowded, since our opponents were our crosstown rivals from North Middle School, the Kings. So this was kind of a home game for both teams.

The lab was my last resort. Maybe I could dump Henrietta

in her coop and track down California Boy later. But the door was locked. Even the Bag had left for the day! If I got benched for being late, I was going to hit Milo Neal so hard that he would land back in Beverly Hills, or Bel Air, or wherever those famous California-types lived. If he was such a big shot, why couldn't he hire a butler to look after his chicken?

The hall clock clicked as loud as a pistol shot. It was 3:58 and I was supposed to be in the dressing room in *two minutes*!

I sprinted to the nurse's office. It was deserted.

What kind of a crummy rip-off school *was* this? What if I had elephantiasis and needed medical attention?

I looked up. It was four o'clock. I was officially late. I made the only decision I could make under the circumstances: Henrietta was going to a hockey game.

★★★

If there's a world record for a half-mile race carrying twenty pounds of hockey equipment and a chicken, I shattered it.

Coach Crenshaw was really mad. "I guess the captain of a last-place team can just toddle in whenever he feels like it! What's the big idea, Lurie?"

Blue-faced and gasping, I could only point to the shopping bag.

"That's no excuse!" roared the coach. "I don't care what's in that—"

And then the pullet's head poked out of one of the air-holes.

"Henrietta!" exclaimed Brendan.

"A chicken?!" cried Coach Crenshaw in disbelief.

"It's Milo Neal's science project!" I wheezed, throwing on my equipment.

"Yeah, but why did you bring it *here*?"

"It's a long story," I managed, lacing my skates at the speed of light. "There was no one else around. Maybe you can find someone else to take her."

"I'm the coach, not the chicken-sitter. Besides, it's time for our warm-up." He clapped for attention. "Everybody on the ice."

The guys stood up on their skates and clattered out of the dressing room. I picked up the bag and got in line.

Coach Crenshaw goggled. "Where do you think you're going with that?"

"I'll leave her on the bench during the game!" I promised.

"Forget it, Lurie!" he said stoutly. "I trust you enough to accept your word that the animal has to be here. But no way is it going to be our trainer! The chicken stays in the dressing room!"

I admit it; I went to pieces. "Oh, please, Coach! If somebody opens the door and this stupid bird gets loose, we'll never see it again. It'll get lost — or trampled — or run over by the Zamboni. And Mrs. Baggio *loves* this chicken! I mean, Milo and the chicken are her whole life! If I lose it, I'll flunk sixth-grade science *again*! And then I'm off the team for sure!"

Good old Coach Crenshaw. He took pity on me. "Okay, but no feathers in the Gatorade."

"Thanks, Coach! You're the greatest!"

The crowd turned out to be mostly Kings fans — probably because they were having a great year, and we were 0 and 5. The South kids who did show up had a good laugh at the sight of me skating the warm-up with a Macy's bag. The other team stared at me like I was nuts.

"Doing your Christmas shopping early?" the Kings' captain sneered at me as we passed near center ice.

A tiny chicken leg reached out of the bag and took a swipe at the guy's shin pads.

The big baby started hollering for the ref. "Hey, he slashed me!"

"I did not!"

"Did so!"

We *did-not-did-so*'ed at each other for a while, until finally the referee said, "Let's see what's in the bag."

"It's . . . extra pucks."

"Then you won't mind me checking them out," said the man.

In resignation, I opened the bag wide.

"*A chicken?!*" cried the Kings' captain in disbelief.

"Is it rubber?" demanded the referee suspiciously. Throwing rubber chickens on the ice was an old-time hockey gag — one that was banned in middle-school play.

"No, it's real," I admitted.

The referee considered this. "Is it your mascot?"

Sue me — I said yes. It was easier than trying to explain.

I wedged the Macy's bag between Steve Tenorio and Lafayette Hughes and went to take the opening face-off.

The Rangers usually had no trouble beating North Middle School. But we were so lousy and this was the best Kings team in years, so we were considered the underdogs.

I won the face-off and got the puck to Joey, who found a streaking DeeVee with a beautiful pass. It should have been a cinch; he had a wide-open path to the net. But instead, DeeVee decided it was time for his patented slap shot. He put on the brakes in a shower of snow and raised his stick so high that he nearly overbalanced and almost fell flat on his back.

I heard Coach Crenshaw scream, "Vincent, don't you dare!"

But it was already too late.

POW!

The shot was as hard as a bullet — and twenty feet above the net. It bounced off the balcony and busted a light on the scoreboard in a shower of sparks. It came back down to the ice just past center, where it started a three-man breakaway for the Kings. Poor Brendan didn't have a prayer. 1–0, North Middle School. Exactly eighteen seconds had ticked off the clock.

"Vincent — you're *benched*!" howled Coach Crenshaw.

"I had to take it, Coach!" DeeVee pleaded. "It was a sure goal!"

The coach waved wildly at the scoreboard. "Is that a one on *our* side? No! It's a one on *their* side!"

"I'll get it next time, Coach! I promise!"

"There isn't going to be a next time, because you'll be *riding the pine*!"

A disconsolate DeeVee sat down to flank Henrietta, and Laffy Hughes came on to join our line.

It was a tough game. The Kings led 2–zip at the end of the first period, and 4–1 by the second intermission. I have to say that two of those goals were pretty soft. The Wall was having another shaky outing in net, and we were heading for 0 and 6 in a hurry.

Coach Crenshaw tried to get us revved up in the locker room, but Henrietta kept squawking and rustling the bag, so he couldn't get everybody's attention.

"If they beat you, they beat you!" roared the coach. "But don't beat yourselves!"

"Maybe she needs more airholes," suggested Brendan.

"Maybe she's hungry," put in Joey.

"*Maybe your coach is talking to you!*" howled Crenshaw.

At that moment, the buzzer sounded, calling us back to the ice.

Our fans — those who hadn't left yet — were silent. All the noise in the arena was being made by the North Middle School supporters — cheers, applause, chants — and what was that other sound? I looked around in confusion. It was coming from the Kings' bench — a high-pitched warbling chatter.

It hit me in a moment of exquisite humiliation. "They're making chicken noises!" I howled in outrage. "They're clucking at us!"

Joey leaned over the boards. "*Shut up!*" he bellowed, which only made the Kings warble louder. Now the noise was mixed with raucous laughter. Worse, they began flapping their arms. That was when Henrietta wiggled halfway out of the bag, probably to check out the clucking.

It put the Kings over the top. They were practically berserk with laughter.

"The Chicken Rangers!"

"Drumsticks on ice!"

"Ranger Fricasee!"

"Why did the Rangers cross the road?"

I have to say the chicken took it better than we did. I was in a blind rage, and the third period hadn't even started yet.

The Kings' captain was still laughing as he skated up to take the face-off. "Cock-a-doodle-do!"

"That's a rooster, you moron!" I exploded. "Ours is a baby hen! A girl!" I was so infuriated that I forgot to take a swipe at the face-off. He took the puck and I lowered my shoulder and let him have it — a beautiful check, all nice and legal. He went straight up and took a swan dive over my shoulder. But I wasn't there to see him come down. I grabbed the puck and charged down the ice. Just past the blue line I hit Lafayette with a perfect drop pass. Then I swooped in and screened the goalie, and Laffy found the corner of the net with a hard shot along the ice. 4–2, Kings.

From then on, it turned into a grudge match. They threw everything they had at us, and believe it or not, we threw it right back in their faces! Steve had just scored to pull us within one, when Lynette Martinez showed up at our bench.

"Where's Joey? I have to talk to Joey!"

Coach Crenshaw stared at her. "*Now?!*"

I pointed to the ice. "He's double-shifting."

As if on cue, a large Kings defenseman smashed Joey up against the boards with a savage body check.

Lynette rushed over. "Joey! *Joey!*"

Joey's helmet was pressed against the glass. He mouthed the word, "What?"

"Joey, I was wrong!" Lynette said emotionally. "I was wrong and you were right!"

"No, *I* was wrong!" Joey shouted into the dirty fiberglass.

"*I was the one who was wrong!*" shrieked Lynette, and for a moment, I thought they were going to start fighting about it. "I'm awful," she went on. "I'm the worst girlfriend in the world."

"You're the *best*!" Joey cried.

"The *worst*! The *worst*!" Remember, soap opera fans, all this was happening in the middle of the play! "I'm so, so sorry, and I want to get back together again!"

"*Yeah?!*" Joey's face beamed like a Christmas tree the first time the lights are turned on. He shook off his checker, kicked the puck free, and galloped down the ice with it, throwing off Kings with a stiff arm.

"Go, man!" I screamed, but Joey didn't need any help from me. He charged the net like a rhino. The goalie went down, smothering the puck under a pad. But Joey kept on digging with his stick. With a cry of pure determination, he muscled the puck loose and fired it into the net. Tie game.

You could almost feel the earth move as we all leaped up to cheer, coming down on our skates at the same moment. Lynette climbed over the boards and made a joyful run at Joey. She had to be restrained by the referee.

"But that's my *boyfriend* who scored that goal!" she wailed.

"Later!" The man escorted her off the ice. "There's still two minutes to play!"

They must have been the longest two minutes in history. Both teams fought exhaustion to break the deadlock. Even DeeVee got another chance to play, as the coaches searched their lineups for fresh legs. With thirty-one seconds remaining, the score was still 4–4. My whole body felt numb, but I was exhilarated. After five terrible losses, it looked like the Rangers were going to come out with a tie against a tough opponent.

Then things started to go horribly wrong. Joey forgot to drop back to cover for a pinching defenseman. DeeVee missed a pass, and the Kings got the puck. I made a U-turn to help out on defense — and that was when I caught sight of our bench.

In all the excitement over the final seconds, my teammates were on their feet, following the action. No one was watching the Macy's bag, and Henrietta must have crawled loose and climbed up onto the boards. There she sat like a hood ornament, spectating along with everybody else.

The dilemma almost tore me in two. Did I try to prevent the Kings from scoring the winning goal or make sure that Henrietta didn't get away? It should have been no contest, right? Hockey versus a stupid chicken belonging to the town snob in my least favorite class. But it must have been temporary insanity — I zoomed toward the bench.

I thought the coach's eyes were going to pop out of his head. "Are you *crazy*, Lurie?! Get back in the play!"

"The bird!" I shouted. "Somebody grab the bird!"

Laffy got his arms around Henrietta just as the Kings' captain unleashed a blistering shot from point-blank range.

"I can't look!" bawled Coach Crenshaw.

CLANG! The drive hit the goalpost and ricocheted into the corner. There was a mad scramble for the puck. DeeVee got there first and golfed it out past our blue line.

At first, I couldn't understand why the whole team was screaming in my face. Then reality sunk in: The puck was bouncing toward me — *and I was all alone behind the play*!

I snatched the puck just before center ice and took off. It was every hockey player's dream — a clean breakaway with ten seconds to play in a tie game. By the time I crossed the blue line I was flying, the roar of the crowd powering me like rocket fuel. I sizzled in on net, raising my stick for a slap shot. Then, at the last second, I pulled the puck to my backhand and flipped it past the goalie's blocker into the net. Final score 5–4, Rangers.

It was a miracle Henrietta didn't get crushed during the celebration. I sure did when my teammates cleared the bench and mobbed me. They lifted me up onto their shoulders and carried me into the dressing room. It was a good thing I was wearing a helmet because my head smacked into that door frame pretty hard. It was a great moment.

Coach Crenshaw seemed just as excited as we were. He was pounding guys on the back, shouting, "See what you can do when you put your minds to it?"

I sat down and slumped against the wall, savoring the thrill. "You're so right, Coach. It's hard to believe we were the same Rangers who lost five in a row."

The mood turned serious as we all thought about our season.

Joey spoke up. "Well, what was different about this game over all the others?"

I looked around. As I scrutinized my teammates' faces, I realized that all eyes had come to rest on the Macy's bag.

"Now, wait a minute!" the coach pulled up short. "Surely you don't think—" He stared at us in disbelief. "The chicken doesn't skate! Right? You won that game! *You!*"

But he had lost his audience. The South Middle School Rangers were focused on the shopping bag and, peering out through a rip, Henrietta.

7

"PSYCHOLOGY TALK" BY KELLY MARIE GINSBERG

I think I have a pretty good understanding of psychology. I mean, when Karen Van Dusen had her accident-prone day — ran into the soccer goalpost, set fire to the science lab, and pushed an entire shopping cart of filmstrips and herself down the back stairs — I wasn't fooled. It was an attention-getting device because her older sister had just become a model, and Karen has a face like a Rottweiler. I read people.

It's just like when Joey Sorrentino and Lynette Martinez started trading insults and fighting. Everybody else said, "Separate these two before they kill each other." But I knew that deep down there was a real attraction. And when Joey flushed

Lynette's best barrette down the toilet, and she responded by dumping soy sauce all over his favorite T-shirt, I knew it was true love. Psychology.

I cured Sophie Tisdale's fear of lipstick, predicted the end of Adam Lurie's scoring slump, and even helped Horace Maminsky get over his strange obsession with peanut butter.

So why couldn't I figure out Milo Neal?

I didn't know whether to kiss him or strangle him. Seriously! He was the one who brought us Henrietta. Yet he insisted on treating her like an animal!

And for a guy who was supposed to be a genius, how could he be stupid enough to entrust Henrietta to Zachary for the weekend?

"Are you crazy?" I bellowed on Monday morning when I found out. "She *hates* Zachary!"

He rolled his eyes at me. "A chicken doesn't have the intelligence—"

"Henrietta is *not* stupid!" I cut him off. "She's a perceptive, sensitive creature, and if she hates Zachary Gustafson, then it must be for a good reason. Maybe chickens have a special radar that can detect a maniac. Have you ever read those sick screenplays of his? Why couldn't you give her to *me*?"

"She went with you last weekend," he offered lamely.

I made a face. "Oh, I get it. She doesn't have the brains

to hate somebody, but she finds it unacceptable to receive the same hospitality two weekends in a row. Half the class wanted Henrietta. Why *him*?"

Milo gave me a sheepish look. "I thought maybe if I gave him a little responsibility, he might stop calling me and coming over to my house."

Pretty good psychology, if I say so myself. You break down a patient's defenses and he tells you what he's *really* thinking. I was about to congratulate Milo on this breakthrough when I caught sight of Zachary at the far end of the hall.

"Follow me!" I tossed over my shoulder as I sprinted over to Zachary. Henrietta *wasn't* with him.

"Oh, hi," he greeted. "What's up?"

"All right," I confronted him. "Where is she?"

He looked blank. "Where is who?"

"Who?" I struggled for control. "Abraham Lincoln. Sonic the Hedgehog. *Henrietta*, you dolt! You were in charge of her this weekend!"

"Oh," he said with a nervous laugh, "that all got canceled. I had a little accident, so I couldn't do it." He showed me the remnants of a small bruise on his cheek.

"Well, who's got her now?" I persisted.

"How should I know?"

I stared in horror. "Who took Henrietta when you got hurt?"

He shrugged. "Nurse Jansen brought me over to Emergency and then my parents drove me straight home after that."

I don't know why I kicked him so hard. I made a mental note to analyze my dreams that night to figure it out.

Milo finally made it to the scene. I turned on him. "I told you it was nuts to entrust Henrietta to this flake! He *lost* her!"

Instantly, Milo looked to Zachary, who nodded, studying his sneakers.

Milo was appalled. "When I phoned on Saturday night, you told me the specimen was one hundred percent."

Zachary struggled to save himself. "Well, she might have been. You know, wherever she was." He hung his head in shame. "I'm sorry, Milo."

Milo was visibly upset. I have to admit I felt some satisfaction seeing Milo the Unflappable show some feeling.

"This is terrible!" he exclaimed. "My experiment is in danger of being compromised!"

"I'll compromise your face if anything happens to Henrietta!" I promised darkly.

"Maybe . . ." I began. That's when I heard the cheering. It seemed to be coming from the cafeteria.

"*Give me a T—*" hollered somebody.

"*T!!*" came a chorus of voices.

"*Give me an A—*"

"*A!!*"

"*What does it spell?*"

"*Henrietta!!*" chanted the group.

We raced past the breakfast line and stopped dead. Atop a cafeteria table perched none other than Adam Lurie, holding the shopping bag aloft. I couldn't see Henrietta, but I could make out the impression of her sweet little beak pressed against the Macy's logo. Adam's hockey buddies and a handful of others made up the crowd.

I looked daggers up at Adam. "You had her all along?"

He shrugged down at us. "Zack was hurt; someone had to take Henrietta. My mom and I made a coop out of a couple of old hockey nets in the garage." He added, "Okay, Milo?"

"Acceptable—" Milo began.

"You should have *called* me!" I cut him off. "Henrietta hardly knows you! She must have been terrified — in your dark, dingy garage, surrounded by total strangers all weekend! You had no right to do it!"

"Hey," said Joey, "she's *our* mascot."

"Mascot?!" It came from me, Milo, and Zachary.

"We finally won last Friday, and Henrietta was on the bench with us. So" — the way Adam said it, you'd think it was the most normal, sensible thing in the world — "she has to be there for the rest of the season." The other Rangers nodded in agreement.

"Adam," said Milo seriously, "as an athlete, you must know that makes absolutely no scientific sense."

"Hey, man," said Steve sharply, "you don't mess with a winning streak."

"What winning streak?" I exploded. "It was only one game!"

"It doesn't matter!" Adam insisted. "If you lace your skates wrong before a big win, you do it that way forever! If your mom wears polka dots in the bleachers, it's law! If you step into your jockstrap left-leg-first, that becomes the next amendment to the Constitution! And that includes keeping a tweety-bird on the bench!"

Have I mentioned my theory about how hockey players are like cave dwellers crawling through the mud pit of a thousand monster-truck rallies? What — I mean, *what* could you say to a speech like that?

8

DOWNLOADED FROM THE FILES OF ZACHARY GUSTAFSON

THE BRAIN EATERS

Scene 11

[INTERIOR: Burning building – night]

FIREFIGHTERS hack down the flaming door and DETECTIVE JEFFERS leaps heroically through the fire to where STEVE lies dying of 34 broken bones, internal bleeding, head wounds, and tonsilitis.

JEFFERS

Are you all right?

STEVE

(gasping for breath)

Forget about me! I'm a goner! You have to stop . . . him . . .

JEFFERS

You mean . . . the brain-eating psycho-monster?

STEVE

I know his secret identity.

JEFFERS

What is it?

STEVE

(beckoning him closer)

To catch the brain-eating psycho-monster, just look for a big . . . a big . . .

JEFFERS

A big what?

But it's too late. STEVE's eyes roll back in his head and he dies.

CUT TO:

The BRAIN-EATING PSYCHO-MONSTER, fleeing through the streets, his six insect legs showing under his trench coat. He spreads terror to all who see his repulsive pustule-covered praying mantis head.

He approaches the university science lab, home of some of the biggest and most delicious brains in the city.

Hungrily, the MONSTER licks his green lips with a tongue coated with glowing acid. Then, before our eyes, he mutates into his secret identity—

Which was . . .

What?

I stared at my computer screen in total despair. Right in the middle of the most exciting, pivotal scene in my screenplay, I had writer's block. I didn't have the slightest idea what the brain-eating psycho-monster's secret identity should be.

This was terrible! I'd never had writer's block in my whole life. And just when Milo and I were starting to hit it off, too. Oh, sure, he was still pretty steamed about last weekend. I think his exact words were, "Go away. I never want to see you again for the rest of my life." Actually, I was pretty impressed I managed to get such an emotional reaction from a quiet guy like Milo. That was one of the reasons I knew we were going to be so close.

I chewed on my pen. I opened and closed every single drawer in my desk. I chewed on my pen again. This time the cap broke and I got ink in my mouth. Several minutes of hacking and spitting later, I was no closer to the solution to my problem.

I was checking myself for permanent blueness when I

caught a glimpse of a darting shape in the bathroom mirror. My throat seized. It was Doomsday — *headed straight for my room*!

"*Dew–ey!!!*" I made a desperate sprint across the hall and burst into my doorway. Doomsday already had his tiny baby hand cocked back, ready to throw a size-D battery at my computer.

I left my feet just as he launched the battery. With a flailing hand I slapped it away, at the same time leaping over my little brother and interposing myself between him and the desk.

But Doomsday still had plenty of ammo. He must have raided the junk drawer of my dad's desk. I blocked the fountain pen with my left hand and deflected the letter opener with my right. The chess queen made a nasty bump on my knee. The magnet and the pencil sharpener were a painful one-two punch as I stopped them with my chest. I won't even mention where the paperweight got me.

I had no choice but to wait until Doomsday ran out of projectiles, since I didn't dare yell for my mother. She'd blame this all on me, just like last Friday. I mean, *everybody* steps on a mop caddy and rolls into a wall. It happens to millions of people. But Mom — my own flesh and blood! — accused me of fighting and banned me from my computer for three days. It totally threw my screenplay off schedule and probably contributed to my writer's block. I couldn't risk it again.

So I took the heat. *And* the pain. *And* the Wite-Out bottle in the face. Finally, the last protractor ricocheted off my solar plexus.

"Ha!" I snorted. "What are you going to do now?"

Doomsday scrunched up his baby face and started to howl.

Mom was on the scene in a nanosecond. "Zachary Gustafson, how *dare* you pick on your little brother! And what happened to your room? It's a pigsty!"

"It's a battlefield!"

"It's a disgrace!"

She folded her arms. I knew I was toast. I made a feeble last-ditch effort. "It was Dewey, Mom! Honest!"

But even as I tried to defend myself, Mom strode purposefully over to my PC and pulled the plug. "This will cost you a week away from your computer, young man."

"A whole week? That's too long! It's not fair! You're messing with my creativity!" But at least I had my deadline, just like the big-time screenwriters. Seven days to figure out the secret identity of the brain-eating psycho-monster.

★★★

". . . and finally, in hockey action on Saturday," came Mr. Delong's voice over the PA system Monday morning, "the Rangers defeated St. Cloud by a score of eight to five. That's four in a row for our Rangers. Don't forget to come to the pep rally after school today. The team will be there — *and* Henrietta."

All through the halls of the school I could hear the cheering. Didn't it figure? My two least favorite things — the hockey team and Milo's stupid chicken — were turning into the heroes of the year. Coupled with my writer's block, it was pretty depressing.

I just so happened to run into Milo by standing in front of his locker for twenty minutes. He tried to walk away but, like any good friend, I stayed loyal. I followed him all the way to the science room.

"I had a nice conversation with your mom on Saturday." Actually, while I'd talked on the phone to Mrs. Neal, in the background I could hear my dearest friend hissing, "Tell him I'm not here! Tell him I've gone out! Tell him I moved to Europe!"

He blushed. "I was kind of busy," he mumbled, throwing open the lab door. He probably wanted to slam it in my face, but that was impossible. The lab was jam-packed with people. Milo crammed himself in behind a tall eighth-grader.

Lafayette Hughes turned around in annoyance. "Hey, what's the big idea — *Milo! How's it going?* Great chicken, dude. First-class poultry, no lie!"

I could just make out the top of Kelly Marie's head near the front of the throng. She waved, "Hi, Milo! Come on in! We're feeding Henrietta!"

Milo melted into the teeming crowd. I tried to follow and bounced off Lafayette.

"I'm a close friend of Milo's," I protested.

"In your dreams, nerd!"

It was like the Hollywood parties I'm going to get invited to when I'm a big-time screenwriter. If you're not on the guest list, you're *out*. That dumb pullet was getting to be like a movie star in this school. Only the beautiful people were allowed to hang around.

The only way I got in there at all was when the bell rang and Mrs. Baggio shooed all the tourists away.

Kelly Marie was on her hands and knees in front of the chicken wire. "See, sweetie?" she cooed right into that blank ugly chicken face. "Everybody loves you."

"Because of the hockey team," Adam reminded her.

As usual, Kelly Marie had this all worked out in her warped mind. "I admit that it *was* the Rangers that brought her to public attention. But it was her charm and personality that won everybody over."

"Chickens don't have personality," Milo insisted. "They exist purely—"

"She does so!" countered Kelly Marie. "She's happy and outgoing, but with a quiet, contemplative side—"

"And she's friendly," added Brendan.

"She's great at Monopoly," Sheila put in.

"Oh, come on!" Milo exploded. "The specimen doesn't

have anywhere *near* the intelligence necessary to play even the most simple board game!"

"Well, I have to roll for her since her little wings can't hold the dice," Sheila conceded. "But if she wants to buy a property, she kind of cackles. And when she lands on Free Parking, she gets *really* excited."

This looked like a perfect opportunity to win back a few points with Milo. "No way!" I said with a wink in his direction. "How could a chicken ever put a hotel on Marvin Gardens?"

With a *cheep* of outrage, Henrietta scratched and kicked with her toes, raising up a cloud of sawdust that drifted through the wire and settled on my shoes.

"Hey!" I blurted. "She did that on purpose!"

"Chickens have no purpose, either," Milo said, covering a smirk. Considering he was my best friend, he certainly seemed to enjoy seeing me suffer.

A shriek from Kelly Marie brought the class to attention. She was hopping up and down like a maniac, pointing at the bird's hind end.

"Kelly, what is it?" Mrs. Baggio asked in alarm.

"Look! It's a feather! A *real* feather!"

Big fat hairy deal. The bird had a feather on her butt. But our whole class abandoned their individual projects to rush over and examine this eighth wonder of the world. Whoop-de-doo.

"There's another one!" crowed Brendan, pointing to a wing.

Even Milo kind of got into it, commenting while making notes, "Specimen maturing acceptably."

"Acceptably?!" Kelly Marie was outraged. "Milo Neal, your big brain must be covering your eye sockets! Don't you see what this *really* means? Our little Henrietta is growing up!"

★★★

I caught up with Milo again at lunch. But when I sat down beside him, he picked up his tray and moved to another table.

I tried again in gym class, seventh period. Cleverly, I made sure we were on the same vaulting horse. As we flew by in opposite directions, I yelled, "We need to talk!"

But I didn't get to tell him when and where because I got out of sync for our next vault. Coach Crenshaw spotted me trying to sneak ahead in line and sent me to the locker room in disgrace.

Out of the corner of my eye I caught sight of Milo turning his ankle on a tricky landing. In a split-second decision, I smashed my face full-force into the changing room door. The nosebleed was like Niagara Falls.

"Gustafson!" barked the coach, watching my towel turn crimson. "Nurse's office! Now!"

So we were sitting on the bench outside the nurse's

office, me bleeding and Milo groaning. I couldn't be sure if he was in agony, because he didn't start making that noise until I sat down beside him.

"How's your leg?" I asked, very nasally.

"You're bleeding on my sneakers," he replied, giving me the worm guts look, complete with sound effects.

I was getting a little annoyed. Didn't he realize that I didn't *have* to have this nosebleed? That I was putting myself through this pain just to get the chance to talk to him?

"Look, Milo, I'm sorry. I didn't mean to abandon your experiment. I had a concussion."

Milo glared at me like no best friend ever should. "That's not what I'm mad about. I'm mad because I phoned to check on the status of the specimen, and you out-and-out lied!"

He had me there. As a total last resort I told the truth. "You and I were just starting to hit it off, and I was afraid this would spoil our friendship. I figured the chicken was probably okay, and maybe I'd never have to tell you."

Milo's expression softened a little. "Yeah, okay, maybe." Then he shook his head in frustration. "But this whole school is nuts! All I'm trying to do here is a science project!"

I shrugged. "And it's going great. The whole school loves Henrietta."

"That's the point!" he exploded. "It's a specimen! It doesn't have anything to do with friendship or hockey or love or popularity! It's a link in the food chain! It exists to be hatched, raised, slaughtered, and eaten! That's my project! Nothing more!"

My ears perked up. "Slaughtered and eaten?"

"What don't you understand?" Milo asked, a little impatiently. "Chickens don't die of old age. They're killed, cooked, and eaten."

I was still in the dark. "Yeah, but you're not going to do *that* part — you know, the killing and the eating?"

"Well, of course I am!" Milo erupted. "What's the point of studying the food chain if we don't complete the link? At the science fair I'm going to serve chicken to the judges while they review the experiment notes."

I goggled. "You mean *our* chicken? Like, *Henrietta* chicken? *Dead* Henrietta chicken?"

"It's the food chain," Milo explained again. "The judges will actually participate in the end of the link. I thought that would be a nice finishing touch."

If Milo had told me that he was an alien and that his nose was about to blast off from his face and burrow down to the earth's core, I wouldn't have been any more surprised. I mean, if Kelly Marie knew this, she'd go supernova. Everybody who had adopted Henrietta as a pet/mascot/hobby/friend — they didn't have the faintest idea that they were looking at an oven-stuffer-in-training! I bet Milo thought it was common knowledge.

That rotten chicken who pecked me, scratched me, and made sure everybody in the world knew how much she hated me — who even gave me a concussion — that fuzzy fiend from the underworld had a date with the frying pan!

I don't get too many moments of ultimate joy, but this was one of them.

Milo interrupted my thoughts. "What are you grinning about?"

"I . . . I think my nose has stopped bleeding."

At that moment, Nurse Jansen appeared, hauled Milo in, and sent out Steve Tenorio with a bandage around his thumb.

The musclehead took one look at my bloody nose and red-stained shirt and grinned nastily. "What happened to you, Zack? Did you get caught in one of your own screenplays?"

But nothing could spoil this perfect day for me. "I'm really happy the Rangers are doing so well with your new mascot," I said, and laughed wildly.

"You're weird!" Steve accused, and walked away.

I was still doubled over when he turned, puzzled, to frown at me.

★★★

All week I walked on air, hugging the secret. I got detention for humming. Every time Kelly Marie opened her mouth about Henrietta, I had to leave the room and laugh into my fist in the hall. When I saw all those idiots, who weren't even in our class, lining up to clean chicken droppings from the floor of the pen, the truth was almost bursting out of me: *Don't get too attached to the chicken. She's not staying.*

I went to the hockey pep rally Monday after school. All the Rangers got a big reception, sure. But then Adam held up Henrietta and the crowd went nuts. A couple of those muscleheads unfurled a banner that said HENRIETTA FOREVER. And I was thinking, Don't count on it.

The Rangers won their fifth in a row, and everyone was talking championship. Oh, I knew what they could serve at the victory banquet!

But seriously — when their good luck charm got sacrificed in the name of science, would Adam and the Rangers start losing again? That would be the icing on the cake — served after a delicious chicken dinner.

When I was in the lab, of course, I played it cool. I didn't want to spill the beans. But every time I looked at that miserable bird I pictured her as a different recipe. Tuesday she was Cajun-style; Wednesday, stuffed and roasted; Thursday, chicken Cordon Bleu; by Friday, I saw fajitas, complete with guacamole and flour tortillas.

Best of all, the end of the week was also the end of Mom's ban on my computer. I'd been so distracted, what with all the happiness and stuff, I hadn't really given a thought to my writer's block and the secret identity of the brain-eating psycho-monster. But I was confident. It wasn't even Saturday yet, and as I drifted off into sleep, *The Brain Eaters* was playing itself out like a movie in my half-dreams.

I saw the psycho-monster stalking through the streets and stopping in front of the university lab. Its hideous features began to distort as it mutated into its secret identity — a form so innocent and harmless that it could move among its victims without creating a stampede of terror. Then, in a split second, it could crack open a dozen heads and be popping down brains like peanuts.

I was just about asleep, but I struggled to stay awake enough to see the end of the mutation — the secret identity. The psycho-monster's new features coalesced and came into focus. The homicidal archevildoer was now — a big chicken!

I sat bolt upright in bed. *A chicken?!*

Fade to black . . .

9

FROM THE DIARY OF MRS. BAGGIO

I must confess that I'm beginning to feel a little uneasy about the chicken project. I suppose I should have seen it coming. But I was so overwhelmed by the thought of *teaching* Victor Neal's son that I fear I missed the big picture: I'm barely tolerated at this school; Henrietta is the object of worship.

Oh, this is nothing new. Put a hamster or a rabbit in a classroom and you have an instant fan club. The students will do anything for a warm-blooded creature that nibbles. And with Henrietta — well, perhaps it was the novelty of a chicken, mixed with the fame of Milo and his father. And now this strange hockey connection. It was spontaneous combustion, an overnight success story. A star was born.

I've never had so many students come into my lab; I've never seen so much interest in science. All books on chickens have been checked out of the school library. Students discuss the nutritional value of birdseed when they used to talk about rock and roll. Volunteers waiting their turn with Henrietta now play my Quizzles and my math games. My gyroscope is spinning again. One hockey player who can barely remember his times tables has me tutoring him on calculating trajectory and acceleration to improve his slap shot. All because Henrietta has brought them to my room. It's a science teacher's dream. Except—

Henrietta will be dead in a few weeks. Milo's project calls for it.

I circulated among my students to make sure they were okay with that.

"It's a fact of life," I told Sheila Martel. "All chickens are raised to be eaten."

"Yeah," she agreed. "Thank God that isn't going to happen with Henrietta."

I raised the same topic with Joey Sorrentino and Lynette Martinez. They both looked one hundred percent blank.

"Chickens are food!" I persisted. "Where do you think *chicken* comes from? They don't carve it off a warthog, you know!"

"But Henrietta's a *school* chicken." Joey lectured me like I needed to be straightened out on the subject. "*Farm* chickens are the ones that you eat."

With Kelly Marie, I just said it right out: "When a chicken gets big enough, you slaughter it and eat it."

She looked me straight in the eye. "If anybody tried that with Henrietta, I'd break every bone in his body!"

I had to face the facts. No one had the slightest idea what was coming at the end of Milo's project. Furthermore, when that information got out, I was going to have a riot on my hands.

Oh, what a pickle!

I even went so far as to approach Milo. "Perhaps it might be nice to have Henrietta in a cage on display at the science fair," I suggested brightly. "Then you could serve Real Dixie Fried Chicken to *symbolize* her place in the food chain."

He was horrified. "That negates my whole experiment! How can I make my specimen an exception to the food chain when the whole purpose is to show that there are no exceptions to the food chain?"

And he was right, of course. Besides, I'm the one who invested so much of my own and the class's time in Milo's project. To make him change it would not only be unfair — it would make *me* look like a proper fool.

So I'm caught between a rock and a hard place. What can I do? Oh, dear, what *can* I do?

10

FROM THE SUPER-SECRET RECORDINGS OF JOEY SORRENTINO

Lynette says it was fate that the Neals got divorced, and Milo and his mom moved to St. Martin, and Milo ended up going to our school. Lynette says it was no accident that Milo got put in the Bag's class, and that he was doing his project on a chicken, and that chicken turned out to be Henrietta. It was destiny. That's what Lynette says.

Me? I agree with her, mostly because disagreeing with Lynette is bad business. The last time I disagreed with her, we broke up. And the time before that. And the time before *that*. But enough of my love life. This is supposed to be about Henrietta.

She's the greatest. Our dog is lazy and he has bad breath, and I'm positive our cat has a split personality.

My brother's hamster is a near-idiot, running on that dumb wheel all day. But when I look into Henrietta's bright chicken eyes, I know I've got a friend who'll never let me down. Lynette says Henrietta and I are on the same wavelength, although I'm pretty sure I heard somewhere that chickens can't swim.

Take last night's Ranger game for example. We were down 6–3 against Minnetonka, and Steve was still out with his sprained thumb, and Adam was in the penalty box for a misconduct, and the Wall was even worse than usual in net, and DeeVee was benched because he took a crazy slap shot and busted the skylight in the Community Center. Our fans were leaving, and Coach Crenshaw was yelling, and the winning streak was going down the tubes.

Then all of a sudden, Henrietta squawked. Not any little baby chirp, but a real grown-up chicken squawk, her first one.

"*Time out!*" bellowed a voice.

"Time out?" echoed the coach in disbelief. "Only I call time out! Who said that?"

It was Kelly Marie, who always sat directly behind the team so she could keep an eye on Henrietta.

"Did you hear that?" She climbed out of her seat and onto our bench, and picked up the old parrot cage that was

Henrietta's home during Ranger games. "She squawked! And she ruffled her little feathers! I saw!"

"What's wrong with the chicken?" called Adam anxiously from the penalty box.

"She squawked!" called half a dozen Rangers in a state of high excitement.

"She's trying to tell us something!" I said breathlessly. "She sees how lousy we've been playing!"

"You don't need a chicken to tell you that!" Coach Crenshaw was starting to look a little upset.

"You guys make me sick!" Kelly Marie snorted. "You don't care about Henrietta as a person! You're not interested that she's growing up! You just want her to help you play stupid hockey!"

The coach blew his stack. "What's so bad about that? We're a hockey *team*! This is a hockey *rink*! We're in the middle of a hockey *game*! What are we supposed to play — *Yahtzee*?!"

The referee skated over. "Rangers, your time's up."

"But Henrietta talked," DeeVee explained, "and we can't figure out what she said."

"I'll tell you what she said!" roared the ref. "She said get your butts on the ice or you're getting a penalty for delay of game! That's what she said!"

Then Henrietta squawked again and, from that moment on, our feet had wings. We scored five goals in five minutes to win the game 8–6. An amazing come-from-behind victory — and we owed it all to our mascot.

Lynette says Henrietta squawked to show that, just like *she* was maturing, *we* had to mature as a hockey team. Man, I'd like to see any dog or cat do that.

★★★

Thanks to Henrietta, November was shaping up to be the greatest month in my life. The Rangers were the hottest middle-school team in Minnesota, and after Adam, I was the top scorer. We had won eight straight since our 0 and 5 start, and we'd already broken the top ten in our division.

Lynette says it's not hard to feel good when everything's going your way. I agree with that, and it's not even because I'm afraid she'll break up with me again. In fact, Lynette and I have been getting along so well that it's almost scary. We haven't gotten into a real screaming fight since the day before yesterday. And even then we only broke up for half an hour or so. It's Henrietta. I swear it.

Here's why. When we got to school every morning, Lynette used to get really cheesed at me because I'd blow her off and go play tennis-ball hockey with Adam, Laffy, and Steve. But now the two of us head straight for the lab to see if the Bag needs any help with Henrietta. This alone avoids at least two breakups a week.

Not only that, but it used to drive her nuts that I'd pick the raisins out of my cinnamon bun at lunch every day.

Now she knows I slip them to Henrietta, so it's okay. And she can't complain that we don't talk enough. We spend hours and hours discussing chickens, reading about chickens, and making ourselves ready for the big day: After weeks of anticipation, our names had finally made it to the top of the waiting list. Milo was going to let us take Henrietta home for the weekend. And we had special plans.

Lynette says it's going to be historic.

11

EXPERIMENT NOTES: MILO NEAL
11/22

> It's not so bad coming home from school Monday through Thursday. I've got homework to do and experiment notes to update. Before you know it, it's time to go to sleep so I can start the process over tomorrow.

> But on Friday, my excuses for being busy are gone. That's when Mom shifts into high gear:

"You should get out more. You're not sociable. You need to be with people your own age. You never see a living soul all weekend."

{This never happened in California, although I was usually by myself there, too. Perhaps it = worry re: new town & school/further study req'd.}

"Why don't you get together with your friend Zachary?" she would suggest over and over. "Or how about that girl who came by? What was her name?"

"Kelly Marie."

"She left you her number. Give her a call."

"They're both weird." That was my standard answer.

> The problem might have been a little easier if I had my specimen to care for over Saturday and Sunday. But thanks to Mrs. B, that was never going to happen. {Why is it such a big deal to "help" me by taking the subj. for the weekend? Joey S and Lynette M practically danced with the cage all the way out of the lab. And it's not just those two. There are thirty-one names on the sign-up sheet — baffling because the experiment will be over long before thirty-one weeks, and subj. will no longer exist/further study req'd.}

> But when I got home that Friday, my mother wasn't in nagging mode at all. In fact, she was waiting by the door, beaming.

"I have the most wonderful news!" she said.

I brightened. "Dad's coming?"

She gave me a sympathetic smile. "No, Milo. Not yet. But guess what? You've been invited to a party tonight!"

I stared at her. "By who?"

"I've got all the information on the telephone pad upstairs. What a nice girl — so friendly. She really sounded excited about having you come."

"Aw, Mom," I groaned, "you know I hate parties."

"How can you say that if you never go to any?" she demanded.

> I never stick my head in the furnace, either, but I know it's lousy.

"I'm not going," I insisted. "I won't know anybody there."

"That's not true!" my mother pounced on it. "The girl having the party must know you, right? Otherwise why would she call to invite you?"

"Because my chicken is more popular than Santa Claus," I explained bitingly, "and definitely a whole lot more popular than me."

"Well, Zachary's going to be at the party," she countered.

> This is why my mother should never go into sales. ZG is not going to put me over the top re: this party. This = a real estate agent saying, "Buy this house — it's built on a nice toxic waste dump."

I said, "How could you know that Zachary will be there?"

She looked a little sheepish. "I phoned him. He says he'll meet you at the party."

"That'll be a trick because I'm not going."

Suddenly, Mom changed tactics and decided to play it cool. "Okay. I certainly can't force you to go if you don't want to, even though you'll be miserable staying around here."

> She personally would be supplying the misery.

"Fine."

"Now, you go and lie around the house like a sack of flour, and I'll call you when dinner's ready."

> I had to admire her willpower. I knew she was dying to run upstairs to get her message pad so she could read me the details of this party. I admit I was a little curious myself. Who was the mysterious hostess? But I would have died before asking.

> The standoff stayed friendly through dinner. Then, while I was loading the dishwasher, I noticed Mom's speech had become short and clipped. Later, in front of the TV, the silent treatment began. But I could see her glancing toward the stairs, which led up to the details of the party I hoped I was missing by now.

{My mother looks totally serene when she's angry. But you can almost hear the hiss of the boiler room filling up with steam just below the surface/further study req'd.}

Finally, I could take it no longer. "*What?*"

She glared at me. "I can accept that you don't want to go to this party. But the least you can do is phone that poor girl and tell her you can't make it."

"Oh, all right," I sighed. "What's the number?"

> She dashed upstairs and returned seconds later with a sheet from her memo pad. I stared.

Lynette Martinez

18 Apple Blossom Lane

7:30 P.M.

I was shocked. "That's impossible!"

"I took the message myself, Milo."

"But Lynette can't be having a party!" I protested. "She's looking after my specimen this weekend!"

It was my mother's turn to sigh. "You and your father — honestly! The world has to grind to a halt for the experiment! Do you really think this Lynette might endanger your chicken?"

> I imagined the kind of party LM might have. I didn't conjure up the image of people in tuxedos playing Parcheesi while a string quartet performed Mozart.

I ran for my coat. "I've got to get over there!"

A wide grin split my mother's face. "Don't forget to bring money. You might have to chip in for the pizza or something."

"I'm not going as a guest!" I roared.

"I should have known," she laughed. "You're going as a killjoy. That'll do wonders for your social life."

"I've got to retrieve my specimen!"

> But I knew Mom was right. In addition to a nerd, a brain, an outsider, and a conceited snob, I was now going to be known as a party pooper.

> Why me?/further study req'd.

12

RANGERS UPDATE: CAPTAIN ADAM LURIE REPORTING

Leave it to Joey and Lynette to throw a party in honor of a chicken.

That's what they called it — a Henrietta Appreciation Bash. Don't get me wrong. I appreciated Henrietta just fine. I mean, we hadn't lost a game yet with her sitting on our bench. But I love her the way you'd love any good luck charm that was working for you — like a rabbit's foot or a horseshoe. This was like throwing a Presidential Gala for a four-leaf clover.

But you didn't pass up a chance to go to one of Lynette's parties. For starters, she had the loudest stereo in St. Martin and the perfect place to put it. The Martinez house had a giant attic converted into a rec room. Strip hardwood made the ultimate dance floor and the place was filled with beanbag chairs. They had the works — video games, a wide-screen TV, air hockey, a pinball machine, and, across a corner by the window, the coolest, most comfortable hammock in the world.

Mr. and Mrs. Martinez had gone into Minneapolis for a wedding, and Lynette had gotten their permission to "have a few friends over." There were forty-five people in the attic when I got there and everyone was in a big-party mood. The dancing had just gotten under way, although the floor wasn't that crowded yet. A lot of the kids were over at the food table, helping themselves to snacks, ice cream, and a mountain of nachos at least three feet high.

The best thing about Lynette's parties was that they were a great place to be seen, especially for a hockey player like me. Lynette and Joey hung out with the cool people — the Rangers, the cheerleaders, mostly eighth-graders, and even a few freshmen from the high school. I was really impressed to see Tony Walters, Brendan's older brother, the *real* Wall. I wish we still had him in goal. Brendan was a nice guy, and he tried really hard, but just seeing Tony brought back memories of last year. The Wall was our MVP and the league's shutout king. He led us to a season of 12–3–2 *and* the championship before the Canadians skunked us 11–zip at Christmas.

Henrietta sat in her cage on that awesome hammock in the corner, watching the goings-on with unruffled calm. It didn't seem to bother her that Laffy, playing DJ, was cranking the music louder with every song. She wasn't alarmed in the slightest that the attic was filling up to capacity and the floor was shaking with the vibrations of so many dancing feet. There was a real cool attitude to this chicken; either that or she was too dumb to notice the joint was jumping.

Just when it seemed like everything was about to hit fever pitch, suddenly Lafayette pulled the plug on the stereo, and Joey and Lynette managed to get the place quieted down.

"Attention, everybody," called Lynette. "We'll get back to the music and the fun, but let's take a few minutes to salute our guest of honor, Henrietta."

Joey lifted the cage from the hammock and held it high. There was a big cheer.

I picked up a couple of wisecracks from the ninth-graders. But when they saw how seriously the rest of us were taking this, they shut right up.

Then Steve and DeeVee and a couple of the cheerleaders circulated through the crowd with large bottles of diet soda, filling up everybody's glasses.

Our hostess raised her drink. "To Henrietta!" she cried in ringing tones. "Mascot . . . chicken . . . friend."

As we all stood there with our glasses held high, Laffy cued the music:

. . . I can fly higher than an eagle!

You are the wind beneath my wings.

I don't think it's disloyal to the Rangers to admit that I'd never felt so stupid in my life. Picture it — sixty people standing around toasting a chicken while the music blared about flying eagles. At least nobody could make fun of me, because everybody I knew was right there, doing the same idiotic thing.

Fortunately, it was over fast. Laffy cut to some decent rock and roll, and there was a stampede for the dance floor.

Joey and Lynette waded into the gyrating crowd, holding Henrietta's cage high between them.

I made a bolt for the hammock in the corner, but Steve got there a split second ahead of me. I grabbed the fabric at two strategic points and flipped, sending him tumbling to the floor. In a flash, I was in the hammock, luxuriating in the perfect comfort.

My joy lasted about three seconds. For there, pushing his way through the crowd in front of the nachos, was none other than Zachary Gustafson. I stared, unable to believe my own eyes. The one thing I thought you could depend on at Lynette's parties was that you would never run into any losers, let alone the world champion checkered-flag speed demon of the Loser-apolis 500!

I launched myself out of the hammock, grabbed the party-crashing dweeb, and steered him away from the roaring floor-to-ceiling speakers. "Are you crazy, Zack? What are you doing here?"

Dweeb-asaurus played Mr. Innocent. "I was invited."

I stared him down. "Well, not really," he admitted. "But my good friend Milo was, and I'm meeting him."

"Milo . . . ?" But then I realized that of course Henrietta's owner would have to make the guest list. Otherwise Lynette would never invite a sixth-grader, aside from Brendan, who was a Ranger.

"Okay, meet Milo," I said grudgingly. "But the hammock is off-limits." Some things had to stay sacred.

I could tell Zachary was pretty impressed by his surroundings. After all, how many chances would a loser like him have to get in on the kind of party Lynette throws? And I have to say that it was getting considerably awesome.

People were arriving in a steady stream, and the attic was jam-packed. You could tell that word of the party had spread around town, because there were a lot of people there who definitely weren't from South Middle School. Some of them looked like high school students — even juniors and seniors. A few looked like extraterrestrials, with nose rings, dog collars, and blue hair. The place was so steamy from all those bodies that even with the window wide open I was sweating. Laffy had the stereo up to nine by now, with the bass maxed out. You could feel each drumbeat in your kidneys. There were so many kids on the dance floor that they were belly to belly, bumping and gyrating, a single seething mass. All arms were raised and Henrietta's cage was being rolled from hand to hand above the dancers.

Barbara Falconi grabbed me by the arm and hauled me out onto the floor, which was a pretty tight squeeze. Suddenly, Henrietta's cage bounced off my head. I looked up and caught a brief glimpse of our upside-down mascot pressed against the bars. I don't claim to be a professor of tweety-birds, but her eyes were bulging, and her neck was drawn back into her feathers — she sure didn't look very happy to me.

I grabbed the back of Joey's collar and turned him around to face me. "Maybe we should give her a rest!" I shouted, pointing at the cage.

"You're right!" he bellowed back. "She *is* the best!"

So much for trying to be heard.

Then I was distracted by a pretty hilarious sight — Milo Neal trying to push his way across the dance floor. He looked like a guy wading through a neck-deep river of molasses. Dancing bodies bumped him, and flailing arms smacked him about the head. But his face was a study of anger and effort, and he forged on. He kept repeating something over and over. Even though I couldn't hear him above the ruckus, I knew what he was saying:

"Where's my specimen?!"

As much as I was enjoying seeing the crown prince of California science in such a panic, I reached up for the cage so I could show it to Milo. After a minute, I felt the metal bars against my hand. I latched onto the cage and pulled it down. But even before I saw it, I knew it felt too light. I stared in horror. The little gate was open and Henrietta was gone.

But California Boy wasn't looking at the cage at all. His horrified eyes were fixed on Tony Walters — the Wall — on the other side of the dance floor. Tony moved to the beat, both arms straight up over his head. His fingertips gripped a familiar bundle of feathers.

I shouted, "*Wa-a-all!*"

But it was too late. The frightened chicken wriggled herself free and began scrambling across dancers' heads, deftly leaping over the sea of grabbing hands. It was amazing — eighty of us and only one of her, and she made it, flapping and scratching. She hopped across us like we were stepping stones, scooted up the slope of the hammock, and disappeared out the open window.

There was a collective gasp that almost ate up all the oxygen in the room. Laffy cut the music and joined the stampede to the window.

Milo and I got there first. We looked down, fully expecting to see a heap of broken feathers on the grass three floors below us. But there was nothing there.

"Did she bounce?" I asked weakly, picturing our hockey season as dead as Henrietta probably now was.

Then we heard that squawk and it wasn't coming from the ground. We looked up and there she was, perched on a branch of the big apple tree in the Martinezes' yard.

"Fascinating," said Milo. "Her wings managed to take her the eighteen inches from the ledge to the nearest branch. The specimen is maturing rapidly."

Lynette and Joey pushed their way to our side.

"Henrietta!" Lynette shrieked out into the night. "You come back here this minute!"

In answer, the bird backed away a few steps on the branch.

Zachary rushed forward — like we needed him! "I've got an idea, Milo!" he babbled. "You hold on to my ankles, and I'll hang out the window and grab the branch, forming a human bridge. Henrietta can just walk across me right back into the house!"

In the golden age of stupid ideas, that one will still be a classic. "Don't tempt me, Zack," I muttered. "If you're going out that window, you're going all the way."

Milo started for the stairs. "Someone get a ladder," he ordered briskly. "The specimen is too frightened to come in on her own. I'll have to go up and get her."

I'm not a big Milo fan, but I had to be impressed by the way this L.A. kid took charge. I mean, Lynette was in tears, Joey was paralyzed with guilt, the high-schoolers were still fooling around, and the rest of us were as useful as a flock of sheep aboard the starship *Enterprise.*

In a body, we all followed Milo down the stairs and out into the yard. We gathered around the base of the apple tree, peering up into the branches. In the gloom, it was hard to pick out Henrietta.

Zachary spotted her first. "There she is!"

High above us, the tweety-bird shifted on her branch, dislodging an old, frozen, wormy apple. It dropped like a bomb, catching Zachary full in the mush.

"Ow!"

Lynette came running from around the front.

"Where's the ladder?" asked Milo.

"We don't have one!" she wailed. "So I called 911!"

I listened. You could already hear the sirens in the distance.

Well, the high school guys — they thought that was just great. To them this was the icing on the cake — you had a wild party, and you topped it off with a police raid. They started horsing around on the lawn, laughing and shouting and hurling clumps of frozen turf at each other.

"Cut it out, you guys!" shrieked Lynette. "This is serious! Henrietta's in danger! Joey, make them stop!"

"Come on, everybody! Chill out!" Joey pleaded.

The roughhousing raged on. I doubt the high-schoolers even heard him. They did calm down a little to watch the fire truck roar up the Martinezes' driveway. Four rubber-coated firefighters leaped down and squeaked over in their humongous boots.

Lynette ran screaming over to meet them. "Henrietta's in a tree and we can't get her down!"

"Don't worry, miss." The fire chief trained his high-powered flashlight up into the branches of the apple tree. It illuminated our mascot, perched on the flimsy branch, terrified and shivering from the cold.

"I don't see her," said the chief.

"Right there!" yelled a dozen of us, pointing. Even the high-schoolers were starting to get involved.

The chief squinted. "Did she climb up there to rescue the chicken?"

"She *is* the chicken!" bawled Lynette.

The man stared. "You called 911 for a *chicken*?"

I stepped forward. "I know it sounds stupid, but she's our mascot!"

"And she's the wind beneath our wings!" chimed in DeeVee.

"She's a link in the food chain," Milo corrected severely.

"She's everybody's friend!" quavered Lynette. "Please, please, *please* get her down!"

The chief scratched his head. "Well, I suppose we can't just leave her there."

So they dragged out the ladder and hauled Henrietta

down from the tree. But they sure didn't look too happy about it. I guess we should be grateful they didn't turn the hose on us.

"Quick, get a blanket," ordered Milo. "The specimen shouldn't be exposed to this kind of cold."

"Here." Joey pulled his sweater over his head and wrapped it around the bird in Milo's arms.

Lynette was trembling with emotion. "I'm never going to forgive you for this, Joey! This is all your fault!"

"*My* fault?" Joey repeated. "It was *your* party!"

"But it was *your* idea!"

"Which I got from *you*!"

In a rage, Lynette tore his signet ring from her finger and bounced it with deadly accuracy off his forehead.

"We're finished!" they chorused in perfect unison and ran off in opposite directions.

I stepped up and put a sympathetic arm around Milo's shoulders. "Look, Milo, we're sorry—"

Stiffly, he shook me off, wheeled, and stalked away, taking his chicken home.

Zachary ran after him, waving the empty cage. "Wait up, Milo, buddy! I'm coming!"

13

"PSYCHOLOGY TALK"
BY KELLY MARIE GINSBERG

Weekend mornings were newspaper mornings at my house. We got the *Minneapolis Tribune* on Sunday, but Saturdays were reserved for the *St. Martin Sentinel*, our local weekly. My dad had the sports and Mom was reading the editorials. I poured myself some orange juice and sat down with the front section.

The *Sentinel* was more of a family tradition than a really good paper because not much ever happened in our sleepy little city. I breezed quickly through the headlines — nothing interesting, as usual, until one word popped off the page at me: CHICKEN.

TEENS CALL 911 TO RESCUE CHICKEN AFTER WILD PARTY

My blood froze. I read on, hoping against hope that the article was about some other chicken.

> A teen party got out of hand last night, and a defenseless animal nearly paid the price. The fire department was called to 18 Apple Blossom Lane to rescue someone named Henrietta only to discover that Henrietta was not a person but a chicken belonging to Milo Neal, son of the famous Victor Neal. The chicken, which figures in young Neal's science project, became frightened when the party grew rowdy and fled via an attic window, marooning herself in a tall apple tree . . .

I dropped the paper as though it burned my fingers. "*Those stupid brainless morons!*"

My mother jumped. "What is it, dear?"

I showed her the article. "And I know who did it, too — Joey and Lynette! *They* had Henrietta this weekend! And that's Lynette's address!"

Dad read over Mom's shoulder. "I remember when we used to do stuff like this back at the frat house," he chuckled. "It's all in fun."

"It wasn't much fun for Henrietta!" I seethed. "Poor little sweetie! She could have been lost or even killed! Not to mention that she was running loose in a party full of crazy people! She could have been stomped on!"

"Now, Kelly," my mother warned, "I hope you're not planning to do anything rash."

I was already lacing my second sneaker. "I'm going to take Henrietta away from those incompetent low-grade nitwits!"

★★★

I knocked on the door of 18 Apple Blossom Lane. The lady who answered looked a lot like Lynette, so I assumed she was Mrs. Martinez.

"Hi," I greeted. "Is Lynette here?"

Mrs. Martinez's brow clouded. "Lynette is grounded for the week. And if you were at that awful party last night, you should be grounded, too."

"Oh, I wasn't even invited," I defended myself. I noted that she was wearing sweats and holding a huge green garbage bag. Obviously, the cleanup from last night was a major operation. "What I really wanted to know . . . uh . . . is Henrietta still here?"

Mrs. Martinez frowned. "I told you — Lynette isn't seeing any of her friends for at least a week." She glanced at the garbage bag. "Maybe two."

"No, no. I mean Henrietta — the chicken."

Mrs. Martinez's mouth dropped open. "There was a *chicken*?" She recovered a little. "Well, I suppose that would explain the feathers and . . . uh . . . other things we found in the rec room."

I thanked her and left, heading double-speed for the only other place Henrietta could be — Milo's house.

Mrs. Neal let me in. "We've been expecting you, Kelly Marie," she beamed, throwing the door wide and ushering me in as though I were visiting royalty.

I stared at her. "How did you know I was coming?"

But then I caught sight of the living room. Draped in various poses around the comfortable furniture were Milo, Zachary, Adam, and Joey.

"Hi," said Adam weakly.

I swooped down like an avenging angel. "Don't *hi* me! I could kill you guys! Twice! Where's Henrietta?"

"In the kitchen with the vet," said Milo. "I think she has a fever."

I looked daggers at Joey. "You and your wacko girlfriend couldn't leave well enough alone!"

"She's not my girlfriend anymore," said Joey, tight-lipped.

I snorted with disgust. "Don't worry. You and Lynette are getting married. Why ruin two houses?"

Zachary spoke up. "How did you know there was a party?"

"The whole town knows! You idiots made the paper! Mrs. Baggio's probably reading all about it right now!"

"She already phoned," said Milo mournfully.

Mrs. Neal appeared carrying a tray loaded with bagels and muffins and steaming mugs of hot chocolate.

"I'm so thrilled that you all came over today," she smiled, setting everything out on the coffee table.

I cocked an eyebrow. Mrs. Neal must have been pretty worried about her son not having any friends. Here we were, in a sickbed vigil for Henrietta, and Milo's mother was acting like this was a tea party.

The guys fell on the food like ravenous tigers. I sipped a bit of chocolate. "You must be *really* broken up over Henrietta," I said sarcastically. "Your appetites are suffering."

"It's not going to help the specimen if we starve," offered Zachary.

"Oh, you too with 'the specimen,'" I exclaimed. "If you sit too close to Milo, he rubs off on you?"

We all rose as Dr. Siltinen, the veterinarian, appeared in the doorway, holding Henrietta wrapped in a wool blanket.

"Well, Milo, you have a pretty sick bird here."

I heard Joey gulp. "Is she going to . . . you know, *die*?"

"She's suffered a severe chill," the vet replied. "I'm prescribing antibiotics to prevent it from turning into pneumonia. If you keep her warm and quiet, she should be back to normal in a few days."

I heaved a tremulous sigh. "Oh, thank you, Dr. Siltinen! You're the greatest—"

But Adam Hockey-Is-My-Life Lurie had to open his

mouth and prove what a low-down two-faced selfish pig he is. "But we've got a game on Monday! She can come to the rink, right?"

"Absolutely not," said the vet firmly. "Cold, damp air is exactly what you have to avoid."

Adam was in agony. "It's not that cold! We'll wrap her up! She'll have a hot water bottle! We'll get a heater! Oh, please—"

With all my might, I stomped on his foot. It shut him up in a flash. If he'd opened his mouth, a shriek would have come out.

"No." The doctor was adamant. "The chicken is not to leave the house for the next seventy-two hours."

"We're playing Mount Carmel," Joey said hopefully. "They're the worst team in the state. Maybe we can beat them without Henrietta."

Henrietta squawked, not her usual perky, energetic sound, but a weak, pitiful mewl. My heart broke in two. So I began a long lecture, heavy on the psychology, about what was wrong with each and every one of those insects — and what would happen to them if they ever mistreated Henrietta again.

14

DOWNLOADED FROM THE FILES OF ZACHARY GUSTAFSON

WE MEET AT LAST

[Scene 56]

[EXTERIOR SHOT: The White House – day]

Finally, the moment has arrived – our first ever contact with an alien race. The galactic spacecraft, which looks a little small, sets down on the White House landing pad.

PRESIDENT ZOT

Citizens of the world, today we get our first glimpse of life forms from outside the Milky Way galaxy . . .

> Instead of opening, the spaceship door disintegrates, an example of the highly advanced technology of the space travelers. The Marine band strikes up a welcoming march. The CAPTAIN emerges with his crew — interstellar chickens—

Chickens?!

I pulled back from the computer in disbelief. Why did I type that? I didn't *plan* for the interstellar visitors to be chickens. That's one of the problems of being a true natural writer. The story comes from your gut, not your brain. Why did my gut want *chickens* to be in *We Meet at Last*? I don't even like chickens. I only knew one, and she would be dead long before the gala Hollywood opening for *We Meet at Last*. First *The Brain Eaters* and now this! Why were all these chickens invading my screenplays?

To get my mind off my writing problems, I spent a lot of time at Milo's place that weekend. Officially I was visiting the sick chicken. It was the perfect excuse to work on Milo a little more.

Unfortunately, the whole world had the same idea. The house was like Epcot Center. It was packed!

Kelly Marie practically lived there, fussing over Henrietta. There were also a lot of hockey players in and out, visiting their mascot and scarfing down the endless trays of snacks Mrs. Neal put out. Not to mention the constant *boom!* . . . *boom!* . . . *boom!* of DeeVee outside on the driveway, practicing his slap shot against the aluminum garage door.

Being around so many Rangers was dangerous for a guy like me, but I took the heat to spend so much time with Milo.

"Dweeb . . . geek . . . suck-up . . . loser . . ."

Nobody actually said it out loud; the words just kind of bubbled up from the background every time I managed to sidle up to the man of the house.

Naturally, Kelly Marie had to stick her nose into it. "This is textbook psychology," she explained to the team. "Zachary represents all your hidden insecurities."

"What a load of garbage," Adam groaned.

Suddenly, Lafayette bounded in through the sliding door and stuffed a mittful of snow down my shirt.

"*Yeeeow!*" I jumped up and down, brushing it out.

"The carpet! The carpet!" warned Milo, giving me the worm guts look. Like I was manufacturing the snow in my belly button.

"See?" Kelly Marie was triumphant. "When you pick on Zachary, you're really picking on yourselves."

"So how come I'm the one with the f-f-frozen stomach?" I muttered, teeth chattering.

"In psychology it's the same thing," she said smugly, and launched into one of her famous lectures.

She got the hockey players so riled that Steve grabbed me by the belt, and Lafayette gave me a killer wedgie.

"Aw, come on!" I complained, my legs dangling as they

held me up. I pointed at Kelly Marie. "*She's* the one you're mad at!"

"Yeah," Steve explained as the two muscleheads carried me out to the backyard, "but you're not allowed to wedgie a girl."

"Sure you are!" I exploded. "Girls can be firefighters and senators and astronauts! They can get wedgies, too!"

As usual, my protests fell on deaf ears. They wrapped the back of my underwear over a fence post and hung me there, struggling and freezing. Through the frosted windows I could make out Kelly Marie — toasty warm — still raving about psychology.

Milo was the one who got me down. I was really impressed by the fact that he saw me hanging for only about five minutes before coming to rescue me.

I decided to play up the friendship angle. "Thanks, pal," I said when I was on the ground again. "You sure came through for me there!"

Milo looked stricken. "I just can't believe *any* of this!"

"I know," I sympathized. "Who would've thought a chicken could get so sick?"

"Not *that*!" he cried. "I mean, why is everybody *here*? The experiment suffered a setback and I'm dealing with it. That's all."

I shrugged. "I guess they're worried about Henrietta."

"Worry has no medical value!" raged Milo. "Kelly Marie

has taken over my house! Joey has red eyes from pining over Lynette and my specimen! My mother just sent him up to take a nap in *my* bed! The hockey team is eating us out of house and home! How is *that* supposed to help a sick chicken?"

Secretly, I was celebrating. Milo *never* opened up like this to anybody. It probably meant we were turning into really close friends. I manufactured a sigh of shared suffering. "These guys, they just don't understand the science way like we do."

In my mind, we weren't freezing in Milo's yard. We were sipping coconut frostees at Victor Neal's pool while Samuel L. Jackson begged me to let him play President Zot. With stuff like that to look forward to, what's a wedgie here and there?

In the meantime, I planned to take my revenge in little ways. On Monday, the Rangers had to play without Henrietta. If they stank, it meant they were going straight down the drain the instant Milo put his project into the final phase.

And I intended to be there — in the front row with my dad's trumpet — to root big-time, heart and soul, rah! rah! for the other team.

Fade to black . . .

15

RANGERS UPDATE: CAPTAIN ADAM LURIE REPORTING

Okay, I admit it wasn't Zachary's fault that we couldn't beat the worst team in the league. We had nobody to blame but ourselves that we wound up in a 5–5 tie with Mount Carmel, the state joke since Coach Crenshaw was a Ranger.

Fine. We played lousy. For some crazy reason we were useless without our mascot. But to suffer the added humiliation of one of our own South Middle School students cheering for Mount Carmel — that loser — worse, the number one expert Professor of Loserology at Loser U — it was too much! It was the end!

So I arrived at school on Tuesday with a mission — Dweebicide. Zachary was a dead loser. Then I was going to find Milo and tell him that Henrietta was coming to our next game even if she was in the final stages of bubonic plague. I didn't care if she was on a stretcher with a breathing tube in her beak and an IV sticking out of her wing. The Rangers weren't setting blade to ice without our chicken.

I found Zachary at a cafeteria table, poring over one of his stupid screenplays. It would have been smart to sneak up on the little Benedict Loser, but I was so mad I just blurted out, "You're dead, man!"

He grabbed the script and bolted. I must say that, for a loser, he was pretty fast. But no sixth-grader was going to outrun a varsity athlete, and I had payback on my mind.

"Heads up!" I called, hurdling some eighth-graders who were working on a big poster. My foot cleared the tall girl's head by a quarter of an inch. I hit the floor running and did a quick spin-o-rama around the band teacher, who was carrying a tuba under each arm. It slowed me down a little, but I still caught sight of Zachary disappearing into the far stairwell. That meant he was probably heading for science class.

I flew down the stairs three at a time and pelted into the lab. There I saw exactly what I expected to see — Zachary doing the Gustafson Shuffle right behind Mrs. Baggio. I was breathing hard and seeing red. My eyes must have been bulging out of my head.

"Adam—" The Bag turned to me angrily. I was nailed for sure when Kelly Marie's voice rose above the general hum:

"Look! It's Henrietta!"

I wheeled. There was Milo, carrying that beautiful, adorable, *essential* chicken!

"She's okay again?" I asked as the class burst into cheers and applause.

"Dr. Siltinen said the specimen has made a one hundred percent recovery," Milo announced. "I've weighed her and considering the—"

"*Hello, sweetie!*" shrieked Kelly Marie, making an end run and yanking the cage from Milo's hands. "Everybody missed you *so much*! You look *wonderful*!"

I figured I'd better get it spelled out. "I mean, she's okay to come to the rink, right?"

"If you're *very* careful with her," Milo said grudgingly.

Henrietta squawked and the whole class crowded around her.

"Look how much she's grown!"

"She's smiling! She's happy to be back!"

"See, Henrietta? I'm wearing your favorite shirt!"

"Look how many new feathers she's got!"

Even the Bag joined the admiration society. She and Kelly Marie placed the chicken back in the pen amidst the get-well cards from almost every homeroom in the school.

The class stood around like proud parents as Henrietta began poking and prodding the cards with her beak and taking the occasional bite out of the daisies Lynette had brought over.

That was when I made my move. I cornered Zachary behind the Mars globe and lifted him up by his collar. "Well, Loser, I hear you're a big hockey fan — for Mount Carmel Junior High!"

Naturally, the dweeb tried to weasel out of it. "It wasn't me! It was somebody else!"

"If you wanted to keep a low profile," I growled, "you should have left the trumpet at home!"

"You've got me all wrong!" Zachary blubbered. "I was *for* you guys! Go Rangers!"

"Well, it's too bad you won't be able to cheer us on anymore," I snarled. "If I see your ugly face within a mile of the rink, get ready to eat a snow cone out of the Zamboni!"

The dweeb flushed with anger. "Who wants to see your crummy old team?"

I lifted him up another foot and braced him against the Henrietta feeding sign-up sheet. "You take that back! The Rangers are going all the way this year!"

"Oh, yeah?" Dweeb-asaurus was getting brave. "You couldn't even win against a last-place team like Mount Carmel!"

"Hah!" I cried. "With our mascot, we're unbeatable!"

Zachary's eyes narrowed. An evil grin appeared on that smarmy face. "Well, how long do you think you're going to have her?" he taunted, pointing over at Henrietta. "Look at her! She's almost full grown! As soon as she's an adult chicken, Milo's going to kill her and serve her up at the science fair!"

This came at a lull in the conversation, so Zachary's last words echoed through the lab as if they'd been broadcast over loudspeakers. A gasp went up like all the air was being sucked out of the room. I dropped the dweeb like a hot potato. All eyes turned from Zachary and me to Henrietta to Milo.

"Milo, is it true?" quavered Sheila Martel in disbelief.

"Of course not!" scoffed Kelly Marie. "How could it be true?"

But I took one look at Mrs. Baggio's stricken face and I knew something was wrong.

"Certainly it's true," Milo said. He seemed totally amazed that we even had to ask. "My project is on the food chain. The specimen is food. I've explained it several times."

"This isn't funny!" snapped Kelly Marie nervously. "Mrs. Baggio, make him cut it out!"

The Bag ordered everyone to their seats. "All right," she said, walking up and down in front of us. "This has gone far enough. We've all sort of adopted Henrietta as class pet. But let us never forget that she is Milo's project. The plan for her has always been the same: Throughout her life we have given her food. That food did not merely disappear. By the science of the food chain, it helped her grow from a chick to a hen. And it will resurface when the meat is eaten at the science fair."

The place went nuts. Everybody started babbling all at the same time. Kelly Marie was out of control, screaming at the top of her lungs. I guess I was pretty loud myself. Sheila was in tears, and Zachary was trying to offer support to Milo, who was shell-shocked. Even in the total chaos, Superdweeb couldn't resist the opportunity to suck up.

The Bag had climbed on top of the teacher's desk and was waving her arms in a desperate attempt to restore order. Fat chance. If St. Martin had been selected by the Air Force for target bombing, the class couldn't have been more upset.

Henrietta darted around her coop, knocking over get-well cards in agitation. You'd almost think she knew that she'd just been invited to lunch as the main course.

As for me, I was the most miserable guy in the place. How many times in the history of sports has a team lost a championship because somebody killed and ate their mascot?

It was Kelly Marie who finally shut us up, and she did it with a voice that would have put an air raid siren to shame:

"Quiet! QUI–ET!!!"

Silence fell. Even the Bag sat down. Kelly Marie faced

Milo in a gunfighter's stance. If looks could kill, California Boy would have made it to the cemetery in plenty of time to greet his chicken.

"Milo Neal," she began in a raspy voice that none of us even recognized. "The science fair is in less than three weeks. Are you telling me that Henrietta has two-and-a-half weeks to live?"

Milo looked pretty shaken as he spent too much time adjusting his Bertrand St. Rene glasses. "More or less," he admitted. "You have to allow time for Arno's Butcher Shop to prepare the meat."

"But class—" Mrs. Baggio made a feeble attempt to regain control.

"Don't worry, everybody!" Kelly Marie overpowered her. "It is *never* going to happen! Not in a million years!"

16

"PSYCHOLOGY TALK"
BY KELLY MARIE GINSBERG

Dear Mr. Delong,

As our principal, you're a pretty busy man, so maybe you don't know that Milo Neal is planning a brutal murder at your school . . .

I paused in front of my dad's typewriter. Was the wording strong enough? I really needed to get his attention. I signed the letter and frowned. Maybe Mr. Delong would think that stopping Milo would be meddling in Mrs. Baggio's class. A lot of principals didn't like to do that. With Henrietta's life hanging in the balance, I couldn't risk it. I had to go to a higher authority.

Dear Mayor Troy,

I'm writing for your help to stop a heinous crime in St. Martin . . .

While sealing the envelope, I thought it over. The mayor was one of those idiots who considered it great PR for the town that Victor Neal's son was growing up here. I remembered his picture in the paper right beside Milo and his mom when they first moved back. Would he have the guts to step in against Milo?

Dear Congressman Kovacs,

I know it's a long flight from Washington and kind of scary with blizzard season coming up. But you are desperately needed here to save a life . . .

I pledged my entire Thanksgiving weekend to writing letters and making phone calls. Milo and his mom went down to Minneapolis to stay with relatives, so there was no point in picketing on their lawn. Mrs. Baggio had Henrietta; I left sixteen messages on her answering machine.

"Kelly!" my father called. "What happened to all the stamps?"

"Just take it out of my allowance," I said readily.

The phone rang and I picked it up. It was Sheila from

science class. "Kelly Marie," she said, "would you be willing to sign a petition to save Henrietta?"

"That's a great idea!" I exclaimed.

"It wasn't mine," she admitted. "I got it from Joey and Lynette."

"Joey and Lynette?" I repeated. "I thought they hated each other!"

"They were both so worried about Henrietta that they realized how short life can really be," Sheila explained. "They got back together and formed SMASH."

"SMASH?"

"Stop Milo And Save Henrietta. Aren't you a member?"

"Sign me up!" I cried. Deep inside, I doubted that a couple of airheads like Joey and Lynette could work up anything that might help Henrietta. But on the other hand, maybe two half-wits make up a whole. Anyway, the more people you had banging the drum, the better the chance of it reaching the right ear. Which gave me an idea:

Dear Governor Hutchinson,

Some say that a society is judged by how it treats its weakest citizen. Well, what could be weaker than a chicken . . . ?

"Kelly," my mom called, "hurry up! We're going over to Grandma's!"

"I'm not going," I replied.

"What?" There were footsteps pounding up the stairs and then my mom appeared in my doorway. "Aren't you feeling well?"

I looked at her earnestly. "Mom, what if at Grandma's I get this brilliant idea that would save Henrietta, but by the time I come home, I've forgotten it?"

She perched on the edge of my desk. "Now, Kelly, dear, we agree that the Neal boy's project goes too far. But that's up to Mrs. Baggio and the school, not to me and not to you. Besides, you're not a baby anymore. This happens. You remember when our spaniel died?"

"Mom, Oliver got run over by a station wagon. Nobody ate him!"

She sighed. "We can bring Dad's laptop computer to Grandma's. So if you have a breakthrough, you can jot it down."

She obviously didn't think I would take her up on it. But when Grandpa placed that cooked bird on the Thanksgiving table and started carving, I pushed my plate aside and powered up.

Dear Minnesota Chapter ASPCA,

Do you handle chickens? If so I have a tale to tell that will simply break your heart . . .

I attended the SMASH meeting at Lynette's house after the Rangers got home from their road trip on Saturday. The players were pretty up because they'd just scored a big win against a strong team from Rochester.

You didn't have to be a psychologist to figure out that Adam and those lunkheads cared a lot more about winning than they did about Henrietta, but I kept my mouth shut. I needed the Rangers on Henrietta's side.

"Milo wouldn't let us take Henrietta to an away game," Steve grumbled. "He's still mad about the party!"

"Look who's talking!" shrilled Lynette. "*He's* going to cook her for lunch and he's worried *we* won't take care of her!"

"So you guys won without Henrietta?" I asked in disbelief.

Steve shook his head. "She was there. But Milo had to come, too."

Adam grinned. "We stuck him on the bus beside Dee-Vee. Three hours of slap shot details."

"Serves him right," I grimaced. "I'd like to send *Milo* to the butcher shop!"

"I say he should be our target," Lafayette agreed. "Let's see him finish his science project with two broken arms!"

"Chill out," said Adam of all people. Since he was such a hockey nut, I figured he'd be screaming for Milo's blood louder than anybody else. "You can't hold it against Milo. He honestly thought we all knew what happens at the end of his project. And, face it — every time we started getting attached to the chicken, he warned us not to. He didn't even want us to name her."

"It's true," said Brendan mournfully. "He must have said it a million times: 'A chicken is not a pet; a chicken is a chicken.' We didn't listen."

"Oh, shut up!" I snapped. "So he told us! That makes it right? Milo doesn't matter! The science fair doesn't matter! Your stupid hockey team doesn't matter! The only thing that matters is Henrietta!"

Dear Mr. Arno,

I happen to be a vegetarian and wouldn't eat meat if you paid me. But sometime in the middle of December, Milo Neal is going to bring you a chicken. I don't know how much money you butchers earn. But whatever Milo is paying you, I'll give you double not to kill it. Just bring the chicken to the above address. And whatever you do, don't tell Milo . . .

I lay awake Sunday night, tossing and turning. I wracked my brain. Had I done everything possible? Had I written everyone who had any power whatsoever to save Henrietta? Could there be a stone left unturned? An avenue unexplored? An authority I could still appeal to?

And then it came to me.

Dear Victor Neal,

I won't take up too much of your time because I know you must be pretty busy being a TV star and a scientific genius.

I am writing because I think you should know that your son has a big brain but a very small heart. And if he kills Henrietta, everybody in school is going to hate him. Please hurry. The science fair is on December 14th, but Henrietta could die any day now. You've got to do something!

Yours anxiously,
Kelly Marie Ginsberg
PS: Henrietta is a chicken.

17

EXPERIMENT NOTES: MILO NEAL
12/07

> I admit I was nervous about fitting in when I moved to St. Martin. But even in my wildest nightmares I never expected to be Public Enemy #1 by Christmas.

> Yet here I was, Milo the Merciless, heartless cold-blooded killer of poor defenseless small animals, chickens a specialty.

{How did I get into this mess? Was it my fault? Was it everybody else's?/further study req'd.}

> I kept analyzing the chain of events to try to detect the link where I went wrong. I mean, I did my proj. following the scientific method step by step. And now the whole school was up in arms over their "darling Henrietta." Logic

says that someone must be crazy here. The question = Was it me?

{In Los Angeles the life of one little chicken wouldn't cause this much ruckus. But this ≠ Los Angeles. I noticed that when the temperature went down to eleven below zero last night!!!}

> Still, the Minnesota winter was balmy compared with the deep freeze I had to face every day at school. It had gone way beyond our little science class. The halls were plastered with SAVE HENRIETTA posters. Mr. Delong and the staff took them all down, but by 9:00 the next morning, they'd be up again. I saw one that featured my picture from the *Sentinel*, doctored up to make me look like a medieval executioner holding a giant beheading ax. Another said MILO with a red line through it, like a no smoking sign. Everywhere I looked, something about "chicken rights" was staring back at me. On Monday morning, we were all welcomed back from Thanksgiving weekend by a giant banner over the front entrance of the school: MAKE FRIENDS NOT CUTLETS.

> Didn't it figure? Even in a windchill of -40°, I couldn't get sick enough to miss a day of school.

> The only person who would walk with me, talk to me, and sit with me in the cafeteria was ZG. Just my luck. If there was anyone in all of St. Martin I'd have enjoyed being ignored by, it was him. He called it "friend loyalty,"

and although I had a bit of a problem with the "friend" part, he was definitely loyal.

"It's not your fault everybody else was too stupid to understand your project," he told me several times that miserable week.

> Heaven help me — I was so shaken up that I appreciated having ZG to confide in.

"I don't know. Maybe it *is* my fault," I said. "Everybody else sees something special in that chicken."

"Not everybody," ZG offered. "I don't."

"Yes you do," I countered. "They see something to love; you see something to hate. I just see a link in the food chain. Why am I the only one?"

"Well," said ZG thoughtfully. "Have you tried?"

"Tried what?"

"Getting to know Henrietta."

"There's nothing to get to know!" I exploded.

> But that day after school, locked in my room, I made an effort. I sat cross-legged on the floor and stared into the cage. What I saw was really quite impressive. The creature that had been a tiny wisp of fluff a scant two months ago was now covered in lustrous white feathers. Her red comb was well-defined, and in spite of the setback, she was plump and healthy. She'd been on a full diet for two weeks now. In fact, my calculations had been remarkably accurate. The subj. was now a fully grown hen, ready for the dinner table—

> Wait a minute. The logical scientific approach was exactly what I was trying to avoid here. I needed to be totally emotional about this if I was going to see what other people saw.

> I said, "Okay, Henrietta—" Yes, I broke my own rule and called the spec. Henrietta, "Okay . . . uh . . . sweetie, strut your stuff."

> She clucked, she twitched, and she bobbed her head up and down like chickens do. There was no recognition of me as the caregiver. None of the personality KMG seemed to see, no sign of the keen intelligence so obvious to JS, not a trace of the fun-loving *joie de vivre* that won LM's heart. I didn't feel inspired like the hockey team. I didn't even observe anything to dislike, à la ZG. She was, all things considered, a chicken — subj., spec., link in the food chain, the wind beneath nobody's wings.

> CONCLUSION: I'm not the one out of step with the band; they're all out of step with me.

> There was a knock on my bedroom door. I leaped to my feet as my mother let herself in. "Milo, may I have a word with you?"

{A word usually meant five hundred thousand million words +/- 10%/further study req'd.}

"Sure, Mom. What's up?"

"I just got off the phone with Mr. Delong," she said worriedly. "He told me what's been going on at school.

And he suggested I talk to you about changing the experiment."

I stuck out my jaw. "How?"

"By eliminating the part where you eat Henrietta."

"That *is* the experiment, Mom!" I exclaimed. "There *is* nothing else! I can't change it!"

"You mean you won't."

I tried to be patient. "If you order a cheeseburger, hold the bun, hold the cheese, hold the meat, you've got a handful of nothing, right? Well, that's what you're left with when you have a food chain experiment that defies the food chain!"

My mother sighed. "Mr. Delong said the whole school is up in arms over your project. Some of the kids are so upset that their parents are calling the office to complain. They've even had a call from the *Sentinel*. Milo, I grew up in St. Martin. It's not like Los Angeles, where something like this would barely be noticed. These are nice, warm people — but if this story gets around, you may never live it down! Please, just this once I want you to give in."

I folded my arms in front of me. "And take an incomplete in science?"

"Mr. Delong said you'd get an A. And they'd still pick you for the science fair."

"It would be an incomplete to *me*!" I insisted. "They

could give me Dad's Nobel Prize and it would still be for an unfinished project!"

She looked at me very seriously. "I admire your integrity, but I think you're making a big mistake over something that's just not that important." And she let herself quietly out of my room.

> Mom has a nasty habit of cutting the legs out from under you just when you think you're on solid ground.

> I looked to the cage and this time I really wanted it. I truly, honestly was dying to see even the slightest indication that there was somebody in there. The specimen twitched and warbled. Nobody home.

> Deep down, I knew Mom was right. I was as cooked as the subj. was going to be. Except — here in St. Martin, all I had of my dad was the stuff he taught me about experiments and scientific method. I was out of his life completely. But if I could win the science fair, that = one huge reminder that I was his son. I would almost be following in his footsteps! Maybe then he'd call more often and come to see me — even invite me back to California for a long visit.

> This was more than a science fair to me. It = a chance to start over with my father.

> Even with all the tension at home and at school, nothing compared to the pure, unadulterated agony of the hockey games. I couldn't very well relinquish my subj. to those

well-meaning lunatics. Which meant that I had to accompany the spec. to the rink. I suppose I could have refused. But I was so hated already, I didn't dare make things worse. There I'd sit, LM despising me on the left, KMG reviling me from the right, watching a sport that made as much sense to me as a pet rock.

So I didn't complain too much when AL told me that Saturday's game would be in Fairmont, about thirty miles away. And when I found out that this match would determine the South Minnesota championship, I allowed myself a faint glimmer of hope. Please, oh please let the team win! Then they'd be happy, they'd no longer need my chicken, and maybe, just maybe that might ease some of the pressure at school.

> The bus ride was pure torture — thirty minutes in a confined space with large people who hated me. It was far worse than the games themselves, where the players' dirty looks were covered by their visors. At one point I heard LH trying to convince DeeVee to take a slap shot at my head.

> I didn't think it was very funny, but it drew a big guffaw from Coach C. "Are you kidding? If Vincent could aim that thing, he'd be in the NHL!"

"I don't have to be here at all—" I announced to the bus.

"Who sent for you?" came a chorus of snarls from above the shoulder pads.

"—and neither does this cage," I finished.

Coach C broke the unpleasant standoff. "All right, listen

up," he ordered. "You all know where we stand. Fairmont's in first place with a record of fourteen and five. We're half a game behind them at thirteen and five with one tie. Which means a tie still leaves us in second place. We have to go for the win."

"We're gonna crush those guys!" roared LH, and the entire team joined in a bloodcurdling roar. The coach beamed with pride.

> Why did athletes feel the need to rampage like gorillas in order to prepare for a game?/further study req'd. I had a vision of the Fairmont Flyers in *their* locker room, beating their breasts and howling in honor of our arrival.

> Their fans were certainly in a state of high excitement. I was appalled by the hostile reaction the Rangers received when they took the ice.

But when I mentioned it to Coach C, he looked at me as if I'd just arrived from Mars. "They're *supposed* to hate us, Neal! We're the other team!"

"Ah," I replied. "Much like the resentment of rival scientists when my father won his Nobel Prize."

> His response was a look blank enough to use as a billboard.

> Before the opening face-off, I had to hold my spec. over the bench so the players could bonk their helmets into the cage and run their sticks along the bars.

"Go get 'em, Henrietta," breathed AL, his face so intense it was almost scary.

"It's all up to you, girl," added JS.

{Was I missing something? How was it possible for my subj. to influence the outcome of a sporting event? Especially when she was in a cage, outside the field of play/ further study req'd.}

> Of course, I was not the best person to judge a game of ice hockey. What I saw best resembled a riot on ice. Upon closer inspection, I discovered the puck, which told the combatants whom to brutalize. When somebody scored, his entire team would perform the Minnesota equivalent of an earthquake. I got the impression that these two schools were evenly matched, since the earthquakes took place equally often on each bench.

> How was it that I could understand high-level science but couldn't make heads or tails of the chaos on the ice?/ further study req'd. I concentrated on the scoreboard. At least that way I would know who was winning. Although it looked like nobody was going to win this game. When the clock ticked down to the final minute, the score was deadlocked 7–7.

> I suppose it was the thought that the season was nearly over that induced me to try to make up with the hockey team. "Congratulations on a well-played game," I called down to the bench. "You can be really proud of a tie against such a strong opponent."

The coach stared at me. "Neal, are you out of your mind?"

"Milo, you big dope!" AL shouted up at me. "A tie does us *nothing*! We need a win or Fairmont takes the championship!"

Coach C shifted into high gear. "Lurie, Sorrentino, get in there! Pull the goalie! Put Hughes in the slot! Tell Tenorio to pinch!"

> No, I don't have a clue what any of that meant. When the puck was dropped, all that strategy boiled down to this: Both teams stampeded the Fairmont net. They met with a resounding crunch that shook the building. There they lay, piled up like sandbags, three feet in front of the empty Flyers goal.

> There was an enormous gasp from the crowd. Maybe they were searching for the puck, which had disappeared under the mountain of fallen players. Silence followed as the Rangers looked on in desperation, their championship hopes down to the final dwindling seconds on the clock.

> And suddenly there it was! At the edge of the pile, just beyond AL's shoulder — the puck!

"Adam, behind you!" I shouted.

> Lying flat on his stomach under two Fairmont players, AL pulled his stick around, sliding it blindly along the ice. It batted into the puck with a tiny clink. Slowly — agonizingly slowly — the puck trickled over the goal line into the net.

The buzzer sounded to end the game. Final score: 8–7 for the South Minnesota champion Rangers.

★★★

"But Adam!" I insisted for the twentieth time on the bus ride home. "It was me! *I* was the one who yelled, 'Behind you!'"

> I don't know why I cared so much. Maybe I felt that if I was going to get involved in anything as meaningless as an ice hockey game, I should at least get some credit for it.

"Milo, give it a rest," AL groaned, absently stroking my spec.'s feathers. For some reason, they had switched places between their trophy and my chicken. The championship cup was locked in the cage. "You weren't even watching the game!"

"At the end I was!" I defended myself. "How else could I have seen the puck in the scramble?"

"Your voice is too high," JS insisted. "The guy who yelled was, you know, *deeper.*"

"A baritone," agreed Brendan.

"No, it was *higher,*" ST argued. "Higher, and kind of raspy, like an old guy."

"It was *me*!" I cried. {These hockey players could be maddeningly stubborn/further study req'd.}

AL handed my spec. over the seat and regarded me with genuine pity in his eyes. "You don't have to *lie*, Milo."

"If you're trying to make us love you, forget it," snarled LH. "Nobody will ever forgive you for what you're going to do to Henrietta!"

I sighed in defeat. "Well, at least she's not your mascot anymore. That ought to make it a little easier."

JS stared at me. "Are you nuts?"

I spread my arms wide. "The season just ended!"

AL faced me. "Milo, we're South Minnesota champions! We have to play the Canadians next Saturday! We can't face them without Henrietta!"

"But — but —" I stammered. I couldn't remember being at such a loss for words since the day my parents told me they were splitting up. "But the science fair is next Saturday. The specimen won't — I mean, she can't—" A chorus of outrage cut me off.

> Next year my science proj. isn't going to involve any type of life form unless it's already dead before it can develop a fan club. The total irony was that, if I had kept my eyes on the scoreboard instead of the ice, I never would have spotted that loose puck. Ergo, I couldn't have shouted to AL, and the clock *and* the season would have expired with the score still tied 7–7. No championship, no Canadians, no date with destiny for my chicken.

> It was undeniable. Victor Neal's son, the genius-in-training, had grown up to be the biggest idiot on the face of the earth.

> Maybe I was adopted/further study req'd.

18

DOWNLOADED FROM THE FILES OF ZACHARY GUSTAFSON

HORRORDOME

[SCENE 4]

[INTERIOR: Goodyear blimp — day]

High above the Enormo-Dome, the brilliant but warped evil scientist DR. DEMENTO finishes tying up the BLIMP PILOT.

PILOT

You'll never get away with this! You're demented!

DR. DEMENTO

No, I'm Dement-*o*!

He stuffs a gag in the PILOT's mouth and throws his head back in terrifying maniacal laughter.

[POINT-OF-VIEW SHOT: Far below, thousands of people, like ants, stream into the 100,000-seat stadium.]

DR. DEMENTO

Poor unsuspecting fools! I'll fill their "Super Bowl" with the hot soup of terror!

As the last few stragglers enter the stadium, he presses a red button.

The giant retractable roof of the stadium slams shut and all entrances seal automatically. A hundred thousand people are trapped!

I rubbed my hands together with glee. This stuff practically wrote itself! This was going to be my best screenplay ever! Dr. Demento was a truly memorable character. I could easily see a whole series of movies: *Horrordome II: The Carnage Continues*; *Horrordome III: The Meadowlands Massacre*; the possibilities were endless.

Perfect timing, too. Pretty soon I'd be close enough to Milo to ask his dad to show my work around in Hollywood. Spilling the beans about Henrietta croaking was one of my smarter moves. I can't believe I didn't think of it sooner! How do you get to be somebody's best friend? By making everyone else in the world hate him! It was friendship by default. Milo was alone like a dog except for me.

I know that sounds cold. But I was a good friend to Milo.

For instance, I told him about the time I wet my pants at Disney World, because friends always share their deepest secrets. He's probably going to tell me something important, too. I went over to his house every day that week. I mean, the guy needed the support. Even his own mother wanted to stop him from whacking Henrietta. I give him credit, though. He was brave. Every single day he tried to talk me out of coming, saying it wasn't necessary and stuff.

"Oh, it's no problem," I told him. "I'm here for you, buddy." He just groaned with gratitude.

School was the toughest of all. It wasn't easy sharing a classroom with a doomed chicken. The air in the lab crackled with tension and heartbreak and anger. Every few minutes, someone would look over at Henrietta poking around in her coop and freak out, or burst into tears, or launch into yet another plea for mercy.

They all knew Henrietta was close to the end, because the science fair was on Saturday. But Mrs. Baggio banned all Henrietta talk, and Milo wouldn't say when he was taking that lousy chicken over to Arno's Butcher Shop. So nobody knew when "it" was going to happen.

I did, of course. I read it right off Mrs. Neal's kitchen calendar last night. There it was, in bright red ink under Wednesday — *Arno's 4 P.M.*

Milo caught me snooping and swore me to secrecy.

"Hey, you can trust me, pal," I pledged.

Zachary Gustafson's word is as good as gold. I only slipped up once, but I think I got away with it.

I committed the strategic error of being in the washroom at the same time as Adam on Tuesday before science. As usual, he started getting on my case about taking Milo's side against his stupid Rangers. I wasn't in the mood for another wedgie, so I told him to mind his own business.

"It *is* my business!" he snapped back. "It's the captain's business to make sure our mascot is safe!"

So help me, I couldn't resist. "After tomorrow," I assured him, "you won't have to worry anymore."

I left him standing there in the can. I was positive he didn't understand what I meant. These hockey players aren't too bright, you know.

Just to be sure, I kept an eye on him in class. He was looking back at Henrietta a lot. Did he suspect anything? Probably not. Everybody was looking at Henrietta — everybody except Milo.

Mrs. Baggio was still trying to run this like a normal class. The science projects were starting to come in, but it was taking forever to present them. Sheila sobbed her way through her project on bats, never once taking her eyes off the chicken coop in the corner.

"*Bravo!*" Kelly Marie leaped to her feet, applauding madly. "That's the greatest science project I've ever seen in my life! Mrs. Baggio, 'Bats' should be our class entry for the science fair."

"It's awesome!" Adam chimed in. "I never knew science could be so exciting!"

By then the whole class was clued in. They were clapping and chanting, "Bats! Bats! Bats! . . ."

I sprang up. "This is stupid! They don't think 'Bats' is any good. They just want someone else to go to the science fair instead of Milo so there's no sense cooking Henrietta!" I sat down amidst a shower of spitballs and jeers.

Mrs. Baggio put on a brave face. "The student who goes to the science fair will be the one who hands in the best work. And that decision won't be made until all the projects are in."

She was in for a long wait because I hadn't started mine yet. It wasn't that I was lazy; I just didn't have the guts to ask Mrs. Baggio to remind me what my topic was. But I wasn't worried. I'd whip something up at three o'clock in the morning on the last day. How hard could it be for the best friend of Victor Neal's son?

[INTERIOR: Enormo-Dome – day]

Halftime at the Super Bowl. The MARCHING BAND is on the field. MAJORETTES are twirling batons. The CROWD is clapping along.

[INTERIOR: Goodyear blimp – day]

DR. DEMENTO prepares for the final phase of his sinister experiment.

DR. DEMENTO

They called me mad when I proposed the transmutation of matter! But I'll show them all! They'll see that Myron Demento is nobody's fool!

> He flips a giant switch.
>
> [INTERIOR: Enormo-Dome – day]
>
> There is a brilliant flash and a thunderclap. The cheering sound has changed to a high-pitched warble. The music stops; the instruments fall to the Astroturf.
>
> The smoke clears to reveal the stadium, filled with 100,000 chickens. Chickens fill the stands. The BAND and MAJORETTES have changed into chickens. Chickens wait in line at the concession stands. In the broadcast booth, chicken COMMENTATORS cluck into the microphones. The TEAMS try to take the field but, now chickens, they can barely move inside their helmets. Chicken REFEREES flop about, lost in giant striped shirts . . .

Whoa!

It was happening again! More chickens! A hundred thousand of them this time!

In a cold sweat, I switched off the computer. Was I losing my mind? Just when I needed to be in peak writing form, my whole style was going to the dogs! Or, at the very least, the chickens! How could I give Victor Neal a screenplay full of chickens?

Okay, calm down, I told myself. It was only the big ruckus at school giving me chickens on the brain. Tomorrow Milo would take Henrietta to Arno's and it was a one-way trip. She'd be gone — from my life *and* my writing. Aloha, my feathered friend.

What a beautiful thought! Only — it had seemed a lot more beautiful when it wasn't happening *tomorrow.*

I struggled into my pajamas, figuring I'd go to bed really early and sleep off this weird feeling. But when I was all tucked in and the lights were out, it wasn't any better. I kept seeing Henrietta — and an ax — and a rotating spit. I should have been overjoyed about this. I hated the chicken and the chicken hated me. This was the perfect ending to a horrible relationship, especially since I wasn't the one who was going to die.

Get a grip, Zachary!

Every time I closed my eyes I saw that silly red craw that wiggled when she walked on those stupid chicken feet; that annoying squawk echoed in my head; those beady eyes stared at me — reproachfully—

And I knew, as sure as Hollywood is in California, that if I let Henrietta die, she was going to haunt me for the rest of my life.

I jumped out of bed and started throwing on clothes. Fade to black . . .

19

RANGERS UPDATE: CAPTAIN ADAM LURIE REPORTING

After tomorrow you won't have to worry anymore.

That was what the dweeb said. But what did it mean? Was Milo planning to back off and let the chicken live? That didn't sound like Milo. And it definitely didn't sound like a twenty-time recipient of the Congressional Medal of Losers. No, Zachary meant I wouldn't have to worry because there would be no more chicken to worry about. Tomorrow was execution day!

Well, I didn't know if Henrietta was special or just some Joe Blow chicken off any farm. But I was sure of one thing: I had to save the team. And saving the team meant saving the bird.

So that's what I was doing when I headed for the school at eight o'clock Tuesday night. Chicken napping.

I knew the janitor's entrance would be unlocked until the custodian left around nine. The tricky part was avoiding Mr. Farr as I crept through the maze of tall storage shelves and slipped into the main hallway of the school. Mr. Farr was a nice guy, but I didn't want to have to explain what I was doing there. This was exactly the kind of caper that could get you kicked off the team.

It went so smoothly that I let down my guard and I almost missed it. For there, in the gleaming wetness of the freshly mopped floor, was a trail of sneaker footprints. I frowned. It definitely wasn't Mr. Farr — the prints were too small. It didn't make sense. There weren't any clubs or teams that met on Tuesday nights. Who, besides me, was sneaking around the school?

Keeping a sharp eye out for Mr. Farr, I followed the trail. It stretched past the gym, through the math wing — I froze. The intruder, whoever it was, was heading for the science lab.

Panicking, I picked up speed and made for the Bag's room on the dead run. As I raced around the last corner, I never saw the foot that tripped me.

To say I flew forty feet would be exaggerating, but not by much.

WUMP!

I hit the ground and saw stars. When my vision cleared, the person standing over me was Kelly Marie.

She was smiling. "Adam," she said proudly, "you came to save Henrietta."

I sat up and faced her. "That's what I was doing before some *total maniac* tried to kill me!"

She hauled me up. "Well, I couldn't tell it was you until you were flat on your face already." It was perfect commando logic.

"How did you know tonight was the last chance?" I asked. "Did the dweeb spill his guts to you, too?"

"I got my mom to call Arno's and say she was Mrs. Neal," Kelly Marie admitted. "They confirmed the appointment for four o'clock tomorrow."

"Right after school!" I gulped. The Rangers were that close to losing our mascot! "Come on, let's go get her."

We ran into the lab together and stood, side by side, staring in shock. The coop was empty.

I was pretty upset, but Kelly Marie went into a meltdown. Her face turned bright red and she began to hyperventilate, each breath making a high-pitched wheezing whistle.

"Not so loud!" I hissed. "Do you want Mr. Farr on our necks?"

"But where's Henrietta?"

"I don't know! How should I know?" I babbled, straining

to keep my voice down. "Unless Milo anticipated our move and took her home a day early."

It took a second to recognize her reaction, because it wasn't rage, or a tantrum, or a psychology lecture. Her lips trembled and tears rolled down her cheeks. Kelly Marie was *crying*!

I hate crying. "Cut that out," I ordered nervously.

"She's *go-o-o-one*!" she quavered.

Tears freak me out. For a moment, I even forgot about the Rangers and how much we needed Henrietta. I was *so* uncomfortable I didn't know where to look — up at the ceiling, out the window, down at the floor — I gawked.

"You're wearing your Doc Martens!"

She lost it on me. "How can you talk about shoes when we've lost Henrietta, you cold-hearted—"

"No, no, no!" I grabbed her by the shoulders. "The footprints I followed were sneaker prints! So they can't be yours! They had to be—"

"Milo's!" she finished breathlessly.

We both looked down. The tracks led from the doorway to the chicken wire, then away from the coop straight into Mrs. Baggio's equipment closet.

I was over there in two strides. "Okay, Milo, the jig's up. Come on out."

There was no answer, so Kelly Marie rushed up and flung open the door. But it wasn't Milo in there, clutching the struggling Henrietta to his chest. Among the beakers and experiment books cowered none other than His Royal Loserness, the gold medalist from the Loser Olympics, Zachary Gustafson.

"Are you taking her to Milo?" I accused.

"I'm rescuing her!" the dweeb insisted.

"Don't believe him," snarled Kelly Marie. "He hates Henrietta."

"Darn right," he said proudly. "But do you think I want to spend the rest of my life with *that* face on my conscience?" To prove his innocence, he handed the bird to Kelly Marie.

As a parting shot, Henrietta took a swipe at him with her claw.

"Ow!"

I clamped my hand over the dweeb's mouth. "Pipe down and let's get out of here!" I grabbed a blanket and wrapped it around our mascot.

Once outside the school, we paused to consider Henrietta's future.

"I'll take her," Kelly Marie said immediately.

"You're the first person Milo will suspect," I told her. "And I'm the second." I turned to face Zachary.

"No way!" cried Kelly Marie. "I refuse to leave Henrietta with someone who hates her!"

"She hated me first!" whined Zachary.

"It's perfect," I argued. "Everybody knows Zack and Henrietta hate each other. Plus he's such a big suck-up that no one would believe he'd ever go against Milo."

"That's not fair!" said Zachary hotly. "Milo and I have a genuine friendship!"

Kelly Marie addressed the bird. "It's okay, sweetie. He may be a complete idiot, but he isn't going to let anybody hurt you." She shook her fist at the dweeb. "Right, Zachary?"

I glanced at my watch. It was almost nine. "Let's get home before our parents start thinking something's up."

I looked into Superloser's shifty eyes. "The Canadians game is on Saturday afternoon. If anything happens to the bird between now and then, *you're* going to take her place at Arno's Butcher Shop."

20

DOWNLOADED FROM THE FILES OF ZACHARY GUSTAFSON

How would Steven Spielberg smuggle a chicken into the house with his mom right there in the kitchen? I tried to use my screenwriter's imagination. In a real Hollywood movie, I would parachute into the reservoir in frogman gear, swim until the pipes got too skinny, and then rocket straight in through my bedroom window using antigravity boots. But in cheapo St. Martin, I didn't have any of that stuff. So I went to the garage, stuffed Henrietta into a cardboard carton, and got psyched up to finesse my way into the house.

Mom was doing the dishes — with her back to the hall — so I made a mad dash for the stairs.

"Zachary—"

Caught!

"I was on the phone with Laura Walters tonight, and she mentioned Brendan is working on a science project. Aren't you in that class?" Then Mom turned around and noticed the box. "Oh — what have you got there?"

"It's . . . it's . . . my science project."

She beamed. "That's great, hon. What's the topic?"

At that moment, Henrietta started scrambling around. Thinking fast, I pretended to lose control of the box to cover the movement. But no one could think fast enough to explain the long feather that came flying out and drifted to the floor.

Mom stared. "Your project is on feathers?"

"Oh . . . of course not . . . ha, ha. That wouldn't be very scientific. It's on" — I wracked my brain — "pens."

She goggled. "Pens?"

"You know," I explained, "like the first pens used to be feathers? A history of pens."

"That's wonderful!" she approved. "In fact, I think Dad has a fountain pen that would be perfect for your display."

I manufactured a yawn. "Maybe I should call it a night, Mom. I'm pretty tired."

I was almost home free, halfway up the stairs, when that miserable chicken squawked.

Mom was on me again. "Did you say something, dear?"

"Just yawning, Mom. Man, I'm beat."

"Be sure to hold the box steady," she cautioned. "I think some of your pens are rolling around."

I sprinted up the stairs and stuffed Henrietta's box under the bed. I felt like I'd just been dragged forty miles by horses. But deep down I knew the hassles were only beginning.

***

Mrs. Baggio made an impassioned speech first thing Wednesday morning. "I know that some of you may think it was kind to steal Henrietta and hide her away. But please remember that a lot of work went into Milo's project, whatever your opinion of it. It isn't fair to have it snatched away at the last minute."

The interrogation continued with Mr. Delong. "Boys and girls, it's important that you realize this is a *crime*. Henrietta is *property*. If she's not returned, we'll have no choice but to call in the police."

Then Milo made a little speech, but he was pretty low-key. He just kind of apologized for upsetting everybody with his project. "When I moved to St. Martin, I didn't want to make people hate me. Considering who my dad is, you know that science is really important to me. So I hope that whoever has my specimen will let me complete the experiment."

You could tell he was pretty fried. His expression was

really downcast, and he headed home just before lunch, mumbling something about stomach cramps. I felt like worm guts, and Milo didn't even have to give me that look down his nose.

Kelly Marie shared none of my guilt. "Give me a break! Even now he's talking about 'the experiment' and 'the specimen.' To say he's a cold-hearted pig is an insult to pigs!"

"Don't blow it," Adam advised me. "The team knows you've got Henrietta, but everybody else is in the dark. So just play dumb. It should be easy for you."

You had to love that heartfelt gratitude.

In the halls at class changes, the name Henrietta was on everyone's lips. The relief was so thick that you could almost spread it on toast. There was a lot of speculation about the identity of the hero who saved Henrietta from the ax.

"It must be Kelly Marie. She's ballistic over that chicken!"

"It's got to be one of the Rangers! They stink without their mascot!"

"Mr. Delong snatched her to keep the peace at school."

"I'll bet Milo did it himself so he wouldn't have to kill her."

"No way! Lynette made Joey do it! The chicken's hidden in her attic!"

Notice that the name "Zachary Gustafson" never got

mentioned by anybody. Like I wasn't cool enough to kidnap a chicken! I hate this school!

Dewey seemed to think that Henrietta was some new kind of fellow baby. He loved to sit under my bed and peek at her through the airholes in the box. When I took her out, he'd try to flap his arms and squawk along with her. She liked him, too. Or at least she didn't try to peck his head off like she did to me.

I figured there wasn't any harm in it. I mean, the kid couldn't talk and tell Mom. And anyway, when Doomsday was mugging at that stupid bird, it kept him from bombing my computer. It was a whole new side of my baby brother. I'd always known he was homicidal, but now I saw he was stupid, too.

My dad came to the same conclusion at dinner on Thursday night. "What's wrong with the baby? He sounds like a chicken!"

My mother laughed. "He's just finding his voice."

"And the thing with the arms?"

I stepped in. "He's a baby, Dad. Babies do stuff like that."

Mom glowed with pride. She thought Doomsday and I were developing brotherly love. If she knew why—

My dad reached into his shirt pocket. "Here you go, Zachary. I brought a couple more pens for your project. Check out the green felt-tip. My boss's husband donated it to the cause."

"How's that project coming, anyway?" Mom asked. "You seem to be spending a lot of time locked in your room working on it."

"Oh, yeah!" I enthused. "It should be ready to hand in tomorrow." *Please don't ask to see it!*

The doorbell rang. My life was saved.

It was Kelly Marie. This was the fourth time in two days that she'd shown up on my doorstep. My folks were positive I had a girlfriend.

I took her up to my room to commune with "sweetie."

"Mr. Delong called the cops on me," she said, absently tapping Henrietta's beak with her Greenpeace pinky ring. "They sent this deputy over to my house to tell my parents I might be guilty of cattle rustling."

"Cattle rustling?" I repeated. "She's a chicken, not a cow!"

"It's just a bunch of legal mumbo jumbo," she shrugged. "Any theft of animals comes under this 1870 law that was written during the Old West days. Ignore it."

"That's easy for you to say," I pointed out. "You're not the one with the rustled cattle living under your bed!"

But she just played with Henrietta. The doorbell rang, and a moment later, another cattle rustler, Adam, joined us upstairs.

"Your folks went out to get some groceries. They took the little dweeb." He looked down at the chicken cradled in Kelly Marie's arms. "Hi, Henrietta. Ready for the Canadians?"

Kelly Marie bristled. "She's not going to that game! It isn't safe!"

"Hey!" Adam stuck out his jaw. "You might have saved this tweety-bird because you love her; *I* saved her for the Rangers."

"But she'll be caught!" Kelly Marie wrapped her arms protectively around Henrietta. "Someone'll see her on the bench and tell Milo!"

"We'll hide her in the spare equipment bag where we keep the extra pads," Adam explained. "No one'll see her."

"It's too risky!"

Adam folded his arms. "Either she goes to the big game or to Milo's." He added, "Tonight."

"You wouldn't!"

The doorbell interrupted the confrontation. I ran to the window and looked down at the porch. "It's Milo!"

"We've got to get out of here!" Adam exclaimed in a panic.

"Why?" asked Kelly Marie. "So we're visiting Zachary. Big deal."

"Get real! I'm on the *team*! I don't hang out with just anybody! A smart guy like Milo would see something was up!"

I started out of the room. "You two sit tight and shut

up. And that goes double for the chicken. I'll see what he wants."

I opened the door and let Milo in. He looked awful.

"Sorry to bother you, Zachary," he said sadly. "I just had to get out of the house. Not even my mom is on my side these days."

I hesitated. For months I'd been waiting for Milo to turn to me as a true friend. Now, finally, it was happening. But I had two cattle rustlers and a hot chicken stashed in my room, and all I could think of was how to get rid of him.

But Milo was already shrugging off his jacket. "Mrs. Baggio phoned me today. She asked me to go to the science fair anyway. She said I should serve Real Dixie Fried Chicken as a symbol of my specimen's place in the food chain."

We sat down in the kitchen.

"I thought she wasn't deciding who goes to the science fair until all the projects were finished," I commented.

"Well, they're all in except one," he replied. "I saw the sheet. Someone's doing infrared astronomy."

"Oh, no!" It hit me like a blow to the head. *That* was my topic! "Are you sure it didn't say, you know — 'Pens'?"

He blinked. "Pens? You mean ancient methods of written communication like hieroglyphics and cuneiform?"

"No, I mean pens — like Bic," I sighed. "And Paper Mate."

"Oh. Well, no, it was definitely infrared astronomy. Anyway, I've decided to go with the fried chicken thing."

"It sounds great," I managed, not really paying attention. I was wracking my brain to come up with a way to convince Mrs. Baggio that infrared astronomy really meant pens.

"I haven't got a prayer without my specimen," Milo groaned. "It's just that, if I won here and did well at state, I might have qualified for the national." His eyes took on a faraway look. "That's in L.A. this year. I could have visited my dad."

"That would be . . . uh . . . really . . . uh . . . great . . . uh . . ." I didn't even know what I was saying. Because over Milo's left shoulder I could see Adam and Kelly Marie tiptoeing down the stairs and sneaking out the side door.

Milo kept talking.

Fade to black . . .

21

EXPERIMENT NOTES: MILO NEAL
12/14

> Riddle: How many Minnesotans does it take to kidnap a chicken?

Answer: Just one. But . . . *who*?

> Okay, it wasn't very funny. But it got me through the three toughest days of my life. Days where every face in the school hall seemed like it could belong to a potential spec.-napper. Days where I couldn't walk past a simple innocent house in St. Martin without wondering if my subj. was being held within.

> The interesting part was that I didn't really care anymore. I no longer lay awake at night wondering if the culprit = KMG, AL, or Sheila M; JS and/or LM; a hockey player, or

some die-hard chicken activist I didn't even know. I forgave them all individually and blamed the town. St. Martin, Minnesota, killed my proj. It was the fault of this small frost-bitten city that I was about to pass off a bucket of Real Dixie Fried Chicken {extra crispy} as a science experiment.

"It's better this way," my mother assured me.

> Better for who?/further study req'd.

> But my sarcastic reply was interrupted by the phone. Probably ZG, to see when I was going over to the Community Center. He had volunteered to hang out with me at the science fair — big surprise. Actually, I was happy to have company. I didn't want to face the judges alone with my non-proj.

"Milo—" my mom called from the kitchen phone.

"It's almost time to go," I reminded her.

"It's your father."

> Sonic the Hedgehog wouldn't have beaten me to the receiver. My dad was usually so busy that these calls could be kind of rare.

"Hi, son. Freezing yet?" {This = his standard greeting ever since we moved to Minnesota.}

"Only since Labor Day," I grinned. The phone connection was fuzzy and distorted. "Where are you?"

"Twenty-seven thousand feet over Iowa," came the reply. "I'm on the plane, Milo. I should make it to the science fair in time for the judging."

> *Yes!!* My heart raced. I hadn't seen my father since September, except on TV. Only — suddenly, I remembered my proj. Victor Neal wasn't going to be very impressed by a few notes and a bucket of fast food. "Uh, Dad, I just want to warn you—"

A burst of static came over the line. "I'm losing you, son. What did you say?"

"Just that my project got kind of messed up," I said, raising my voice. {Why does it always feel as if shouting will improve a bad connection? It has no scientific basis/further study req'd.} "It's kind of a long story—"

But I don't think my father could hear me. He said, "Blasted phone!" and the line went dead.

"He's coming?" my mother asked.

> When I nodded she smiled. A *real* smile. I appreciated that.

> For four months I'd been dying for my dad to visit. And now he was finally coming — just in time to see me disgrace the Neal family name in the field of science, which = his life's work.

> For some crazy reason, I couldn't wait to tell ZG. Out of all the people I knew in Minnesota *and* California, he'd be the only one to see the irony.

22

RANGERS UPDATE: CAPTAIN ADAM LURIE REPORTING

The first scary thing about playing the Canadians was watching them arrive. Have you ever seen twenty gorillas get off a bus? It gives you a sick feeling in the pit of your stomach. And when you see the occasional little guy in there, you're thinking how fast or how good he must be, or what an amazing shot he must have to make the best junior high team in Winnipeg.

If you think I was nervous, you should have seen Brendan. I was afraid he'd melt onto the blacktop of the Community Center parking lot.

"Are you sure these guys are our age?" he babbled, his face green. "Maybe they sent a high school team by mistake! Look, that one has a mustache!"

"It's just a little dirt on his face," I said quietly.

"See? They don't wash! They're like cave people! That one looks like Arnold Schwarzenegger! I can't play these guys! They'll score fifty on me!"

"Don't talk like that!" snapped Steve. "We won the championship with you!"

"You won the championship *in spite* of me!" Brendan corrected bitterly.

"You're the Wall," I insisted. But deep down I knew he'd never be the real Wall — never measure up to his brother. He was trying; he was a great kid. But that didn't stop pucks. Watching the Canadians lumbering into the Community Center, I realized those giants were going to eat Brendan for lunch.

Laffy cleared his throat carefully. "I talked to Coach Crenshaw after school yesterday. He said these guys are the Red River Junior High Rebels. Remember St. Boniface who skunked us last year? Well, the Rebels beat them by five goals."

"Thanks," said Joey sarcastically. He looked terrible. Tension over Henrietta and the big game had brought about another breakup with Lynette.

"Look," I said, "none of this stuff should be a great shock. We knew the Canadians were going to be awesome. What did you expect? A bunch of shrimps in ballet tutus?"

"No," Brendan replied, "but—"

"Let's all calm down," I interrupted. "Go home for lunch. I'll see you guys back here at game time."

My confidence was all fake. Lunch may as well have been fried Styrofoam for all I tasted it. I couldn't relax. And I was practically a wreck by the time I arrived at La Casa Loser to pick up Henrietta for the game.

I found Zachary the same way. "My mom's on the warpath," he admitted, his face turned away from Henrietta's flapping wings as he pulled her box out from under his bed. "She found out I got a D-minus-minus on 'A History of Pens.'"

I unzipped the spare equipment bag, which was Henrietta's golden carriage to the ball. "What did you expect? It was garbage."

"*I'm* pretty happy with it," the dweeb told me. "I expected to get an F."

I picked up Henrietta. She seemed to be in a peculiar mood today, flapping her wings and resisting my grip. "What's with the bird?" I grimaced, stuffing her in the duffel.

He shrugged. "She's like that every day for me."

Crash! All of a sudden, a little Hot Wheels car came flying out of nowhere and bounced off the computer on Zachary's desk. My eyes shifted to the doorway. There stood Dewey Gustafson — the microdweeb — his arm cocked back to throw another car.

"*Doomsday!!*" Zachary hurled himself in front of the computer. While in midair, he reached out an arm and knocked down the flying toy.

"Go, Zack," I laughed. Whoever would have expected such a big loser to pull off a slick athletic move? Seriously, that was highlight-film stuff!

But the baby wasn't done yet. He had a whole pile of cars at his feet, and he threw them all at the computer. I watched in amazement. Dewey fired a convertible at the printer. *Smack!* Zachary's hand shot out to slap it away. He stopped a fire engine with his chest. He deflected an ambulance with a high-flailing sneaker. *Nothing* got by him!

"Come on, Adam," he panted. "Grab him!"

But I was really enjoying the acrobatic display. "Nice save!" I cheered. I realized it *was* a save, just like a hockey goalie's. Only I'd like to see Brendan do *that*. Heck, I'd be interested to see if his brother Tony could pull off some of Zachary's moves!

Then I caught sight of an old pair of skates in the corner of the dweeb's closet and it hit me like four thousand pounds of wet cement. The Rangers needed a goalie. Man, our *own* goalie thought we needed a goalie! And here, before my very eyes, was the greatest natural stopper of all time.

Sure, he was untrained. He'd probably never strapped on pads in his life! But desperate times called for desperate measures. If we were going to have any chance at all against the Canadians, Zachary Gustafson — the Grand Poobah of the Loyal Order of Losers! — was going to stand in goal for the South Middle School Rangers! Unbelievable but true.

I grabbed his little brother to stop the attack. "Hey, Zack," I began. "Got any plans today?"

It took him a minute to catch his breath. "Well, I'll probably drop by the science fair and see how Milo's—" He stopped and looked at me in suspicion. "Why?"

The microdweeb started kicking at my ankles, but I ignored him. "How would you like to be a hero and fight for the honor of your school?"

Zachary made a face at me. "I'm not going to hold the chicken. She'll peck my eyes out."

"It's got nothing to do with the chicken," I insisted. "You're going to be the Rangers' new goalie!"

He couldn't have been more shocked if I'd told him he'd been elected homecoming queen. He just gawked at me, so I kept on going. "Yeah, I know you've never played before, but trust me, you're *awesome*! I watched you protecting your computer. You've got all the moves! It sounds crazy, but you can do this!"

He stared at me while all this sunk in. Then a slimy look took shape on his used-car-salesman features. "I'm banned from the rink, remember? Besides, what makes you think

I want to help out your stupid hockey team? I don't recall you muscleheads going out of your way to be nice to me."

"That's ancient history," I said quickly. "Come on! And bring your skates—"

But Zachary wasn't finished. "I'm having a vision!" He closed his eyes like a fortune-teller. "Three words! Dweeb and geek and—"

"We were just joking—" I offered lamely.

"Loser!" He spat it out. "Wait, I'm having another memory—"

"Aw, come on—"

"Wedgies," Zachary said angrily. "I remember a lot of wedgies. Now get your hands off my brother, take your chicken, and beat it!"

There comes a point in every cool person's life when he has no choice but to get down on his knees and beg a dweeb. There was no question that this was my time. I took a deep breath and swallowed a smorgasbord of pride. I apologized for everything any Ranger had ever said or done to Zachary. Then I swore on the legends of Gordie Howe and Wayne Gretzky and all the hockey greats that no Ranger would ever so much as look funny at him — starting today until the end of time.

"Even if I stink," Zachary added, and I knew I'd won.

"You won't." I unhanded the baby and shouldered the spare equipment bag.

★★★

The Canadians game was a major tradition, so the Community Center was bustling. The arena was right across the foyer from the exhibition hall, so there was a huge traffic jam as hockey fans streamed around the science fair nerds, who were maneuvering bulky projects through the crowd into the fair.

Zachary tried to run into the exhibition hall. "Just let me talk to Milo."

"No time," I said, putting an iron grip on his dweeby shoulders.

"Hey, Milo!" he called into the busy hall, waving his arms. But I dragged him across the foyer and into our dressing room.

Coach Crenshaw was in the middle of a lecture about how he didn't want us to get spooked by playing without Henrietta. I rushed in and hoisted the spare equipment bag so the guys would know our mascot was there. A huge sigh of pure relief went up.

"Good," the coach approved. "I'm glad you guys have gotten over that crazy superstition. I want to hear everybody say it: 'The chicken doesn't skate.'"

"The chicken doesn't skate," we repeated.

"*Squawk!*"

The coach frowned, and I thought we were nailed for sure, when the team finally noticed Zachary. To say that he got a standing ovation would be a lie. The guys were ready to run him out of town. *And* me for suggesting he might be our goalie.

"Are you nuts?"

"He cheered *against* us!"

"Get that creep out of here!"

"Come on, Lurie!" Coach Crenshaw added. "We did fine with our team the way it is! We're South Minnesota champions! We don't have to panic and make a bunch of crazy adjustments at the last minute!"

The babble of protest swelled up again, but Brendan quieted everybody down with a shrill, "Let's listen to what he has to say!"

Desperately, I collected my thoughts, searching for a way to convince everybody that this world-class loser should be a Ranger. "I know it's weird, but you've got to believe me! He could be the best goalie we've ever had! Better than Brendan — even better than Tony!"

"*The Wall?!*" My teammates recoiled in amazement.

I looked from face to face. "I'm as loyal as anybody, but you all know we're going to get killed today. Give the dweeb — I mean Zachary — a chance."

"It's our only hope," Brendan added.

At first I thought Coach Crenshaw was going to put up an argument. Instead he just said, "Do it."

I started strapping Brendan's goalie pads onto Zachary's skinny legs.

"Aren't you going to tell them about our deal?" he whispered as I tightened the Velcro straps. "You know, no more wedgies?"

"Later," I muttered nervously.

If my teammates had been skeptical before, *now* they were on the point of revolution. Stupid Zachary could barely stand in all that goalie equipment. Once on the rink, he skated in tiny staccato steps, like a four-year-old who was just learning. When we put him in net for his warm-up shots, he fell, crashing hard to the ice. We picked him up, dazed and wobbly, but he couldn't manage a goalie's crouch. Instead, he slumped, with his glove and stick arms hanging limp at his sides. He made no move to go after the easy practice shots the team slid by him.

"Lurie, have you gone crazy?" the coach rasped at me. "This kid's not a goalie! He can barely stand on his feet!"

I skated over to Zachary. "No, no, *no*!" I shouted. "Pretend the net is your computer and the puck is all that stuff your baby brother throws at it!"

The buzzer went off, signifying the start of the game. For me, it was like hearing the church bells of my own funeral.

"We need more time!" I pleaded to the ref, but he waved me into position for the national anthems.

I skated to the circle, feeling like my intestines had been hollowed out by piranhas. My deepest fear had just come true: In my crazed desire to have a chance against the Canadians, I had destroyed my own team.

23

FROM THE CLIPBOARD OF COACH CRENSHAW

I knew we didn't stand a chance against the Canadians. We *never* have! Oh, sure, back when I was a kid we squeaked by them once. But what nobody remembers was that there was a teachers' strike in Winnipeg that year, so they had to send us a team from this little farm school outside the city. Maybe that was why I was desperate enough to put Gustafson in goal. Besides, everyone knew Lurie would saw both his legs off before he'd hurt the team.

Or so I'd thought. Gustafson wasn't a goalie! He could barely stand on his skates! That's when the extent of my blunder came crashing down on me.

"Walters!" I bawled. "Get some pads on!"

"But Coach," he protested. "Zachary's got my jersey."

"I don't care if you play *naked*!" I growled. "Hurry!"

The players were livid. All through both national anthems: "He stinks, Coach!" "He can't even skate!" "Why's he in there, Coach?"

"*Squawk!*"

I froze. "What was that?"

A few *What was that?*'s bubbled around the bench. I looked around. Between the music and the nervous buzz of the crowd, maybe I was hearing things. The arena practically vibrated with anticipation.

Come on Walters!

But he didn't make it before the anthems ended. We were going to have to play the first couple of shifts with Gustafson.

The referee dropped the puck. The Rebels' captain won the draw and plowed over Lurie like he was a speed bump.

"Stop him!" I cried.

The kid made a beautiful deke, and Tenorio missed his check. The captain streaked in, raised his stick, and fired a blistering shot.

Gustafson didn't move. At first, I thought he didn't even see the puck hurtling for the top corner of the net. Then, almost like a mechanical response, his glove arm snapped up and grabbed the puck out of the air.

"*What a save!*" bellowed a voice, and I realized in shock that it was mine.

Lurie picked himself up off the ice and rushed our goalie, joyously crying "Za-a-ack!"

The face-off moved to our end. Gustafson made an impossible stick save, knocked away a sure goal with his blocker, and pounced on a dangerous rebound.

"Did you see that?" Sorrentino was bug-eyed. "He froze the puck right off their captain's stick!"

"He's not human!" breathed Walters, who was dressed to play but thrilled that he wasn't needed.

"I always knew he wasn't human," grumbled Hughes. "I just never realized he was a goalie."

"Hey!" came Ginsberg's righteous voice from the seats above our bench. "Just because Zachary isn't one of the 'beautiful people,' doesn't mean he can't be a good player!"

I turned to face her. "I thought you only cared about the chicken. Why are you here *now*?"

"Are you kidding?" she cried, a little too loudly. "I'm a Ranger fan! Go team go!"

"*Squawk!*"

I turned to face my team. "Guys, what's going on?"

A roar from the crowd snapped my attention back to the game. I looked to the ice just in time to see Gustafson snatch a booming shot right out of the air. I couldn't believe this was the same kid who couldn't do a single chin-up and refused to climb the ropes in gym because of his fear of heights.

He was putting on a superstar performance. The Rebels were all over us. The shots-on-goal counter showed 23–2, but the kid stopped everything. The first period ended with the score 0–0.

I couldn't resist. In the locker room I lifted Gustafson up, equipment and all, and enfolded him in a big bear hug. "You're amazing!"

His reply was to the team, not me: "This means no more wedgies, right? Adam said."

I couldn't let it go. "Where did you learn to play like that?"

He shrugged. "It's pretty easy. I mean, there's only one puck out there. Doomsday can throw things five or six at a time."

"*Squawk!*"

This time I wasn't hearing things. There was no game noise, no roar of the crowd. Only one thing on earth could warble like that, and it wasn't the Zamboni.

"All right," I demanded, "where is she?"

Dead silence. "No girls in the locker room, Coach," Lurie said finally.

I glared at him. "Milo Neal's chicken is in this room. I heard her!"

"Maybe you heard, like, some *other* chicken," Hughes suggested.

"A stray," Sorrentino added hopefully.

"Maybe the building is infested." *That* was Vincent.

"With *chickens*?!" I exploded. "Look, guys, I understand, okay? She's a great mascot. I'm a Ranger, too. But I have to be a teacher first! That bird is stolen merchandise! Holding her is a *crime*! I can't have that on my team, and neither can you!"

But the guys stonewalled me. I searched all the lockers, the shower stalls, and the laundry bin.

"*Squawk!*"

"Oh, come on!" I shouted in frustration. It was a chicken, not a microdot! How could they possibly keep it hidden?

The buzzer sounded and the crowd cheered us back to the ice. When Gustafson came over the boards, the noise level went through the roof. He got a standing ovation.

I tried to concentrate on the game. Really, I did. But I just couldn't get that fugitive chicken out of my head. We went on the power play; I thought about Henrietta. A questionable off-side call; I scanned the bench, looking for hiding places. There was a scramble in front of the net — *missing chicken*. Gustafson was flat on his back — *Henrietta* — under at least two Rebels. The puck went to this huge kid, who flipped it — *kidnapped chicken* — right at the net. Out of nowhere, a glove reached out of the pile of people and caught it. *Where was that stupid chicken?!*

"Great shift, guys!" cheered Tenorio as the exhausted skaters climbed over the boards.

"Did you see that?" gasped Lurie. "Zack picked one right out of the top corner!" He threw off his helmet, wrapped his head in a large towel, and bent over the spare equipment bag, catching his breath.

"Careful!" I barked when I saw the towel dangling to the floor off the bench. "You're going to trip somebody with that!"

"Sorry, Coach." Lurie stood up.

A second later, when I glanced down the bench, it was Sorrentino crouched under the towel. The next time I looked, there was Tenorio in the same pose. Were my players really *so* exhausted? I squinted at Tenorio doubled over the spare equipment bag. Tenorio wasn't gasping. He'd been off the ice for a while. What was he — what were all of them doing under that towel?

Ohhhhhhh . . .

Suddenly I knew how detectives must feel when they crack the big case. It all came to me — the towel wasn't for drying; it was for hiding. Hiding the duffel. And what could be in the duffel? You didn't have to be a rocket scientist to figure it out.

I saw that Lurie had noticed my interest. "Adam," I said softly, "hand over the bag."

He looked at me beseechingly. "Coach, you can't. Not now."

"The chicken doesn't skate," I reminded him.

"Yeah, I know, but maybe she *sort of* does. You know?"

The weird thing was, I *did* know. I hesitated. I could lose my job if I didn't deliver the chicken to Mr. Delong right away. But these were the *Canadians*! And thanks to Gustafson, we had a chance. Heck, at this point in the Canadians game we were usually down by five or six goals. Call me crazy, I reached for the duffel.

"The bag," I ordered.

Lurie was in agony. "Coach — *please*!"

I looked him in the eye. "I need to count the backup elbow pads," I said stiffly.

The kid stared at me for a moment, and then a slow smile took shape behind his breath-fogged visor. "Yes, sir, Coach!" He placed the duffel on the floor in front of me. The whole team gathered around breathlessly.

As I bent down and unzipped the bag, Sorrentino draped the towel over my head. Sure enough, that goofy chicken head bobbed up at me. "Hello, uh, Henrietta," I began. How do you talk to a chicken? "Milo says you're a brainless bag of oven stuffer, and now's the time to prove him wrong," I said, hoping my wife never found out about this. "So how about a goal—"

That's when I heard Lurie yelling, "DeeVee! *No!*"

I snapped up just in time to see Vincent at the Rebels' blue line. His face was bright red, a study in pure concentration; his stick was raised back so far it was pointing straight up at the heavens.

"Vincent!" I bellowed. "Not a slap shot! Not *now*! I'll bench you for the rest of your life!"

POW!!! He hit the puck with the force of a meteor slamming into a mountain. The enormous effort landed the kid flat on the ice.

"No!" I shouted. But I could see right away that there was something different about this slap shot. Instead of taking off for Jupiter, it stayed low. The puck sizzled in like a cruise missile, about three inches off the ice. It streaked past the defensemen, shot past the goalie, ripped clear through the mesh of the back of the net, and split the boards with a mighty *crack*! The red goal light flashed on.

The crowd erupted with a deafening roar. My players cleared the bench and I'm not embarrassed to say, so did I. Vincent was just getting back to his feet, but we knocked him down again and piled on, howling with joy. I have to admit I was as bad as any of the kids.

Vincent looked up at me. "I'm sorry, Coach. I had to take it—"

Lurie cut him off, laughing with glee. "DeeVee, you big dope, you *scored*!"

Vincent sat up and stared at the puck, which was still

wedged in the boards behind the torn net. "*I* scored?" he barely whispered.

"Yeah!" It came from everybody.

"With my slap shot?"

"Yeah!" I could see the emotion twist that crazy kid's face — I knew he was thinking about the countless hours of firing tennis balls against his garage door, the arguments with me and his teammates over that confounded slap shot, the games spent riding the pine because of it. He might never score again, but this was Donald Vincent's moment. He burst into tears.

It was the most touching scene in all my years of coaching. Vincent bawling uncontrollably, Lurie trying to dry the kid's tears through the visor, the others slapping Vincent's helmet and shoulder pads, the roaring crowd, thunder in our ears. Right then I knew why I became a coach.

"All right, break it up!" The officials began pulling us apart. When the referee saw me he gawked. "Crenshaw, what are you doing out here?" Then he spotted Vincent's tear-streaked face. "Injured player?"

I grinned. "More like a lifelong dream fulfilled."

He looked at me in disgust. "You're supposed to be keeping them in line, not egging them on!"

When I got up, I caught sight of Mr. Delong watching disapprovingly from the bleachers. But at that moment, I wasn't a teacher; I was a *Ranger*!

"*Number one!*" I bellowed, and my players gave me a cheering escort to the bench.

In the stands, Mr. Delong shook his head at me. I didn't care. We were destined for greatness today. I could feel it in my bones!

24

DOWNLOADED FROM THE FILES OF ZACHARY GUSTAFSON

If you live long enough, you become what you despise the most. In my case, that happened when I became a member of the South Middle School Rangers. Worse, I was the star.

That might explain why the crowd had been chanting "*Zack Attack! Zack Attack*!" ever since the start of the third period. They went totally gaga every time I touched the puck. It was more than a little weird to be suddenly awesome at something you didn't even like — almost like getting elected president when you weren't running. But to be honest, this goalie gig was not such a big deal! Compared to the barrage my brother, Doomsday, fired at my computer, the Rebels were nothing special.

They were a lot better than us, of course. That was pretty obvious. I was making saves four, five, even six at a time before my defensemen could clear the zone. When I wasn't flopping around stopping pucks, I checked out the shots-on-goal counter. 51–2 . . . 64–3 . . . 72–4 . . . was this even fair? I looked over at the Rebels' goalie. He was enjoying peace and solitude. Me? I was Mr. Bull's-eye in a shooting gallery. Which gave me a thought for a new screenplay: *An alien species on a distant planet. Every year, a random citizen is selected for target practice for the flaming poison acid-dipped flesh-goring arrow archers. Then this race of mutant highly intelligent chickens*— a booming slap shot bounced off my goalie mask with the force of a battering ram. I had to be on my toes to pounce on the rebound.

Lafayette hauled me to my feet and slapped me on the back. "Way to go, Zack!"

"Great save, buddy!" cheered Steve.

That was another weird thing about today. All those guys who picked on me and gave me wedgies — all of a sudden they *loved* me! They *pampered* me! And boy, did I rub their faces in it! I sent them to the bench for towels. I made them clean the snow off my skate blades. I was constantly getting my stick retaped. I asked for Gatorade at almost every whistle. Not because I wanted it, but because I couldn't resist the sight of those big hockey muscleheads breaking their necks to cater to my every whim.

This was a big mistake, which became obvious as the clock ticked down to the final minutes. Hockey games didn't have bathroom breaks, and I'd polished off about four bottles of Gatorade!

By the four-minute mark, it was a noticeable pressure. Within sixty seconds, I was grimacing behind my mask. Remember — you can't cross your legs when you're wearing goalie pads. When the clock stopped with 1:58 still to play, I felt like my back teeth were floating. A single thought dominated my brain: *I'm not going to make it!*

"Time out!" I headed off the ice, not so much skating as running on the toes of my skate blades.

"We've *used* our time-out!" Adam yelled at me.

"Gustafson, get back here!" That was Coach Crenshaw. I heard him just as I leaped off the ice and hurled myself into the rest room. I was going to catch a lot of flak over this, but I wasn't making my own decisions at that point. The Gatorade was definitely in charge.

Have you ever gone to the bathroom in full goalie equipment? It's like dismantling a car engine. Ninety percent of that stuff has to come off. It's a major operation! By the time I got back to the ice, both teams were standing around waiting, the refs were glaring at me, and Coach Crenshaw's eyes looked like they were about to pop out of his head.

"That's a *double* delay-of-game penalty!" the referee

roared in my face. "One for calling a time-out you don't have, and one for *taking* it!"

"*That's-not-right-a-two-man-advantage-it's-like-giving-them-a-sure-goal-we-don't-stand-a-chance-why-don't-you-just-hand-them-the-game-on-a-silver-platter-it's-not-fair!*" Coach Crenshaw, Adam, and I all screamed it out so fast, it was impossible to tell who said what. But referees are like the weather — they don't change no matter how much you complain.

"Aw, Zack!" Adam seethed.

It looked pretty grim. I mean, the Canadians had nearly eighty shots at me *at even strength*! With two extra players, it was going to be open season on Zachary, and all the hunters had bazookas. Then the Rebels pulled their goalie for an extra skater. That meant they'd have six attackers — against only three defenders and, gulp, me.

It was total chaos — like a hundred Deweys, all throwing blocks at the same time. My three teammates — Adam, Joey, and Steve — formed a triangle to protect the net. But they were trying to stop up Niagara Falls with a cotton ball. Four-inch armor plating wouldn't have protected the net from the offensive barrage the Rebels unleashed at me.

It was all happening too fast to think about what was going on. My mind shut down and a kind of weird automatic pilot took over. My catching glove was just a blur; my blocker and stick worked in perfect unison; my legs were everywhere; hard shots slamming into the goalie pads resounded like drums. Slap shot! *Stick save!* Backhand! *Off the chest!* Wrist shot! *What a catch!* Scramble in front of the net! I dove on the puck. How did I know what to do? No idea! Hey, I'd only been a goalie for an hour or so. The shots-on-goal counter showed 89–4. And through it all the crowd chanted, "*Zack Attack! Zack Attack!*"

Fourteen seconds to play. I huddled with Adam, Joey, and Steve, but we were gasping and choking too much to say anything. Actually, words weren't necessary. The situation was obvious — even to a non-hockey fan like me: If we held out against the onslaught, we'd beat the Canadians for the first time in thirty-five years. If we let them tie it up, we were probably going to get creamed in overtime.

Fourteen seconds. What was fourteen seconds? A lifetime, that's what. It stood between me and no more wedgies. Respect at school. Power, even. Why, as a hockey hero, they'd owe me big.

The puck was dropped. The Rebels' captain won the draw and passed back to his defenseman.

Pow! A booming slap shot was headed for the net. But with all the traffic in front of me, I couldn't see a thing! Then, at the last instant, I caught a hint of black. Desperately, I went into a full split, kicking out my leg. The puck caromed off the toe of my skate.

"Rebound!" shouted Joey.

The puck was just sitting there, fat and inviting. I hurled

myself at it, but the Rebels' captain had the same idea. *Crunch!* I bounced off that sasquatch like a Ping-Pong ball, and careened right into Adam. The two of us landed in a heap behind the net.

No one was yelling "Zack Attack" now. They were just yelling.

The wheels of time seemed to grind to a halt to give me a chance to savor the exquisite agony of the moment: There were two seconds left on the clock. The Rebels' captain had the puck right in front of a totally empty net. His wrists twitched as he prepared to pop in the tying goal.

"*No-o-o-o-o!!*" screamed Adam beside me.

Suddenly he grabbed me by the suspenders of my hockey pants — one final giant wedgie to end all wedgies! He lifted me up, up, and over the top of the net. And as I came down in a perfect swan dive, I swung my goalie stick at the puck.

Thwack! What a beautiful sound. I hit the puck about a trillionth of an inch before it crossed the goal line. And just as I landed face-first on the ice, the buzzer sounded to end the game. Final score 1–0 Rangers. *Miracle.*

The Community Center seated fifteen hundred people. And when they all leaped to their feet at the same time, it almost created a wind. The roar of celebration was that much louder because it was thirty-seven years in coming. My teammates — those rotten Rangers, those muscleheads who made a career out of bugging me — they lifted me up on their shoulders and carried me around the ice for a victory lap.

"Remember," I shouted down at them, spelling out the deal, "no more wedgies!"

But you couldn't talk to people who were screaming with joy. Adam's face was so pink that if you put lace around it, it would have been a valentine! This was probably the greatest moment in the guy's life! And there was DeeVee — still crying! Coach Crenshaw was kissing guys on the helmet! It was disgusting! Lynette leaped the boards and threw herself into Joey's arms. So I guess the on-again off-again was on again. And all this happiness was because of me! I was underwhelmed.

Lynette was the first pebble of the avalanche. They started coming over the boards like army ants, howling and cheering. Pretty soon you couldn't see the ice for the swarms of people. It was like New Year's Eve — everywhere you looked it was a party — friends dancing and singing, proud parents hugging their sons, teachers congratulating the coach, a chicken darting through the forest of skates and legs—

A *chicken*?!

I screamed, "*Henrietta's loose!*"

Plowing through the crowd like a harvester through a field of wheat came Kelly Marie. "Where? *Where? WHERE?!*"

From my perch atop everybody's shoulders, I pointed. Henrietta was scrambling and skittering her way across the rink. A buzz of recognition shot through the crowd.

"Is that a chicken?"

"It's the Neal kid's chicken!"

"The *missing* chicken!"

"Grab her!"

"*No!*" screamed Kelly Marie. "You'll hurt her!"

Mr. Lurie snatched up the bird, but Henrietta flapped wildly and broke free. Everyone made a try for that slippery chicken, *including* the team, so I got dumped on my face. I wasn't the only one. People were diving for Henrietta, slipping on the ice and knocking each other over. If I ever switched my screenwriting style over to comedy, I'd have tons of ideas for my first movie, called *Henrietta vs. The Fifteen Hundred Stooges.*

Out of the sea of grabbing, diving, falling players and spectators rose Henrietta, flapping her wings furiously. She got just enough lift to land her on top of the boards. Then she jumped down and scooted out of the arena.

"*She's getting away!*" shrieked Kelly Marie.

I was the first one over the boards and hot on her tail feathers. Running on skates in full goalie equipment was no easy matter. But I could feel fifteen hundred people swarming behind me. If I stopped, I'd be trampled by the thundering herd. So I chased the bird across the foyer, my skate blades making hideous grinding sounds on the terrazzo floor. With a sinking heart, I realized that Henrietta was heading straight into the exhibition hall and — oh, no! — the science fair!

"Don't go in there!" I shouted. Like she was going to listen! Talk about the worst thing that could possibly happen! That science fair was scheduled to be her funeral! She was supposed to be there not as a guest but as *lunch*! If it came out that I was one of the kidnappers, Milo would never speak to me again. Not to mention that Adam, Kelly Marie, and I would probably get suspended and maybe even arrested as cattle rustlers.

Science fairs were definitely not designed for a hockey team on skates. I stopped short to avoid plowing into display tables and experiments, and everyone else piled up behind me, gridlocked in the doorway. I dropped to my knees and crawled after Henrietta under the tables. Hopping and hustling, the bird led me on a merry chase *beneath* the science fair, navigating through a maze of table legs. For once, I was grateful for my equipment, which was saving me a lot of scrapes, bangs, and bruises. I hadn't crawled this much since I was Doomsday's age. It was murder! I didn't get to stand up until Henrietta emerged from under the experiment tables.

I rolled out into the aisle, leaped to my feet — and found myself staring into the world-famous face of Victor

Neal! I was awestruck. The real California famous guy! He looked exactly like on TV — better even, because we didn't get the Science Channel, so I usually saw him scrambled.

I was so profoundly shocked that it took a second for me to realize I was standing right in front of "The Complete Life Cycle of a Link in the Food Chain." Milo and Mrs. Baggio were opposite me, offering a bucket of fried chicken to two men wearing JUDGE badges.

"Zachary?" Milo blurted, squinting into my face through the bars of my goalie mask. But he was distracted by a loud squawk. There was a mad flurry of white feathers and Henrietta, the lost specimen, flapped her way straight up Milo's chinos and into his arms.

Milo's eyes bulged behind his Bertrand St. Renes. "Where did she come from?"

Victor Neal laughed. "What do you care so long as she's here? Talk about timing!"

Milo turned urgently to the judges. "Would it be possible for my project to be judged last? That would give me about an hour."

The men exchanged shrugs. "Sounds fair enough if there's a good reason," said the senior of the two.

"I'm taking the specimen to Arno's Butcher Shop," Milo explained. "I should have just enough time to cook the meat and we can truly complete the link in the food chain."

Victor Neal snapped to attention. "Milo, what do you mean? You're not still planning to kill that bird?!"

Milo looked confused. "Of course I am. The experiment—"

"Milo, *think*!" his father cut him off. "You've been around that chicken for four months now! It's not a specimen anymore — it's a *friend*!"

"Dad!" Milo couldn't believe his ears. "You of all people should know that a chicken doesn't have the necessary intelligence to be capable of friendship! It's — it's *bad science*!"

"Bad science," retorted Victor Neal, "is ignoring what's right in front of your nose! That chicken got frightened in the crowd and came running right to you! She *knows* you! And you want to eat her? Have a heart!"

Milo flinched as if he'd just been slapped. The poor kid was destroyed. All he ever wanted was to live up to his dad in science, and here was that same dad, wailing out on him! That was when I said my first words ever to the great Victor Neal. But they weren't, "Hi, I'm Milo's best friend in the world," or, "Hey, I understand you hang out with lots of Hollywood bigwig types," or even, "Wait here while I go get the fifty pounds of movie scripts in the steamer trunk in my closet." I didn't say any of that stuff.

Instead, I turned on the great man and barked, "Wait a

minute! Milo's worked like a dog on this project to make you proud! You don't even visit him for four months, and now you show up just to *yell* at the guy?"

What have I done?! My blunder stretched in all directions to infinity. I had been praying, hinting, *scheming* to finagle a meeting with this man ever since I first laid eyes on Milo. And what did I do with this golden opportunity? I chewed out this Nobel Prize scientist in public in his own hometown. Good-bye Hollywood.

Victor Neal was giving me the worm guts look — at least now I knew where Milo got it. His expression would have put out a forest fire.

Timidly, Milo said, "Dad, I don't think you've met my friend Zach—" He fell silent, looking nervously down at Henrietta. She was making strange clucking noises and wriggling around in his arms. I'd been scratched and pecked more than anybody, but I'd never seen her like this before.

"Maybe she's just frightened by all the people," offered Mrs. Baggio. "Hold her tight."

Then the bird started cackling and shaking. Milo's eyes filled with wonder. He said, "Oh . . . oh . . . oh, wow . . ."

He reached under Henrietta and pulled out a gleaming white egg.

Victor Neal snapped his fingers. "That's it! There's your food chain, Milo!"

"You're right!" Excitedly, Milo turned to the judges. "It still counts, doesn't it? The chicken was raised, consumed food, and eventually *produced* food."

"It's even better," Mrs. Baggio added breathlessly. "Henrietta will provide eggs for a long time."

The senior judge threw his head back and laughed. "You're a lucky kid, Milo Neal!" he exclaimed. "It happened at the last second, but your link in the food chain is complete!"

"*FREEZE!!*"

The crowd parted to admit Kelly Marie, approaching like a gunslinger. Only instead of a six-shooter she had the exhibition hall fire extinguisher with the nozzle pointed at Milo. I was fascinated. It was a true screenwriting moment — the standoff. All the best movies have them. You don't get a lot of standoffs in St. Martin, Minnesota. I waited, not even breathing.

She addressed our teacher first. "I'm sorry, Mrs. Baggio."

"But Kelly Marie—" exclaimed Milo.

"*Quiet!*" she thundered. "Now hand over that chicken! And no sudden movements!"

"Now, just one moment, young lady!" Victor Neal stepped out in front of his son.

Kelly Marie panicked. She yanked the pin and a mountain of foam exploded out of the nozzle right onto Professor Neal. It all happened in the blink of an eye. One second

Milo's father was standing there. The next, he was a statue of white fluffy suds.

"Dad!" cried Milo.

"Don't shoot!" ordered Mrs. Baggio, which was kind of like shutting the barn door after the horse was already long gone.

"Henrietta's fine," I told Kelly Marie. "She just laid an egg. *That's* the food chain they're talking about. You just slimed Victor Neal!"

"Really?" Ever the quick-change artist, Kelly Marie enfolded her victim in a big hug. "I knew you'd come when you got my letter!"

"Miss Ginsberg, I presume," said Milo's dad, spitting foam.

Sheepishly, Kelly Marie used the sleeve of her sweat-shirt to wipe the suds from the famous face. The crowd of hockey players and spectators who had been filing into the hall recognized Victor Neal and burst into applause.

The astronomer put an arm around his son's shoulders, sharing some of the foam. "I'm sorry, Milo. Really I am. I should have come sooner, but you know my schedule—"

"It's okay, Dad."

"No, it's not," his father persisted. "Your friend Zeke is right—"

"That's Zachary," I chimed in. "Have you ever met Steven Spielberg?"

I wasn't even miffed that they both ignored me. Great screenplays have heartwarming moments, too, and this was one of them. Arm in arm, father and son walked off to get reacquainted. It would have been a five-hanky moment if one of the characters wasn't covered from head to toe in fire extinguisher foam.

Fade to black . . .

25

DOWNLOADED FROM THE FILES OF ZACK-MASTER GOAL-STOP-SON

HENRIETTA: CHICKEN OF VALOR

[Scene 48]

[INTERIOR: Science Fair — day]

Could this be the end of Henrietta? The HOCKEY PLAYERS cry into their face guards as the oil in the electric wok heats up and begins to sizzle, a stir-fried grave for a beloved friend.

[CLOSE-UP: MR. ARNO, sharpening his cleaver.]

VICTOR NEAL

There's a way, son. There's always a way. Don't lose hope. Be brave like this valiant chicken, and look within yourself for the solution that will let Henrietta live to cluck another day!

HENRIETTA

Squawk!

MILO

(bravely)

Oh, yes, Dad!

[VIEW ON HENRIETTA: An egg comes out of wherever eggs come out of on a chicken.]

I sat back from my computer. That last part wasn't very professional. Oh, well, I'd ask Milo where the eggs come from when he and Henrietta got back from the state science fair in Duluth. With the chicken laying an egg every day, he must have been a pretty big expert by now.

Things were pretty dull with Henrietta in Duluth. Mr. Delong officially declared her the school mascot for all teams and she was going to live in the pen in Mrs. Baggio's room. Why waste a perfectly good chicken coop? In theory, the bird belonged to all of us equally. But in reality she was Kelly Marie's sweetie. Oh, sure, the usual band of chicken wackos were still hanging around — Joey and Lynette, Sheila and Brendan. Even Milo called her "Henrietta" now, instead of "the specimen." *I* was the only one she hated, and I had a giant scratch on my nose to prove it.

The excitement of the big game was pretty much over by now. Yet every once in a while, some goofball would say, "Hey, we beat the Canadians!" and bang, it was celebration time all over again. Frankly, I was getting a little sick of all that yahooing.

But I shouldn't complain. That hockey game changed life a lot for me. I was now on the guest list for all of Lynette's parties. As co-MVPs, DeeVee and I got to share the hammock. Third-graders asked for my autograph on the street. High school guys *talked* to me. I wasn't a dweeb anymore. I was Zack-master Goal-stop-son, the Zack Attack, the Super-Wall.

Adam pestered me twenty-four hours a day. "Aw, come on, Zack! You've got to join the team. With me in eighth grade, you in net, and Henrietta on the bench, we'll be *awesome*! We'll go undefeated and *destroy* the Canadians!"

"Well, I'm not really sure. I'm pretty busy with my writing." Oh, I'd probably do it, but I got a major kick out of stringing the guy along. I didn't intend to sign up for hockey until five minutes before the opening face-off next October. Let him sweat; let them all sweat. Payback for a lifetime of wedgies.

"Please, Zack! It's my last year! I won't sleep till I know you're on the team!" The musclehead even tried to get me to take French with him next semester. Want to hear the logic? So when we were in the NHL together, we could give interviews *en français* in Montreal. Well, okay, maybe my goalie talent is headed for the NHL — but I'd better get drafted by the L.A. Kings. Because there's no way I'm going to let hockey stardom interfere with my screenwriting career!

★★★

South Middle School gave Milo a hero's welcome when he and Henrietta won the state science fair. It was Mrs. Baggio's first state winner ever. Kelly Marie, of course, gave all the credit to the chicken. I could see Milo didn't care so much about the trophy. He was thrilled that he'd get to go to the national finals and be with his dad.

I went over to help him pack and say bon voyage. Kelly Marie was already there, trying to convince him that Henrietta had to fly first class. You should have seen her face when she found out her sweetie was going in a box in the baggage compartment.

While Milo was showing her out, I took the opportunity to stick a few of my screenplays into his suitcase — you know, the really classy ones like *Terror in the Sewer*, *Horrordome*, and, of course, *The Brain Eaters*. If things got dull, maybe Professor Neal would need something to read. I'd be friends with Milo no matter what; but it seemed stupid to pass up a perfectly good Hollywood connection.

It paid off, too. Victor Neal got hold of *Terror in the Sewer* and actually gave it to a friend who worked at Paramount.

Mom almost blew a gasket when I got a letter on real studio stationery. I mean, she was just now getting used to me being a sports hero.

The Paramount guy wasn't that smart because he rejected *Terror in the Sewer.* But he encouraged me to keep writing. He also suggested that I tone down the blood and guts and death, and try to concentrate more on my own experience.

So here I was, hard at work on *Henrietta: Chicken of Valor*, telling the story of the last few months . . .

MILO

(holding up the egg)

This chicken has taught us all a valuable lesson . . .

(organ music swells)

. . . that you should never give up! That it's always darkest before the dawn! And that it takes a brave heart to be a chicken!

He is interrupted by the ringing of VICTOR NEAL's cellular phone.

VICTOR NEAL

(flipping open the phone)

Neal here . . .

VOICE ON PHONE

It's no use, Vic! The planetary high-magnification Cosmo-scope has detected a giant asteroid hurtling toward the Earth!

[EXTERIOR: Outer space]

The out-of-control planetoid streaks past the rings of Saturn, narrowly misses the moons of Jupiter, rips the atmosphere away from Mars, and plows right into Earth.

KA-BOOM!!! Our planet is vaporized in a humongous celestial fireworks display. Five billion perish, not including animals and plants. It is the end of all life as we know it.

ROLL CLOSING CREDITS

Okay, I know it didn't happen exactly that way. Like, Victor Neal might have had a cell phone, but it didn't ring. And all that stuff about the Earth getting destroyed, obviously.

Like it or lump it, that's my style.

Fade to black . . .

The TOILET PAPER TIGERS

For the 1992 World Series Champion
Toronto Blue Jays,
and the fans of the 1977 Jays,
who cheered even when there was no light
at the end of the tunnel.

CHAPTER 1

Coach — Professor Pendergast

Our coach had a great mind for science, but he was a total goose-egg when it came to baseball. I still can't figure out what would make a sixty-year-old guy who worked in a particle accelerator (whatever that is) want to coach Little League — and then forget to show up the day they were drafting players. By the time Professor Pendergast made it to the coaches' meeting, there were exactly nine players left — us. The Feather-Soft Tigers, sponsored by Feather-Soft Bathroom Tissue Inc. Didn't it kind of figure? The warmed-over leftovers of the league were going to be the toilet paper team. All coached by a man who thought a foul ball was a line drive into some farmer's manure spreader.

Everybody in Spooner loved Professor Pendergast. The particle accelerator was great for the town, and all the employees agreed that there was no nicer boss than our coach. So we were pretty thrilled to be Tigers — at first. Even when the professor told us our uniforms weren't ready, nobody thought it was a big deal. Hey, one practice in sweats never killed anybody.

Only there was no practice. Nobody even said the word *baseball*. Instead, our coach talked about the lepton, which is this science thing that he's supposed to be an authority on.

"What do they look like?" I asked. Not because I cared, but because the sooner we got all this lepton stuff out of the way, the sooner we could start playing.

"Oh, you can't see a lepton," the professor explained. "Not even with an electron microscope. They're far too tiny."

"If you can't see it, how do you know it's there?" asked Kevin Featherstone. His dad owned Feather-Soft Bathroom Tissue Inc.

The professor glowed. You could tell he really got into this physics stuff. "In the particle accelerator, we can create collisions that produce leptons that last for as long as three one-billionths of a second!"

In other words, he was a professor of nothing. He sure wasn't a professor of baseball.

"So," I ventured, "who do you think is going to be our leadoff batter?"

Professor Pendergast looked at me like I was some kind of idiot. "Well, I imagine it will have to be one of you boys," he replied, and the conversation switched back to leptons.

Tim Laredo shot me a nervous look. Tim and I and Tuba Dave Jablonski were the only three guys who had played Little League before. Okay, we weren't experts, but we were pretty sure this wasn't what you should be doing in the very first practice.

I decided to take another stab at mentioning you-know-what. "How about a practice game?" I suggested.

Our coach brightened further. "Excellent idea!" He pointed in the general direction of the field. "Now, some of you boys go all the way out there — uh, some of you go partway out there and the rest of you — well, uh, stay here."

We stared at him.

"Don't you even know the positions?" asked Tim.

The professor pointed to home plate. "I know that pentagonal surface is significant—" He scratched his head. "Hmmm . . ."

"Well—" I didn't want to be rude, but somebody had to ask! "Why did you sign up to be a coach when you don't know anything about baseball?"

"My granddaughter is going to be staying with me for

the summer," he admitted. "And I thought this would be a good way to get to know some young people . . ." His voice trailed off. Maybe he finally realized that it wasn't exactly fair to turn our whole season into garbage so some girl wouldn't be bored. "I'm sorry—"

I should've been on my way home to convince my parents to demand our money back. But Professor Pendergast looked really upset and I thought — here was the guy who'd done so much for our town. A renowned genius living in Spooner, Texas, but was he ever snobby or stuck-up? No! And *we* were mad because he didn't know much about baseball.

All of a sudden I heard myself bellowing, "Three cheers for Professor Pendergast!"

We hip-hip-hoorayed ourselves hoarse, and the professor was so happy he loaded us all up into his minivan, and took us to the Six Flags Amusement Park. He gorged us with hot dogs and cotton candy and took us on the Enormo-Coaster. It was fun. It was *great*. But it wasn't baseball.

Only a third of us threw up.

***

At our next practice the *professor* didn't even show up! When I got there, the only other person around was this girl. She was about my age, with blonde hair, and wore Day-Glo orange sunglasses, a New York City T-shirt, army fatigues, and pink high-tops.

She flipped up her sunglasses and barked, "Name!"

"Uh — Corey Johnson," I said, mystified. "Where's Professor Pendergast?"

"Oh, P.P.'s going to be late. He's showing some Korean scientists around the particle accelerator. I'm handling things until he gets here."

"Who are you?"

She grinned broadly, and held out her hand. "Kristy Pendergast. 'Tsup?"

"'Tsup?" I repeated, shaking her hand weakly. It took me half the season to figure out that *'tsup* was Kristy's way of saying *what's up?* which, I think, meant *hello.*

"Yeah! How you doin'? *Que pasa?* What's shakin'? How's it goin'? 'Tsup?"

I jumped on the only thing that made sense. "Pendergast?" Then I remembered why our coach volunteered for his job in the first place. "You're the professor's granddaughter!" I said, snapping my fingers.

"Word," she approved.

I stared at her. "Word?"

"You know, check, *sí*, affirmative! Yes," she added when she saw my mouth drop open in total confusion. "I'm visiting for a few months. I'm from New York, dude! The parental units are doing the Europe thing this summer, so I'm chilling out down here with my main man P.P. Now — Johnson — Johnson —" She checked her clipboard. "Okay, you're starting in left field."

"*What?*" I blurted. "I'm a pitcher!"

Kristy shrugged sympathetically. "So's this kid Kevin Featherstone. Sorry, bro'."

"But shouldn't we hold a tryout to see who's better?" I demanded.

"Earth to Johnson; Earth to Johnson," Kristy chanted. "Featherstone's the sponsor. He puts up the bucks — his kid plays where he likes."

I couldn't believe it. "Mr. Featherstone said that?"

Kristy was shaking her head and clucking sadly. "You just don't get it, do you? You rural dudes expect life to be fair. You should spend a few days in New York. Reality sandwich, man. Left field."

At that moment, Kevin showed up. "You're the pitcher," I told him, choking on my reality sandwich.

"Yo, Featherstone," Kristy greeted him. "'Tsup? Kristy Pendergast. I'm in charge here."

Notice how she promoted herself from "handling things" to "in charge"? Well, by the time the Tigers were all there, she was "assistant manager," "batting coach," "trainer," and "public relations chief."

I have to admit she was fair. She was just as annoying to everyone else as she was to me. Ernie MacIntosh's glove was too small; Luis Bono was the catcher and should have been wearing cleats; Caspar Howard's socks were drooping;

this wasn't right; that wasn't right; they do it better in New York; blah, blah, blah. I sat there, burning inside. Who died and left her king? I was just about ready to start a dugout revolt when the professor walked in.

"Grandpa! You got here just in time! That's terrific!"

The professor's face lit up at just the sight of her. "How's my little princess? Have you been getting along with my team?"

"Oh, yes, Grandpa!" she smiled sweetly. "We're all great friends!"

Wait a minute. What happened to *yo*, and *'tsup*, and *P.P. my main man*? It looked like, when the professor was around, the reality sandwich turned into a snow-job casserole.

The first order of business was our uniforms, which were ready at last. They were white, with FEATHER-SOFT TIGERS printed in blue. Between the words was a roll of toilet paper. On each sheet was a picture of a tiger holding a baseball bat.

We all packed into the washroom hut to get changed.

"Can you believe that girl?" I complained. "Bad enough that our coach is a zero, now we have to put up with Kristy!"

"Why does she talk like that?" asked Ernie MacIntosh.

"Oh, she's much cooler than us!" I said sarcastically. "She's from New York. All New Yorkers talk that way."

"No wonder New York has so many problems," Ernie

decided. "No one can figure out what anybody else is saying."

Tim pulled off his sweatpants. "Hey, you don't think that, since the professor can't really do it, Kristy might try to coach us herself?"

"*No!*" I exclaimed in horror. "Absolutely not! Under no circumstances is that girl—"

Suddenly, there was a click and a brilliant flash blinded us. When the dots cleared away from my eyes I saw it. A camera was stuck in through the open door. *And we were all standing around the bathroom in our jockstraps!*

I cried out, "Hey—" but the hand disappeared. The door shut behind it.

We suited up in seconds and rushed outside to find Kristy patting her camera.

"What'd you do that for?" bawled Ernie.

She was totally calm. "Yo, man, haven't you ever heard of team pictures?" She snickered. "I hope I got everybody's good side."

"Give me that camera!" I snarled through clenched teeth.

She frowned. "I heard you in there dissing my main man P.P."

"Dissing?" I repeated.

"Disrespecting!" she translated. "Somebody has to keep you jerks in line."

"You think you can push us around because you've got a picture of — of *that*?"

"Not at all." She replaced the lens cap on her camera. "Of course, you guys wouldn't want a picture like this to fall into the wrong hands—"

"Not our mothers!" blurted Tuba Dave in agony.

I lunged for the camera but Kristy deftly held it just outside my grasp. "No more cracks about my main man P.P.," she said firmly.

"Well, he isn't exactly a baseball expert!" I said feelingly.

"You know, you dudes are all starting junior high this September." Kristy mused. "Wouldn't it be *unfortunate* if a copy of this picture just so happened to get pasted on every locker in the school?"

My breath caught in my throat. A gasp of horror rose from my fellow Tigers. We'd all heard rumors about how tough it was to be a seventh grader at Spooner Junior High. If Kristy's picture got around, we'd be laughingstocks!

I looked her straight in the eye. "You don't have the nerve."

She laughed in my face. "Get real, bro. I'm from New York."

Ernie was the first to crack. "What do we have to do?"

"Check it out," she replied. "My main man P.P.'s a great guy. But his head is all balled up with leptons and stuff. So it's been a long time since his last chow-fest with the reality sandwich."

Unbelievably, I thought I understood. "Well, at least we agree on one thing," I said grudgingly. "We all like the coach. But when it comes to baseball, he's hopeless."

"He doesn't expect the World Series," she went on. "He just wants a normal team — win a few, lose a few, have some fun. Dig?"

"And we would be thrilled to oblige," I said sarcastically. "I'm pretty sure we can handle the 'lose a few' part. But we may need a little help with the 'win a few,' like maybe some experienced coaching."

"You don't need experience! You've got the ultimate advantage! All the competition is from Spooner, and all the other one-horse towns around here. But the Tigers are running on brain power that's straight from New York!"

There was a babble of protest.

I said, "Forget it, Kristy. Nobody's going to let you coach this team."

"Hey!" she said. "Cool your jets. Mellow out. Calm down. Take five. Make like a melon and chill. I'm just a fan. An interested party. A sports buff. A booster."

Then she patted her camera, and it made me think of the picture that was held inside, locked on a piece of film. I thought back to the washroom. How had I been standing? Could you see my face? What else (gulp!) could you see?

"Well, what are we waiting for?" I announced. "Let's practice."

***

Professor Pendergast was about as useful as air-conditioning in the Arctic. It would be unfair to say he didn't know which end of the bat to hold. He did. (The thin end.) But when Tim Laredo popped one straight up a thousand miles, our coach considered it a home run. He thought a hit was anything that made contact with the bat, including the "hit" that ends up in the bleachers behind you, the "hit" where you never make it to first, and the "hit" that somebody catches. Bobby Ray walloped a monster home run that was out of the park by half a block. Professor Pendergast thought it was a passed ball.

"At least that's a baseball word," Tim told me in the field. "When I dropped a long fly, he called it a touchdown, 'cause it touched the ground."

Kristy, our "booster," was a pain in the butt. She started out in charge of equipment, but somewhere in there, she found time to bug everybody on the whole team. She drove me so crazy about my batting stance that I actually threatened to beat her over the head with the bat. I am *not* a violent person!

"Yo, man," was Kristy's mild comment. "You say something like that to a New Yorker, you've got to be prepared to do it."

"I've never been to New York," I told her. "But if it's full of eight million people like you, it must be the worst place on earth."

Ernie pulled me aside. "What are you — crazy?" he hissed. "You can't talk to her like that! If she gets mad she'll develop The Picture!"

"Don't be stupid," I said peevishly. "You want to be her slave for life?"

"I can't remember exactly when the flash went off," moaned Luis. "I might have been bending over to tie my shoes."

"What a day to wear bunny rabbit underwear!" added Bobby Ray.

"What do you care?" Tim asked him. "You go to school in Eaton."

Bobby Ray shook his head. "Eaton Junior High comes to Spooner for shop and home ec. I'm dead."

"I sure hope my birthmark doesn't show," put in Tuba Dave.

"What birthmark?" asked Ernie.

"Well, you can't see it *now*!" Tuba Dave exploded.

What a practice! Six of us couldn't hit. Four of us couldn't catch. Nobody could handle a routine grounder. And when Kevin was on the mound, no one was safe! Talk about wild! He didn't just bean the batters; he nailed me in the on-deck circle!

"Sorry," Kevin called.

Before chewing him out, I reminded myself that this was probably the guy's dream. Why else would he get his dad to pull strings to make him pitcher?

"I guess this really means a lot to you," I commented, tossing him the ball. "Pitching, I mean."

Kevin looked surprised. "Not really."

I frowned. "Well, then, I guess your dad's the one who wants you to pitch."

He shrugged. "Dad doesn't care. He just wants me to be part of the team. Actually, I thought *you* were going to be our pitcher."

By the time I found Kristy, my face was burning hot, and it had nothing to do with the weather.

"'Tsup, Johnson? You look a little purple. Grape City, man."

Mutiny City. "Kevin doesn't care who pitches!" I rasped. "Kevin's *father* doesn't care who pitches! You lied!"

"Chill out," she said blandly.

But by then, the professor was on the scene. "What's the trouble, Princess?"

I was triumphant. Now Kristy couldn't shoot me down without showing her grandfather what a tyrant she was.

"I think I should get the chance to try out for pitcher," I said.

The professor beamed. "Of course!" He pointed to the outfield, where some of the guys had paired up to play catch. "See? Everybody's pitching. You pitch to your partner, and then he pitches back to you."

"But that's not pitching!" I protested. "That's throwing!"

"Well, perhaps you can try out for thrower," suggested our coach. And he walked away, leaving Kristy grinning so wide — I can still see it in my mind. It almost killed me.

"You won't get away with this," I told her, my eyes mere slits.

Kristy was totally calm. "I'm considering becoming a photographer when I grow up. What do you think? Do I take great pictures, or what?"

I was so furious that I couldn't be trusted with a bat. I went to sit in the bleachers. It was too painful to watch the practice, so I watched the professor. He was smiling and applauding, while the guys scrambled around like chickens with their heads cut off. He didn't even know enough about baseball to realize this wasn't it!

Finally, when the whole disaster was over he said, "Boys, I'm very proud of you."

Kristy came over, smiling her used-car-salesman smile. "Wasn't that a wonderful practice, Grandpa?" To me she whispered, "Yo, man, you guys need help!"

★★★

By midnight, I still hadn't cooled down. I lay in my bed shaking with rage. Kristy hadn't even been in town a whole day yet, and already my summer was ruined!

The worst part was there was nothing we could do about it! The guys would never dare go up against her because they were so spooked by The Picture. That meant we also couldn't get our parents to complain. She'd blame us and develop the film. And trying to explain anything to the professor was impossible. He'd never believe the truth about his "little princess." We were trapped, unless . . .

I jumped up and ran to my desk. Maybe *we* couldn't stop Kristy Pendergast, but if the league complained, the professor would have to do something. I found my league pamphlet and checked the name and address of the president.

Dear Mr. Lopez,

I think you should know that a terrible person named Kristy Pendergast is ruining the Feather-Soft Tigers by bossing everybody around, and not letting people pitch. She is the granddaughter of the coach, who is a really nice guy, except he thinks she's great. Please help. The whole team is going down the drain.

Signed,
Anonymous

I sat back and reread my letter with satisfaction. When Mr. Lopez read this, he'd make the professor tell Kristy to mind her own business. And the beauty of it was that Kristy would never know who did her in.

I went back to bed and slept like a baby.

CHAPTER 2

Catcher — Luis Bono

No one thought it was a big deal when our catcher, Luis Bono, took a fastball right in the mask during the warm-up before our first game.

Actually, we were all kind of impressed that Kevin had managed to get one over the plate. The ball sizzled in from the mound, hitting the gap in the bars of the mask right between Luis's eyes. There was a muffled *twang*, and the ball stuck there, jammed in the mask.

"Yo, bro', looks like a giant insect eye! Attack of the praying mantises!" laughed Kristy.

I took comfort in my letter to the league president, which had gone out yesterday.

Wouldn't you know it? Professor Pendergast, the brilliant lepton scientist, couldn't figure out how to get a baseball out from between the bars of a catcher's mask. And it was really in there. Even Tuba Dave, our strongest player, couldn't pull it out.

"Did anybody get the license number of that truck?" asked Luis, dazed.

"What a bunch of hicks!" exclaimed Kristy, pulling a hairpin out of her ponytail. She grabbed the mask from Tuba Dave's hands, jammed the hairpin under the ball and, with a twist of the wrist, it was all over. The ball popped out, play ball.

Our opponents were Chet's Texaco Oilers from across town. Kristy started out by humiliating us, mounting a cardboard sign on top of her grandfather's van. It read:

OILERS STINK

Mr. Rudolph, the umpire, made the professor take it down, and we got an official warning. We were in agony since Mr. Rudolph was vice principal of Spooner Junior High. I was sort of hoping to get on his good side. That way I could warn him to take down the eight hundred photographs of a baseball team in their jockstraps that just *might* show up on Day One of school. But now he was mad at all the Tigers, thanks to Guess Who.

"Oh, I didn't do it, Grandpa," said Kristy innocently. And our coach, a great scientific mind, believed her. She still had red paint on her hands!

Our parents got to see all this, since the spectators were beginning to arrive. *Every guy* whose folks were there got the old "poor sportsmanship" lecture after the game. So none of us were upset that only twenty people showed up — mostly parents and brothers and sisters of the two teams.

It wasn't exactly the World Series. The other team stank, but you couldn't smell them over the reek that was coming from us.

The Oilers started at bat, and we knew we were in trouble early. On the first pitch, Luis saw a ball coming at him and went a little nuts. He dove out of the way, knocking Mr. Rudolph flying.

"Okay, kid," panted the umpire, scrambling to his feet and dusting himself off. "Calm down."

But the second pitch produced the same result. This time, Luis tackled the batter, who jumped up and was ready to make a big deal out of it.

"What are you — crazy, kid?"

"*Me* crazy?!" cried Luis. "You were supposed to hit that!"

The batter and Mr. Rudolph both regarded Luis oddly. Kristy stuck her nose into it, which was like running up to a fire with a bucket of gasoline.

"'Tsup, dudes? Luis, you okay?"

Outraged, our catcher pointed at Kevin on the mound. "He keeps throwing those right *at* me!"

"He's the pitcher, stupid!" growled the batter. "And you're the catcher!"

Kristy gazed at him blandly. "Are you going to shut up now, or only after I pull your right nostril back and hook it over the button on your left hip pocket?"

Mr. Rudolph stared at her. "Who *are* you?"

And Kristy retreated into the dugout.

Ever wonder if a baseball game could be played without a catcher? Luis ducked, dove, leapt, and rolled, and not a single throw reached his mitt. We allowed eighteen stolen bases! There were so many runners out there, it looked like a track meet! Luis's mom even came out onto the field to try to calm her son down. It didn't help.

At one point, in the second inning, with the Oilers up at bat and leading 3–zip, bases loaded, Luis saw a fastball in flight and covered his mask with his mitt. The ball bounced off his chest pad right onto the plate. The guy scoring from third almost killed himself on it. Ernie MacIntosh charged in from first base, too late to tag the next guy coming home, so he tried to throw to third. I got this ball in left field. The Oilers scored a grand slam without a hit! All errors! I wonder if that's ever been done before.

"Splendid! Splendid!" was the professor's comment.

Our coach pretty much cheered his way through the

whole thing. It was too bad that he went to the bathroom in the bottom of the fourth because he missed our hit. Bobby Ray Devereaux managed to smack a line drive between the shortstop and the third baseman. Bobby Ray got greedy, though, and went for second base. He was out by a mile, but Kristy launched off the bench like a Polaris missile.

"Kristy!" I hissed. "*No!*"

Too late. "What are you — *crazy*, Ump?" she howled, kicking dirt all over Mr. Rudolph's shoes. "You're missing a great game here! Get some glasses!"

By the time the professor got back, his sweet little granddaughter was in the parking lot, ejected in disgrace.

"Where's Kristy?" he asked.

There were a lot of "ums" and "uhs," because nobody wanted to tell the hero of Spooner that his little princess was Godzilla.

"She — uh — went out to get some air," Ernie improvised. Ernie was not known for his ability to think under pressure.

Then, believe it or not, the game got stupider. Tuba Dave popped straight up, and the ball came down and hit him on the head. So his folks escorted him home with a headache. Since we only had nine guys to start with, we had to borrow a second baseman from the other team. We complained that the new kid wouldn't be trying a hundred percent. But even I have to admit that he was our best player. He almost set up a double play, except that Ernie missed the perfect throw to first, and the play turned into an inside-the-park home run. Well, sort of inside-the-park, because the ball rolled under the bleachers into some high grass, and we couldn't find it.

After twenty minutes of searching, the other team wanted to go home. So Mr. Rudolph called the game in the fifth inning. Final score: Oilers 9, Tigers 0.

"Boys, you did splendidly well," beamed Professor Pendergast.

"But, Coach," I protested, "we got creamed!"

"It's not whether you win or lose," proclaimed our coach. "It's how you play the game." Ever wonder why they never say that to the guys who win?

"But we didn't play well either," Tim pointed out. "We didn't just lose. We stank and lost. We're hopeless."

"Even my dad walked out," added Caspar.

The coach surveyed our long faces in genuine alarm. "You're not having fun."

It was amazing. Our chances of ever even scoring a run, let alone winning a game, were way below zero. Yet all we could think of was how upset Professor Pendergast looked.

"Of course we had fun," I lied and forced myself to smile. "It was — a blast."

"Yeah!" Kevin enthused. "Sure, we didn't get any runs,

but we had some — uh — interesting defensive plays."

The professor wasn't convinced. So we had to celebrate our terrific disaster. We gave him a cheering escort to the parking lot. The other team thought we were nuts.

There wasn't much finger-pointing or name-calling. Nobody accused anyone else of being the goat; we were all goats. But I figured Luis had to be at least the leader of the herd.

"What happened to him?" I asked after our catcher had jogged home. "He was fine at practice."

It took Kristy to remember the incident during the warm-up. "You hayseeds know nothing about psychology," she explained. "He's gun-shy from that fastball he almost ate."

"But he had a mask on!" I protested.

"He still got it right between the eyes, man! When he sees a baseball on the way, it brings it all back!"

"But he's our only catcher!" wailed Tim.

"The mind is a delicate thing," lectured Dr. Kristy Freud, famed New York psychiatrist. "We can't just say 'Get over it, or else.' It could turn him into a vegetable!"

"*Really?*" Tim was wide-eyed.

She nodded intently. "Or he could snap the other way — like one of those guys from the movies, with a chain saw!"

"Aw, come on! This is stupid!" I protested. "We've all known Luis for years! He's not going to start going after people with chain saws just because he got a ball in the face!"

"His father owns that equipment rental place," put in Ernie worriedly. "He could get a chain saw easy."

"We have to be gentle," Kristy decided, "build up his confidence, show him we care. We'll help him with his problem, but we'll make sure not to put any pressure on him."

"Our next game is in three days," I pointed out.

"Oh, well, if he's not cured by then, he's dead meat," said Kristy.

★★★

Stage One of the plan, according to Kristy, was me.

"*Me!?* Why *me*?"

"You're his teammate, his trusted friend," she insisted.

"We're not best friends! We happen to be neighbors!" I protested. "If I bang on his door and ask to have a catch, it'll be the first time ever! He'll think I'm nuts!"

She rapped on my head with her clenched fist. "Hello? Anybody home? We've got to get Luis to admit he has a problem before we can treat it. If you guys are tossing a ball around, you can start making like a pitcher, throwing harder and harder, until it brings out the old fear."

"What's so great about that?" I demanded. "The old fear cost us a ball game."

She rolled her eyes. "Then we have an open rap session. You know — hey, Luis, 'tsupwitchoo?"

’Tsupwitchoo? It took me a while but I nailed it down: What’s up with you?

I figured it was okay to go along with Kristy here. After all, the Tigers sure wouldn’t get any better with a catcher who was afraid of the ball.

We walked together over to Luis’s place, and I rang the bell. I glanced over to Kristy for reassurance, and she was gone.

“Psssst! Over here.” She was crouched in the middle of a honeysuckle bush, flashing me the thumbs-up signal.

“Get back out here!” I rasped. But by then, Luis was at the door. “Oh, hi,” I said, grinning like a jackass. “I just wondered if you wanted to have a catch.”

“Not really,” said Luis.

Like a computer, my mind raced through Kristy’s instructions. There was nothing to cover “not really.” “Hang on a second. I’ve got to go talk to this bush.”

Kristy jumped out into the open. “Hey, Luis, ’tsup? Johnson and I thought maybe you’ve got something you want to tell us.”

“About what?”

She shrugged expansively. “*Any* subject. World politics! Black holes! Stamp collecting! Why you can’t catch a baseball worth beans—”

“Cut it out!” I exploded. “Look, Luis, we saw you having some problems yesterday. We’d like to help.”

Luis looked miserable. "You've got to find someone to replace me."

Kristy shook her head. "No can do, baby. You guys are the last nine losers in this league."

"I can't understand it!" Our catcher looked haunted. "Every time I see the ball coming at me, I figure, 'This is the one that's going to knock my head off!' I had a dream last night. All the best pitchers were there — Roger Clemens, and Nolan Ryan, and Dennis Eckersley, and Dwight Gooden — and they were all throwing at my head!"

"That's cold, man," Kristy sympathized. "But don't sweat it, because we're all in this together. We'll see you through. Just like the Three Musketeers — all for one, and one for all."

On the way back to my place, she curled her lip in disgust. "Sheesh, what a wimp!"

"Hey!" I exploded. "What about the Three Musketeers? What about 'We're all in this together'?"

"Hey, man, Roger Clemens never threw anything at *me*!"

"I'll talk to the professor," I mused. "We could move Luis to left field. You're lucky if you get a ball a week out there, and they sure won't be line drives, and—"

She was shaking her head pityingly. "In New York, you get over your problems by facing up to them, not by hiding out in left field. You pick up the reality sandwich, hold your nose, and take a bite so big you could choke on it, man. That's what Luis has to do!"

"I checked with the luncheonette," I said sarcastically. "They're fresh out of reality. How about liverwurst?"

"Lose the comedy routine," said Kristy. "It's time for Luis to confront his deepest fear."

"Roger Clemens hitting him with a baseball?" I asked incredulously.

"Well, obviously, Roger Clemens isn't going to come to a one-horse town like this." She shrugged. "So I guess you'll have to do it."

"Are you nuts?" I exploded. "I can't just walk up to the guy and bean him with a baseball! It's — assault with a deadly weapon!"

"It's a baseball," she said calmly, "not a hand grenade. And you won't be throwing your hardest. It'll hurt; it may give him a bruise. But the guy'll see he's still alive, and he'll be cured."

"Forget it," I told her and started to walk away.

Kristy reached into her pocket and pulled out a small black film canister. "Hey, Johnson! There's a Fotomat at the mall, right?"

I stopped in my tracks. "What's on that?"

She shrugged. "Family stuff — pictures of my dog, our trip to Niagara Falls, a bunch of naked baseball players—"

"*We weren't naked!*" I cried out.

"There's one way to find out," she smiled serenely.

"You wouldn't."

In answer, she strolled off in the direction of Spooner Mall. I followed, making a long speech about how the jig was up.

"You want us to think you're so tough? Well, forget it! You're all talk and no action. One hundred percent hot air. I'll bet there wasn't any film in the camera! I'll bet the lens cap was still on! I'll bet the batteries were dead—"

She marched through the crowded mall to the Spooner Fotomat, and handed in her canister.

I was mesmerized by the developing machine. An endless procession of photos passed by the window on the conveyer belt. Practically every shopper paused to check out the pictures. I swallowed hard. In a few short minutes, *we* would be on that conveyer — in our underwear, jockstraps or worse — for full public viewing. And wasn't that my mother's entire bridge club heading this way?

"*No-o-o!*" I cried out.

The Fotomat guy looked at me like I had a cabbage for a head.

I chickened out totally. "I'll do it! I'll hit Luis with a baseball!" I babbled at Kristy. "Just don't develop The Picture!"

She snatched back the film, and grinned. "You're the boss, bro'."

★★★

Kristy decided that tonight would be the perfect time. Luis always helped out at his father's store in the evenings, and that was when we went to do the deed.

"I hope you can do this," Kristy was warning me. We were crouched between two parked cars in front of Bono's Equipment Rentals. "Don't break the store window! They cost, like, zillions of dollars!"

"Hey," I said sharply. "I'm a pitcher. Just because *somebody* stuck me way out in left field doesn't mean I can't put a ball exactly where I want to."

The look on her face clearly said she didn't think I was that good. And that's when I vowed that I was going to bounce a perfect strike dead center off Luis's forehead.

Inside, Mr. Bono was closing up, so I bore down, just like the big league pitchers. I made the whole universe shrink down to that one little doorway. Then I shrank the doorway down to that one little forehead that was going to be there in a minute. I couldn't miss. It was the only thing in the universe to throw at.

There was the sound of the bells on the door, and the forehead was there! I sprang up, and let fly the perfect pitch — not too hard, not too soft, straight as an arrow.

Direct hit!

Wrong forehead!

Terence Laredo, Tim's sixteen-year-old brother, known to all of us as Terence the Terrorist. He stared at me, veins bulging, one hand clutching his right eye, the other holding — yes, a chain saw.

"*Why, you little—*"

I didn't hear what he called me, because I was running too hard. And, at that, I was a good three steps behind Kristy.

I should be grateful. When he caught me, he didn't use the chain saw.

"'Tsup?" panted Kristy, turning to face Terence. "Kristy Pendergast from New York. That's quite a sprint you've got there! Adrenaline city, man! Ever time it without the chain saw?"

"*I'm gonna have a black eye because of you!*" the Terrorist roared at me from an altitude of about half an inch. He'd had onions for dinner. Yeccch.

"A black eye?" Kristy gazed into his face, which was already starting to swell. "I don't think so. Which eye?"

"*This one!*" He hauled off and belted me with a hammer punch that almost took my head off.

"Oh, that eye," said Kristy.

The worst part was Luis saw the whole thing, and figured out what we'd been trying to do, and why.

Face it. I should have killed Kristy. But she was the one who dragged me home and made up the story for my parents about how I walked into a door.

"You took it like a man," she praised, holding an ice pack against my eye. "Very New York."

I kicked her out of the house.

***

The crank call came just before the eleven o'clock news that night. "Come to the game an hour early tomorrow," the muffled voice intoned. "This means you."

"Kristy, why are you bugging me so late?"

"Oh, hi. 'Tsup? I'm just calling to make sure everyone's there, because we're going to cure Luis once and for all."

"What are we going to do?" I snarled, eye throbbing. "Pelt him with spears? Shoot him with a bazooka? Launch a missile down his pants?"

"You'll see." Click.

If it hadn't been so late, I'd have phoned all the guys to tell them not to show up. But the next day, there we were, milling around like sheep, waiting for Kristy's orders. It was amazing what The Picture had done to all of us.

"What happened to your eye?" asked Ernie. My shiner was in full bloom by now.

"Terence the Terrorist attacked me with a chain saw," I replied sourly.

"He came after me, too!" added Tim, wide-eyed. "Because you're my friend! He rubbed my face up and down the carpet, made me eat a shoelace, burned a hole in my jean jacket, and deducted six inches from my half of the room! I got off easy."

"'Tsup, guys?" Kristy appeared, Luis in tow. "Okay, we all need to form a circle around me and Luis."

"Why?" I asked suspiciously.

From her hip pocket, she produced a well-thumbed paperback entitled *Hypnotism*.

"Aw, come on! That's stupid!" Tim protested. "Hypnotism doesn't work!"

"Yo, man, Luis agreed, so don't hassle it!"

"Yeah," I said bitterly. "Luis agreed because you threatened to develop The Picture."

"*Not* true," Kristy said righteously. "It was pure team loyalty."

It's the Kristy disease. I mean, I'm positive everybody else knew this wasn't going to work. But she just kept shooting her mouth off. And pretty soon, there we were, in the shady part of the clubhouse, sitting around in a circle, hypnotizing Luis.

Guess what she swung back and forth in front of Luis's face! That stupid film canister on a string! Just in case we needed a little reminder of why we were at her mercy! Then she began to chant, "You are getting sleepy — very sleepy — so-o-o-o sleepy — your eyelids are becoming heavy — your eyes are closing—"

Ernie yawned.

"Not you, stupid!" hissed Tuba Dave.

"Sle-e-e-e-py — sle-e-e-e-py —" Kristy continued. "Now, on the count of three—"

"I'm not hypnotized yet," Luis interrupted.

"Are you sure?" asked Kristy. "You might be hypnotized and not even know it."

Luis shrugged. "I don't think so."

Kristy gave him one of her disgusted looks that said a New Yorker would have been in a deep trance hours ago, but we hicks weren't even smart enough to go under.

So she started over with the "You're getting slee-e-e-e-py," and she went on for about five minutes, which is a long time when you're bored stiff. Then finally she said, "Repeat after me: 'I am in a blissful state.'"

"I am in a blissful state."

It wasn't Luis. Ernie sat there, his eyes closed, his chin on his chest.

"You hypnotized the wrong guy," said Luis.

"Make him bark like a dog!" begged Tuba Dave.

"He's just faking it!" I exploded. "Come on, Ernie, the joke's over."

"The joke's over," Ernie chanted after me.

"This is fresh!" raved Kristy. "Okay, listen, Ernie: you are a better hitter than Babe Ruth."

We all laughed, and Ernie woke up.

"How do you feel?" Kristy asked intently.

"Hungry," said Ernie. "Anybody got a Baby Ruth?"

"Luis, man, you're not relaxed enough," Kristy decided, "which means you've got to concentrate on not concentrating. You dig?"

Luis looked worried and tried to watch the film canister as it swung back and forth.

I was burning inside. Bad enough we were the worst team on the planet; now we were going to get no warm-up, and no batting practice, and all because Professor Pendergast had a granddaughter from New York!

"You're getting sle-e-e-e-py — very sle-e-e-e-py —" she continued in her mystical voice. "Sleepy — and sleepy — and ple-e-ease hurry up and get hypnotized before my arm falls off — ve-e-e-ery sle-e-e-py —"

I was about to stop her when Tim whispered, "Look — he's asleep."

And sure enough, there was Luis, out like a light.

"How do we know he isn't faking?" asked Ernie.

"Simple," said Kristy. She hovered over Luis's ear and whispered. "Luis's mom has stegosaurus breath."

Tim nodded, wide-eyed. "He's hypnotized for real all right," he said positively. "Nobody could just lie there and listen to dinosaur jokes about his mother!"

"Okay, Luis, listen up." Kristy continued in her normal voice. "You're not afraid of the baseball. You're a great catcher, and nothing can hurt you."

"Nothing can hurt me," Luis repeated.

"Now, when I snap my fingers, you're going to wake up. You won't remember any of this, except how grateful you are to your good friend Kristy from New York."

"From New York," echoed Luis.

Then she snapped her fingers, and Luis opened his eyes. "I'm sorry," he said. "I guess I'm just not the type who can be hypnotized."

"But you *were*!" I blurted. And that rotten Kristy belted me right in the ribs.

"Oh, that's okay," she grinned, winking at everybody. "Win some, lose some." She turned to the rest of us. "Come on, dudes! You're missing batting practice!"

We came out of the clubhouse, and there was Mr. Rudolph, the umpire, fast asleep on our dugout steps.

"Oh, no!" exclaimed Ernie. "You don't think he heard us, and now we're going to get thrown out of the league!?"

"What?!" snorted Tuba Dave. "You think there's a Little League rule that says 'No Hypnotizing'?"

"Wait a minute," Kevin began slowly. "If he was eavesdropping on us, and he heard us hypnotizing Luis, maybe he accidentally got hypnotized, too."

I turned to Kristy. "Can that happen?"

In return I got a diabolical grin that stretched from ear to ear. She leaned close to Mr. Rudolph. "Okay, Ump, this is the way it is: Everything Kevin throws is a strike;

everything the other guys throw is a ball. Got that? Okay, when I snap my fingers—"

"You can't do that!" I exploded. "It's not honest!"

"Big talk from last place!" sneered Kristy. She turned back to the umpire. "You won't remember a word of this—"

"Don't listen to her, Mr. Rudolph!" I interrupted. "Call a fair game—"

"Ignore this Goody Two-Shoes!" Kristy urged. "The Tigers are the greatest; everybody else is a bunch of bums!"

"You can't show any favoritism!" I insisted. "Everyone has to have an equal chance—" I fell silent. Mr. Rudolph was awake and glaring at me.

"Johnson, are you saying I'm not a fair umpire?"

He hadn't been hypnotized! He was just having a nap!

"Uh — no, sir. I — uh — just—" I looked around. Kristy was nowhere in sight.

"I never show favoritism!" Mr. Rudolph roared. "I call 'em as I see 'em, and what I see now is a smart-mouthed kid trying to influence my officiating!"

Professor Pendergast arrived. "What seems to be the trouble?"

"Oh, Grandpa," said Kristy in her best Little Princess voice. "Corey insulted the umpire!"

I had to make a formal apology. I choked it out through my reality sandwich.

But I had to hand it to Kristy. Luis was okay! We got

killed, of course, 8–1, but Luis was solid as granite behind the plate. He never even flinched. Maybe there *was* something to this hypnotism mumbo jumbo.

"Hey, Luis!" I ran up to him after the other team had finished their celebrating. "Sorry about yesterday. And, wow! You were great!"

"Thanks." He looked at me intently. "But my mom *definitely* doesn't have stegosaurus breath!"

"What?" He was *under* when Kristy had told him that! There was no way he could remember it! Unless— "You weren't hypnotized, were you! You faked the whole thing!"

Luis looked faintly embarrassed. "All you guys wanted it to happen so much. And that Kristy — well, she has The Picture, and she just doesn't take no for an answer—"

"She won't be around forever," I predicted with a wink.

"Well," Luis went on, "I just figured if you were willing to go to all that hassle to cure me, I owed it to the team to get cured, even if it was kind of lying."

"And the next time Kevin pitched to you you wouldn't let yourself get scared?" I asked.

"Well, not exactly." He looked embarrassed. "I think I really got cured when you threw that baseball at Tim's brother."

I grinned. "You saw that it didn't kill him, and you felt okay?"

"No way! A great big tough guy like that can take way

more pain than me! But when he smashed you right in the face, I thought, How much worse could a little baseball be?"

On cue, my eye throbbed. I didn't mind the pain. My black eye had helped the Feather-Soft Tigers.

"Yo, Johnson!" was Kristy's parting shot. "Don't think I won't remember who cost us this game. We had the ump totally hypnotized until you stuck your nose in, with your small-town-fair-play-nice-guy wimporama!"

I thought of Mr. Lopez, who might have been reading my letter at that very moment.

It wouldn't be long now.

CHAPTER 3

Second Base —
Tuba Dave Jablonski

Tuba Dave Jablonski was a great hitter who never got a hit. No pitcher could get a ball behind Tuba Dave. To us he was King of the Line Drive. To the other teams he was "Easy out! Easy Out!"

The problem was that Tuba Dave, who swung a bat like Ty Cobb, ran bases like Ty Cobb's grandmother. He would smack the ball clear to the outfield and still not give himself enough time to waddle to first base before the throw. And since he only hit *line drives*, he never had the height or the distance for a home run.

Talk about depressing! Here was Tuba Dave, hammering pitches that would have been doubles and triples for any of the rest of us — and the poor guy never even got on base.

"He's totally uncool!" Kristy had the gall to say over the phone. "He's *so close* to being a star, but instead he's the crummiest player in the league! That's like having the biggest, hypest, most delicious quadruple chocolate cake, but you can't eat it because you know somebody spit in the pan!"

"He's a great hitter!" I said defensively. "He just needs a little more practice base running—"

"More practice isn't going to help!" she cut me off. "Less Tuba Dave is going to help."

"Lay off!" I exploded. "So he's big. So what? He plays tuba in our marching band. Ever lift a tuba? Ever try to march with it?"

Kristy dismissed this with a snort. "My main man P.P. isn't coaching the marching band. Unfortunately, he's stuck with you losers. Which is why Tuba Dave is going on a crash diet starting tomorrow!"

I was torn. Part of me cried out that this was none of Kristy's business. On the other hand, this could help the team! I did stick up for Tuba Dave a little, though. "Listen," I cautioned her. "A guy's weight — that's a totally personal thing. You've got to be careful not to humiliate him in front of the whole team."

She sounded wounded. "Yo, would I hurt a guy's feelings?"

★★★

I arrived at practice the next day to find the dugout jammed full of diet booklets. There was the *Scarsdale Diet*, the *Prune Juice and Banana Diet*, the *Manchurian Bush Diet*, *Stir-Fry Your Way to a Brand-New You*, *Eggplant Extravaganza*, *Tummy Trimmer*, and a diet that I found just plain scary: *Starving: No Food, No Fat*.

I turned on Kristy in horror. "I thought we agreed not to embarrass the guy! Get these out of here—"

In response, she flashed a dazzling smile, not at me, but at Tuba Dave, who had just walked in. He tossed his glove to the bench and stared at the library of diet literature littering our dugout.

"It's not what you think," I began, but Tuba Dave looked at me, and I could tell he was hurt.

"You know I've been trying to slim down," he said.

I nodded, hating myself.

Tuba Dave picked up a printed brochure that blazoned: *Help at Last with Your Eating Problem*. "I don't have an eating problem," he told us. "I eat great."

"Sure you do!" blurted Ernie. "I mean — not that great! You know — just great enough!"

We all joined in a babbling chorus of approval for the way Tuba Dave ate. All except Kristy. She placed a bathroom scale on the dugout floor. "Okay, Slick," she told Tuba Dave. "Weigh in."

Tuba Dave folded his arms in front of him. "No."

Casually, Kristy jiggled the film canister, which she now wore on a string around her neck.

Totally defeated, Tuba Dave stepped onto the pad. "A hundred and seventy-six pounds?!" He turned accusing eyes on Kristy. "That's impossible! The scale must be broken!"

But Kristy had gathered up the diet booklets, and held them, fanned out like a deck of cards. "Choose your weapon, bro'."

"*Aw!*" Like a condemned man, Tuba Dave reached over and pulled out the smallest of the brochures. He gaped in horror:

Discover the Diet Secret of Ancient Greece! Delicious HORTA, stewed crabgrass from the Peloponnesus.

"Look at it as an adventure, bro'," Kristy advised. "Check it out. Greek food from the land of the Parthenon, Mount Olympus—"

"Yeah, but *crabgrass*?" cried Tuba Dave, looking very pale.

"*Horta*," Kristy amended. "Very cool. You picked the best one."

It was too much for our second baseman. He ran off at top speed (about as fast as a quick walk for the rest of us).

"Oh, well," I said to Kristy. "You're not the first person to bomb out at putting Tuba Dave on a diet."

"Too bad," she commented mildly. "He's going to look pretty flabby on eight hundred lockers."

We caught up with Tuba Dave in the parking lot.

"You've got to do it!" begged Ernie.

"Not in a billion centuries!"

"But she's going to develop The Picture!" wailed Tim.

"Let her!"

"What?" Ernie was horrified.

"I was way in the back!" said our second baseman. "Maybe you can't even see me!"

Ernie turned on Kevin. "It's all your fault!"

Kevin stared. "*My* fault?"

"If your dad had gotten our stupid uniforms ready on time, there wouldn't *be* a Picture!"

"Time out!" I shouted, signaling the T. "Just play along with the diet," I told Tuba Dave. "It'll only be for a few days." I dropped my voice to a whisper. "Kristy'll be off our backs pretty soon."

Tuba Dave looked bewildered. "How do you figure that?"

"I wrote a letter to the league president."

"You're a genius," cried Ernie.

"Shhh!" I hissed. "I didn't sign it. She must *never know* it was one of us, or she'll develop the you-know-what!"

Tuba Dave grimaced. "All right, I'll do it. But it better be only a few days."

***

As it turned out, you couldn't get crabgrass just anywhere. I mean, there was plenty of crabgrass around, just not the right kind that goes into authentic Greek *horta*. We went to nine stores before we found the perfect mixture of grass, dandelion greens, and clover for the recipe. We reported to the Jablonski house just in time to spoil Tuba Dave's dinner.

Mrs. Jablonski had made this great meal with roast chicken and mashed potatoes — *my* mouth was watering, so you can imagine how Tuba Dave felt. The family was around the table. Pieces of chicken were being piled up on his plate. And suddenly, there was Kristy, lecturing his parents about how Tuba Dave was on a new diet, from now on this was all he could eat, and wasn't it wonderful?

I couldn't wait for the Jablonskis to boot her out of the house. But Tuba Dave's parents had been pushing him for a diet for years, so they thought this was a great idea. In fact, Mrs. Jablonski put her own dinner on hold to help Kristy stew up the first batch of *horta*.

"Hang in there," I said to Tuba Dave.

He nodded miserably. "I was sort of hoping the store would be all out, and they'd have to send away to Greece. By boat."

I won't try to build any suspense — the stuff was *disgusting*! We all tried it except for Tuba Dave's little sister, and she was the smart one. I don't much like broccoli and cauliflower, but I have to admit that *horta* was in a class by itself. Long blades of wet grass in a tasteless, watery clump. Unbelievable! Even the adults took a few bites, proclaimed, "Interesting," and turned their attention to the chicken. Tuba Dave only managed a third of a bowl — and I know for a fact he was starving!

As soon as we got out of there, Kristy rubbed her hands together with glee. "He's going to lose weight even faster than I thought! Did you taste that stuff? I'd rather eat garbage!"

"What a terrible diet!" I agreed.

"Are you kidding?" she chortled. "It's the greatest diet in the world, bro'. It's money in the bank. Tuba Dave's going to be burning up the base paths in a couple of weeks!"

I felt a twinge of guilt. Sure, Kristy *was* awful, but she was A-one right that Tuba Dave needed this diet. I actually found myself toying with the hope that Mr. Lopez would take a while before coming to our rescue so Tuba Dave could get thin. It meant more time with Kristy, but that was a small price to pay for making a hitter out of our second baseman.

Kristy put Tuba Dave on daily weigh-ins. By the next practice, he'd *gained* a pound. By our next game, he was up to one-seventy-nine. We lost big, with our expanding second baseman smacking three should-be hits, and never once getting near first base.

Mrs. Jablonski said Tuba Dave was eating his *horta* three times a day, no snacks, no cheating.

Kristy was unconvinced. "No one gains weight eating crabgrass. He must be backsliding. We'll have to watch him."

And when she said "we," she meant *everybody*. She divvied up Tuba Dave's life into time slots and handed them out. I went over to hang around the guy every morning. Tim and Ernie switched off on the afternoons. Different combinations of the three of us and Kristy made sure Tuba Dave was never alone in the evening. When we couldn't keep up the pace, Kevin and Luis helped out. Mrs. Jablonski reported on mealtimes. And Tuba Dave's kid sister was our spy for late night and early morning.

"He's still eating that gross green stuff," Annie Jablonski whispered out her bedroom window to Kristy and me, hiding in the bushes below. "The only other thing he puts in his mouth is that stupid tuba."

From down the hall, we could hear the oompah-pah of Tuba Dave practicing.

"Dessert report," continued Kristy, all business.

"Just us," shrugged Annie. "David hasn't touched a thing."

"Make sure," Kristy ordered. "Weigh all the chocolate in the house, and subtract what you and your folks eat. Then, if the numbers don't match, we nail his butt to the wall."

"How's he been otherwise?" I asked anxiously. "All this diet stuff must be getting him down."

"He's been kind of normal," said Annie. "He talks about the Tigers all the time. Oh, yeah, he's been practicing his music a whole lot. He seems pretty happy."

"Aha!" Kristy snapped her fingers triumphantly. "That proves he's been cheating. Nobody could be happy on a diet of green slime three times a day! This dude should be nasty and rotten and evil! He should make Genghis Khan look like Mr. Rogers!" The oompah-pahs reached us once more. "Instead he's playing a *tuba*! Man, all this practice isn't even helping! Listen to that! It sounds like he's strangling a walrus!"

"Hey!" I interjected angrily. Tuba Dave was a great tuba player, but tonight I had to admit Kristy was right. Our second baseman really wasn't his powerful booming self on the instrument. The sound was weaker — and kind of warbly. "Maybe eating crabgrass messes up your tuba playing. That would explain the extra practicing."

"Something stinks here." Kristy folded her arms in front of her. "I mean, something besides the *horta*."

"Well, I hope it goes on forever," said Annie positively. "David's being extra nice to me, taking out the garbage for Dad, doing all the shopping for Mom—"

"That's it!" cried Kristy.

"Pipe down!" I hissed.

"Don't you get it?" she insisted. "Tuba Dave's doing the shopping! He's buying extra stuff for himself!" She surveyed the house and backyard. "He's got a stockpile hidden around here somewhere, Annie. He's figured out you're watching him, so he waits for you to fall asleep, and then it's major chowtime." She regarded the nine-year-old intently. "When is it safe to search the place?"

"Wait a second!" Now, this was going too far, even for Kristy. "It's one thing to put the guy on a diet and slap him with around-the-clock surveillance. It's something else to break in and search his house. That's illegal!"

"We won't be breaking in," Kristy explained. "Annie will be letting us in. Right, Annie?"

Tuba Dave's little sister smiled conspiratorially. "He's got a tuba lesson at ten tomorrow. He never misses it."

Kristy clapped her hands together with determination. "He's toast!"

★★★

We scoured Tuba Dave's closet. We riffled through his underwear. We even took down the guy's light fixture to make sure there was no food up there. Nothing.

But Kristy wasn't done yet. She must have had CIA training. We went through the Jablonski house with a fine-tooth comb. I doubt Tuba Dave would be storing food in his father's golf bag, but that didn't stop Kristy. She checked bookcases for sandwiches jammed behind *Encyclopaedia*

Britannica. She opened up the furnace filter! The cedar chest! Mr. Jablonski's toolbox! Then she started opening air ducts!

"Okay," she conceded finally. "No food in here. He must be hiding it outside."

I figured she meant the garage and the garden shed. And yeah, we searched those places. But she also had me beating the bushes and digging holes in the flower beds to look for buried bags of supplies.

"Listen, this is stupid!" I said. "Nobody keeps food outside. The animals would get at it."

Talk to a wall. "If you don't have the guts for this kind of work, Johnson, you shouldn't have signed up for Little League!"

"Forgive me!" I raged. "I didn't read the fine print, where it says you have to have detective skills!"

"Wimp City!" She pointed to the giant oak tree that dominates the Jablonskis' backyard. "Okay, up you go."

I stared at her. "The guy can't even waddle to first base. How do you figure he's got a smorgasbord twenty feet straight up?"

She shrugged her famous New York shrug. "If I was eating nothing but crabgrass, I'd swim through molten lava for half a potato chip. Now, alley-oop!"

"It's your idea, *you* do it!"

She jiggled the film canister around her neck. "I'm the

photographer; you're the tree climber!"

We were so close to being rid of her! I couldn't let her develop The Picture over one lousy tree. So I scrambled up the big oak. "Now what?" I called down.

"We search *that*!" She was pointing up directly above me.

What *was* that thing? Curiosity got the better of me, and I began to climb up toward it. It was big enough to be a package of food in a brown knapsack. But how would Tuba Dave get way up there? The tree was starting to groan and shake under *my* weight, and I was half of *him*.

"Status report," called Kristy.

"I can't tell yet." I was close, but the sun was bright, and the sharp contrasts of light and shadow made it difficult to see. And then I hoisted myself up on a high branch and looked.

The suspected food stash was a crow's nest, complete with three baby birds.

I was thrilled. I was going to have the privilege of informing the great Kristy that she had *made a mistake*! I might even use one of her phrases, like "reality sandwich," or "Earth to Kristy." I laughed with the pure joy of it. And that was why I didn't hear the mother crow, swooping down to defend her nest from my "attack."

She was the size of a B-52, and red-hot steaming mad. She made a dive-bombing run on my face. I must have cried out, because Kristy yelled, "What is it? Did you find the food?"

But *I* was the food. The mother bird pecked at my head, flapped in my face, and clawed at my shirt. I had to get out of there, but the only direction was down. I tried to swing away from her, but at that moment, there was a sharp cracking sound, and my branch was no longer attached to the tree.

I was falling feet first right at the fence, but I didn't panic. I could come down on the top rail, cushioning the impact by bending my knees. Then I'd simply hop down to the ground. I bounced off the top of the fence like a superball, my legs springing me high into the air. That's when I looked down and saw blue water instead of green grass. Oh, yeah. The Jablonskis' neighbors had a pool.

If I had performed that well in the county fair belly-flop competition last fall, I'd have either won first prize or been split open like a sack of oats. The water broke my fall, along with my stomach, in a giant tidal wave splash.

Kristy fished me out using the bug dipper and pried the broken branch out of my hands. "You're wasting your time playing baseball," she commented blandly. "You've got a great future as a daredevil. Captain Gravity, man!"

"There was a crow up there!" I quavered.

"You got off easy." She shrugged. "If that had been a

New York crow, it would have had your head off and been stuffing eggs down your neck."

What a great comfort it was to know things could have been even worse.

***

Get this: At our next practice, Tuba Dave weighed in at a hundred and eighty-one, *up* two more pounds!

Ernie was wide-eyed. "*Crabgrass* is *fattening*?"

Tuba Dave himself shrugged it off. "It's just my nature," he explained. "I'm big-boned."

"If his bones are as big as his butt," Kristy whispered in my ear, "then he borrowed them from a brontosaurus!"

"Shhhh!"

"I've got to give you credit," Tim told the dieter. "That *horta* stuff is so gross! I never thought you'd stick to it."

"Oh, it's all a matter of willpower," Tuba Dave lectured. "And once you get used to it, *horta* isn't all that bad."

Did he really mean that? Or was he just talking big because he knew Kristy was on the way out?

"He's lying his head off, man!" Kristy hissed at me. "And we're going to prove it!"

I was disgusted. "The last time *we* proved something, I almost drowned!" I snarled.

But by then the professor had arrived. I trotted out to left field to shag fly balls, and the subject seemed to be closed.

★★★

There was this great old baseball movie on TV. I'd looked forward to it all day. I cleared it with my parents that the set was mine for those two hours. I laid out the pillows so the couch would be just right. I got food and a big bottle of Coke. No sooner were the credits over than Kristy showed up.

"Go away," I told her, not even looking up from the screen.

"No can do, bro'."

"If you won't go away, please shut up. I'm watching a movie."

She stepped right in front of the television. "Tuba Dave is growing, even as we speak."

I was furious. "I don't care if Tuba Dave reaches critical mass! Step aside or die!"

Well, I guess it's pretty obvious by now what the outcome would be. She jiggled her film canister and I ended up going with her. Like common criminals, we went over to Tuba Dave's house and shinnied up the drainpipe into his room. Annie was there to let us in.

"Thanks, kid," said Kristy. "Now, the plan is we hide in the closet, and when he goes for his food stash, we nail him."

"Wait a minute!" I exploded. "It's only nine o'clock! When's he going to go to bed?"

"He won't be up for a while yet," said Annie. "He's watching this old baseball story on TV, and he loves it. He says it's the best movie he's ever seen."

We hid in the closet. That is, *I* hid in the closet. Kristy made herself at home. She stretched out on the bed, leafing through Tuba Dave's comic book collection; she fooled with his computer, played a few games, and erased half his hard disk by accident; then she pulled on a pair of his jeans, just to show that she could fit a truck in there with her.

"Get in here!" I hissed. "The movie's almost over!" I could tell, because the Jablonskis were applauding downstairs. I had missed the greatest movie in the world. I *dreamed* about the day Mr. Lopez would come to banish Kristy from my life.

She really took her time putting away Tuba Dave's rock polishing kit and joining me in the closet. I was having a fit, because there were already heavy footsteps coming up the stairs.

She flashed me a dazzling smile. "You worry too much, bro'."

I shut the door a split second before Tuba Dave came into the room. I found this next part a little hard to believe. Here it was, eleven o'clock at night, but was Tuba Dave getting ready to go to sleep? No. He pulled his big brass tuba out from under the bed, inserted himself into it, and began to oompah loudly. Kristy and I watched through the crack in the door. He was blowing his brains out — *at this hour*! And the weirdest part was how really bad he was, and getting worse all the time. I remember school concerts where he was the star of the band, blasting clear and true over all the other instruments. Now here he was, puffing and warbling and wheezing and choking! His face was bright blue — he looked like he was suffocating!

Kristy covered her ears. "Man, I'm no tuba expert, but this is toiletsville!" she whispered.

Listening to bad tuba playing is not my favorite thing. And Kristy Pendergast drove me nuts anyway, so being shut in a closet with her was special torture. I couldn't stand another second.

"That's it!" I hissed in a fury. "I'm leaving!"

Kristy grabbed my arm. "What are you — nuts? He'll see you!"

He could hardly miss. I'd be walking out of his closet. "This has gone on long enough!" I said determinedly. "The guy's not cheating! He's eating his crabgrass! The diet doesn't work!"

"He's backsliding!" she insisted. "I'm positive!"

"Let go!" I ripped my arm from her grasp, but she just grabbed me around the midsection and held on. But I was determined to get out of there. I mustered my strength for one giant surge, and that was when Kristy let go. I came out of that closet like I'd been shot from a cannon, busting the door clean off its hinges. I caromed right into Tuba Dave. The three of us — me, him, and the tuba — went flying. The crash shook the foundations of the house.

The tuba skittered across the carpet, and out of the bell poured a truckload of M&M's. Billions of them, a universe of candy, a technicolor oompah.

I was thunderstruck. I'd never seen so much chocolate in my life. I didn't know there *was* this much chocolate! The M&M's factory must have been empty!

Kristy bounded onto the scene. A "'Tsup?" died on her lips as she looked at the sea of multicolored candies.

"I can explain," Tuba Dave began weakly. But the explanation was all too obvious. Tuba Dave hadn't been sticking to his diet at all. He'd been sucking hundreds — no, *thousands* — of M&M's through the mouthpiece of his tuba! No wonder the instrument didn't sound right! He was using it as a giant chocolate straw!

Kristy found her voice again. "You're busted, mister! Who do you think you are — Willy Wonka?"

"It was just a little snack," whined Tuba Dave.

"Little!?" I repeated. "There must be five million calories lying right under our feet! There isn't this much candy in Spooner! How did you get it all?"

Our second baseman hung his head in shame. "I ordered direct from the factory. I told them I was a supermarket chain." He gestured to the floor. "This was meant for Oklahoma."

Then Kristy launched into this long speech about loyalty, honesty, team spirit, respect for the professor, and self-sacrifice. She talked as though, if Tuba Dave didn't stick to his diet, he might as well be selling vital U.S. defense secrets to the enemy.

"So you see why this is so important," she finished, popping a handful of M&M's into her mouth. "Mmmm, these are great."

"Yeah, they sure are," Tuba Dave agreed hopefully and snatched a handful. They never got to his mouth. Kristy grabbed his wrist, and shook until the fingers opened and the candies fell out. Then she took the pillow from his bed, pulled off the pillowcase, and began filling it with M&M's from the floor.

"Come on, Johnson," she ordered. "We're confiscating these on behalf of the Feather-Soft Tigers."

What could I do? I grabbed a handful and joined in.

★★★

Two days later, Annie Jablonski reported that her brother never smiled, was mean to her all day long, and was picking constant fights with their parents.

"How about his music?" Kristy inquired.

"His tuba's in the shop," she replied. "He blew up yesterday and threw it in the neighbors' pool."

I know how the tuba must have felt.

"He's turned into a monster!" she exclaimed. "Every time Mom brings him his *horta*, I want to hide under the table! I'm afraid he's going to go berserk and kill us all!"

It made Kristy glow with pride. "He's following his diet."

But to Tuba Dave, Public Enemy Number One wasn't his mother, or his sister, or even Kristy. It was me.

"*You lied!* She's not gone! She's still here! And I'm gonna *starve*!"

I guess I felt a little guilty. And for the first time another thought crossed my mind: Where was Mr. Lopez?

CHAPTER 4

First Base — Ernie MacIntosh

Around the same time that Tuba Dave went on his diet for real, summer school started. Our first baseman, Ernie MacIntosh, was on the roster as always. Last year it had been for geography. The year before that, Spanish. This time it was one of the biggies. Good old Ernie had flunked math.

"So Mom says I have to miss all our morning practices to go to school," Ernie informed us, his distaste apparent.

"No big deal," said Kristy. "Cut school."

"Okay," shrugged Ernie, and that seemed to be the end of it.

"Wait a second!" I interjected. "What happens when you flunk again?"

"Oh yeah!" exclaimed Ernie in sudden realization. "There's a pretest to decide if you need to stay in class for the whole summer. If I flunk it, Mom says I have to quit the team!"

"*What?*" shrieked Kristy. "'Tsupwitchoor mom, dude? Is she nuts? Didn't you tell her we've only got nine guys and we even stink with *them*?"

"She just said my education is more important than—"

"Yeah, yeah, yeah. We've all heard the lecture. Man, this is *wack*!"

"Wack?" I repeated.

Kristy tried again. "You know — bogus! Toiletsville! Nonhype! Unchill!" She threw her hands up in exasperation. "*Bad!*"

"Maybe you could study really hard—" Tim began.

"It's not that," Ernie explained. "I get the math right, but the numbers wrong."

"But the math and the numbers are the same thing!" Kristy said reasonably.

I stuck up for Ernie. "I was in his class last year. We studied together." I shrugged. "I can't explain it. He knows how to do everything, but when it comes to the test, he gets all the wrong answers."

Ernie looked sheepish. "It's just that — well, I guess I'm not that smart—"

"Starting today," said Kristy with authority, "you're smart."

"What are you talking about?" I asked suspiciously.

"You've got just as much brains as the next idiot," Kristy praised our first baseman. "You don't pass because nobody ever really put the screws to you. Check it out. If you flunk that pretest, I'm not just going to develop The Picture for every locker in the junior high. I'm also going to blow it up to poster size and hang it in the mall, and send a copy to your mother, both your grandmothers, and all your aunts!" And with that, she walked away.

I followed. "What are you, crazy? How can you do this to the poor guy?"

She looked me squarely in the eye. "By the time it's all over, he'll thank me."

When I got back to the dugout, no one was thanking Kristy. A council of war was in progress.

"Remember," Tim was saying. "If she prints up that picture, our lives are ruined for three years of junior high!"

"Longer, even!" Tuba Dave lamented. "In high school it's the same people. We can only hope they forget—"

"They won't," interrupted Ernie. "My great-grandfather wet his pants in kindergarten, and they *still* bug him about it at Spooner Retirement Lodge!"

Kevin snapped his fingers. "I heard about that. Our neighbor's great uncle was in the same class."

"Think about it," Tim went on. "The jokes, the gags—"

The wedgies!" Ernie exclaimed.

"We won't get dates for the senior prom!" added Luis.

Ernie looked at me reproachfully. "I thought you complained to the league president."

I shrugged. "I guess Mr. Lopez is a really busy guy. He'll get around to us."

"But if he doesn't show up before I flunk the pretest, she'll develop The Picture!" Ernie wailed.

Tim spoke up. "*If* she has the film. There are nine of us and only one of her."

"We can't beat up a girl!" I argued. "Even if she *is* from New York!"

"We don't have to beat her up," Tim reasoned. "Two of us'll grab her. Somebody opens the canister, exposes the film, and our problems are over."

"The professor's going to be late today," added Kevin. "We'll never have another chance."

I thought it over. We weren't going to *hurt* her — just expose that film. Kristy definitely had it coming after the way she tried to blackmail us and push us around. Look at what Tuba Dave was going through! And me! My black eye was the result of Kristy's "brilliant" plan to help Luis.

"Let's do it."

Kristy was standing out by the mound, wearing her New York bored look — like if invaders from outer space were having a barbecue in center field, she wouldn't bother turning around to watch.

We approached from the rear.

I called out, "Hey, Kristy," and when she turned around, Tim and Ernie grabbed an arm each, and Tuba Dave went for the film. She sweep-kicked Tuba Dave's feet out from under him, and pushed Tim backwards over him. Bobby Ray came forward, but Kristy used her free hand to pull his jersey over his head, blinding him. He blundered right into Ryan. Then she flipped Ernie off her right shoulder, sending him crashing to the ground at the feet of Caspar and Luis, knocking them down like bowling pins. At the same moment, she pulled off Kevin's glasses and stuck them on my face! Neither of us could see! We both tripped — him on Caspar and me on Tuba Dave. By the time I got those glasses off my nose, the nine of us lay in a heap, and Kristy was lazing on the pitcher's mound like she didn't have a care in the world.

It was totally humiliating. Picture it — nine guys, beaten to a pulp by a girl who didn't really even fight. Just a push here and a trip there.

"Please don't tell the professor," I gasped.

She smiled at us. "I'm proud of you guys. You've got guts."

Yeah. They were scattered all over the grass.

★★★

The next day, Ernie sprinted all the way from summer school to the ballpark to show us his practice quiz. He got 14 out of 30. The poor guy was so hopeless at math he didn't even know he was flunking.

"What's this? You're having problems with mathematics?" said Professor Pendergast. "I'd be happy to help you with it."

Of course! You have to know *tons* of math to be a physicist! Here we were with an actual genius as our coach, and nobody even thought of asking him to work with Ernie.

"Gee, that'd be great!" Ernie exclaimed. "How about right after practice?"

"Excellent," approved the professor. "We'll have the house to ourselves. Kristy has gone swimming this afternoon."

That got a big cheer. A whole practice without the little princess!

Our coach was all choked up. "It's wonderful to see she has such good friends."

What?! "Oh, yes!" I managed, crossing my fingers behind my back.

The practice began with new signals for bunt, steal, and hit-and-run, which was kind of stupid because we hardly ever got on base. So my mind was wandering, and that's when it hit me.

"She's *swimming*!" I hissed at Tim.

"Too bad there aren't any great white sharks at the pool," Tim whispered back.

"That's cruel," was Tuba Dave's opinion. "What did a

great white shark ever do to you?"

"Listen," I insisted. "You can't take a roll of film under water, right?"

"So the canister must be just sitting there at the professor's house!" Tim finished excitedly.

We zoomed through our workout in record time. Then I rode back with Professor Pendergast and Ernie. We explained that I was helping Ernie as well.

"Oh, by the way," I added, as though it had just dawned on me. "Kristy has a picture of ours — kind of a team portrait. But we forgot to pick up the film."

The professor directed me upstairs to the guest room. "I'm sure she won't mind. It's the second door on the left."

It was all I could do not to whoop with victory as I sprinted up the stairs and into the room. My jaw dropped. The walls were completely plastered with posters of New York City — the World Trade Center, Empire State Building, United Nations. I looked up. Four different views of the Statue of Liberty gazed down at me.

Then I saw the film canister on the dresser. I nearly wept with joy. No more getting pushed around. No more threats of public humiliation. We were free!

I picked up the canister and pulled off the cap.

Whoooosh!!

A thick cloud of black smoke exploded out of the film can right into my face. I began to cough madly.

"Corey, are you all right?" came the professor's voice from downstairs.

"It's just allergies!" I choked out, running to the bathroom. I opened my mouth under the tap and gulped water straight from the sink. That's when I looked in the mirror. My head was caked with gray soot. Desperately, I splashed water in my face. *The stuff didn't come off!* I tried soap. Nothing! Not even when I scrubbed until my cheeks stung!

Heart sinking, I reached inside the canister and pulled out the broken casing of a smoke bomb. On the side was written BIG APPLE NOVELTY CO., NYC.

That rotten Kristy had gotten me again. She had hidden the film and left the smoke bomb in the canister as a booby trap.

I began to panic. What if this guck didn't come off? What if it was permanent?

"'Tsup!" Kristy rolled in from swimming. She looked at me. "Either a volcano erupted on your face or you found the film can."

"That is the dirtiest, sleaziest, most underhanded thing I've ever seen anybody do!" I seethed.

She laughed. "Glad you liked it."

For her, she was pretty nice. She only busted my chops for about ten minutes before fixing me up. She washed my face with vinegar and the soot came right off. I stank like a salad, but otherwise I was good as new.

We headed downstairs to find Professor Pendergast just as stumped with Ernie as Ernie was stumped with math.

"He understands all of the concepts perfectly," the renowned expert explained, shaking his head. "But he can't seem to arrive at a single correct answer. Most baffling." He raised an eyebrow and sniffed. "Has someone been eating cole slaw?"

Kristy covered up a laughing fit with some coughing. Personally, I didn't find it very funny.

★★★

Ernie's pretest was tomorrow afternoon, and things were looking grim for the Toilet Paper Tigers. If the professor couldn't help him, surely nobody could. He would flunk the test, his mom would pull him off the team, and Kristy would develop The Picture. Then we'd all be ruined in Spooner for junior high, probably high school, and maybe even the rest of our lives.

"As I see it, we're up the creek," I told the guys at an emergency meeting before practice. "All we can hope for is a miracle on Ernie's test."

Ryan Crisp spoke up. "There's one thing we haven't tried."

All attention shifted to our right fielder. Ry was always so quiet that if he had an idea, it had to be important.

"Money," said Ry. "New York is the money capital of the world. Maybe if we offer to *buy* the film—"

"A bribe!" I exclaimed. "It's so sleazy, she'll probably go for it!"

We emptied our pockets. Piggy banks were opened, secret stashes tapped. Allowances were paid in advance. Loans were worked out with brothers and sisters. Annie Jablonski gave Tuba Dave a floating line of credit indexed to the prime rate. He didn't understand it, but he didn't care. We had ten minutes to put our hands on every red cent we could — rolls of nickels, bags of pennies, anything!

Ernie had his summer school books with him so he was elected to be the accountant, since he was the only one with any paper.

"Seventy-six dollars and eleven cents," he reported.

"*What?*" I squawked. "It's got to be more than that!"

I peered over Ernie's shoulder as he added the long column of figures. ". . . fifteen . . . twenty-three, plus eight makes thirty-one carry the three, two plus three is six, plus nine—"

"Wait a minute," I interrupted. "Two plus three is *five*. Two *times* three is six."

Ernie was wide-eyed. "It *is*?"

The other Tigers cracked up, and started razzing Ernie. But I thought back to Ernie complaining about getting the math right and the numbers wrong. 2 x 3 and 2 + 3 probably come into just about every single math question there is. If you had them mixed up, it didn't matter how smart you were — you'd *always* get the wrong answer!

But how could a genius like Professor Pendergast miss something so easy? The answer was simple. The professor was so smart himself — in a million years he'd never think that someone might make a mistake like two plus three equals six.

"Take your money back," I commanded the others. "We're getting an A on that test."

$$2 + 3 = 5 \qquad 2 \times 3 = 6$$

He wrote it two hundred times in his notebook. He chalked it on the dugout wall. It was everywhere — the tops of his sneakers, the bottom of his jersey. We quizzed him all through the practice. As we ran by first base we'd yell out, "Two times three!" and Ernie would have to give the answer. That night, Tim, Tuba Dave, and I tag-teamed a marathon study session at Ernie's. Kristy came by and we wouldn't let her into the house. It was beautiful!

Game day was also pretest day, so Ernie was a wreck. When I stepped up to the plate for batting practice, $2 + 3 = 5 \quad 2 \times 3 = 6 \quad 2 + 3 = 5 \quad 2 \times 3 = 6$ was printed all the way down the length of my Louisville slugger.

It had been a big morning at the particle accelerator and Professor Pendergast was celebrating like a teenager. The big event: two leptons had smashed into each other, creating this thing called an antilepton that had lasted for — get this — a *trillionth* of a second. I guess people impress easily in the scientific community.

Tim was having the same thoughts. "He should get a Nintendo or something."

Kristy returned from releasing a large collection of insects into the opposing dugout.

"If you get caught, we could have to forfeit the game!" I hissed.

She shrugged it off. "How many games have you won so far?"

But then I got a hit, and Tim got a hit, and Tuba Dave crunched the ball into the outfield. He never made it to first, of course, but Tim and I both scored. 2–0 Tigers. Our very first lead.

"Is this good? This is good isn't it?" cried the professor, as the rest of us jumped up and down, cheering ourselves hoarse.

Their pitcher was pretty bad, but then Kevin took the mound to show everybody the true meaning of stink. He threw twenty straight balls, walking the first five batters. Tie score, 2–2.

"'Tsupwitchoo?" Kristy stormed the mound. "See that flat thing on the ground in front of Luis? It's called the plate! The ball goes over it! Dig?"

He must've dug, because he floated one over the plate an orangutan couldn't miss. The batter murdered it for a grand slam. 6–2 for the DiStefano Plumbing Orioles.

"There goes my no-hitter," complained Kevin as the game was stopped to search for the ball.

"An antilepton! Who'd've believed it?" was the professor's comment.

For the first time ever, we fought back. It was great! I'd swing my bat — and the ball would actually be there! I got a single and a double, Luis belted a home run, Ryan and Ernie both got hits. Even Tuba Dave looked a little closer to the bag when they threw him out at first.

We managed a little defense, too, although it was mostly Bobby Ray, who was awesome at shortstop. At the end of the sixth the score was tied 8–8. The Feather-Soft Tigers were going to extra innings.

The professor was so used to losing that he tried to go home. I guess he was pretty anxious to see if the particle accelerator could crank out another antilepton. But when we explained that we might actually *win*, he was so happy he forgot about science. We were pretty hyper ourselves.

"This is what we waited for all winter." Tim grinned.

"What a great game!" agreed Luis.

I didn't say anything because I was watching the Orioles make a pitching change. All of a sudden it hit me.

Little League rules said no pitcher could go for longer than six innings. Kevin had to be replaced, too!

I ran across the dugout bellowing, "Professor!"

Kristy put her hands over her ears. "Mellow on the volume control, dude."

I told our coach about the Little League rules.

He looked confused. "How can Kevin *throw out* his arm? It's attached."

"Listen up, dudes," announced Kristy. "Tuba Dave is pitching."

I choked. "*What?* He's not a pitcher! *I'm* a pitcher!"

"That moves Kevin over to second," she finished.

Boy, did I blow my stack! I got in Kristy's face and started screaming, "*It's not fair! You just don't want me to be the pitcher! It's none of your business who's the pitcher! You can't make me not be the pitcher . . .*" And I kept on howling while Caspar struck out, and Ryan and Luis grounded out to end our half of the inning.

I folded my arms in front of me. "I refuse — I absolutely *refuse* — to go along with this!" And I stood my ground while the rest of the players took the field. The problem was that when Mr. Rudolph came and ordered me to take my position, the only open spot was in left field. Well, I couldn't fight with the umpire in the middle of a game. So I went, biting back my rage.

"Play ball!"

Tuba Dave gave up a hit to the leadoff man, but the second Oriole popped straight up to Luis. The next guy hit a dribbling grounder along the first base line. It was an easy double play, which would make three outs. The inning was over!

But there was Ernie, droning over and over, "Two *times* three equals six . . . two *plus* three . . ." He picked up the ball on "three," so he threw it — *to third base*!

The runner was the second most shocked guy in the place. The most was Caspar Howard, our third baseman. Totally bewildered, he tossed it back to Ernie, who stepped on the bag, and the batter was out.

"Excellent!" cheered the professor.

"The *other* guy!" cried Kristy. "Get the other guy!"

They'd forgotten about the lead runner, who was rounding third.

Befuddled by too much studying, Ernie threw to second. By the time Kevin got the ball on its way to Luis, the winning run was halfway home, and nothing could stop him.

Suddenly, out of nowhere, a pink high-top sneaker was on the base path between the runner's feet, and he was tripping, tumbling, sliding in a cloud of East Texas dust. Luis made the tag easily.

"I *saw* that!" Mr. Rudolph ran after Kristy, who was strolling casually back to our dugout.

"*Tripped* him?" exclaimed Kristy in her best "little

princess" voice. "Grandpa, I would *never* do that! Did you see me trip anybody?"

The professor went for it, hook, line, and sinker. I wish I could say the same for Mr. Rudolph. He counted the run, and we lost, 9–8.

★★★

The next day, I went to summer school to stand with Ernie when the results of the pretest were handed down. Wouldn't you know it — Kristy was already there.

"He better've passed, after he cost us that game!" she growled.

"I don't remember Ernie getting caught interfering with a base runner," I pointed out coldly.

"It was our only chance, bro', and whose fault was that? What kind of idiot mixes up three, the number, with third, the base?"

Probably the same kind of idiot who thinks two plus three equals six.

Ernie burst out of a classroom like a freight train. "A-minus!" he shrieked with joy, waving his paper in the air. "No more summer school!"

I was thrilled for the guy. I was about to shake his hand when he threw his arms around Kristy and *kissed* her right on the cheek! "Thanks a million!" he said, from the heart.

"Don't sweat it, bro'," she replied. "Anytime."

After she'd left, I turned on our first baseman. "Are you

crazy? How can you thank *her*? After what she was going to do to you — to *us*! And she still might do it!"

Ernie shrugged. "If it wasn't for her I'd be off the team. I don't think she's that bad."

And he walked away, leaving me clawing at the walls.

Come on, Mr. Lopez! Hurry!

CHAPTER 5

Right Field — Ryan Crisp

The problem with losing a close one is that you keep going over it in your mind. When you get creamed 20–0, nobody thinks, If that line drive had only drifted foul in the top of the third . . . But when you were tied after six innings, one little break could have made the difference. Who could resist replaying the game over and over? Every called strike, every close tag.

The one that really bugged me came in the bottom of the fifth. One out, nobody on base. The batter hit a long fly ball to right field — directly at Ryan Crisp. It was an easy out, right? Wrong! Our right fielder was asleep! I didn't know it was even possible to sleep standing up if you weren't a horse! The ball came down right on his head. At least it woke him up, but by then the "easy out" had turned into a triple. The next Oriole popped up to me — which would've been three outs if Ry had caught that ball. But no, the inning was still alive, and the runner tagged up and scored. And we lost. Again.

Now, I'm no crybaby, and I realize the rest of us didn't exactly play like stars either. But it was the coach's job to say something to Ry. And since our coach was still celebrating the antilepton, I figured I'd bring up the subject — gently, with tact.

"You know that ball you took in the head?" I began.

Ryan blinked. "Sorry. I lost it in the sun."

"Oh." This was going to be harder than I thought.

"Let me try," said Luis. "Ry, all the other fielders were awake—"

"I've got a new glove," Ry explained. "And the pocket is stiff." I think he expected us to believe that was why a fly ball had bounced off his head.

"Put it this way," Tuba Dave took a stab at it. "You know how some people are into sleepwalking? Well, let's just say there was such a thing as sleep-fielding—"

He was interrupted by a snort of disgust. We wheeled to find Kristy standing there. "Lose the jive, dudes! Cut to the chase! Get to the point," she added for those of us who didn't speak New Yorkese. She turned on Ryan. "You were asleep, man! Crashed out! Catching Z's! A-snooze! Sawing logs! Chilling with the sandman! 'Tsupwitchoo?"

"The ball took a bad hop," Ry offered.

"Yeah," Kristy agreed. "Off a hollow sphere! So let's make sure it doesn't take any more! Go to bed early!"

"I can't," said Ry. "Tonight's the night I stuff envelopes for Merkel's Department Store."

"Well, tomorrow night, then."

Ry shook his head. "Tomorrow I sweep up at the print shop." He looked thoughtful. "And Wednesday I wash dishes at Sal's Diner. And Thursday I'm on envelopes again. And Friday—"

"All right, all right," Kristy interrupted. "I get the picture. How about sleeping late in the morning?"

Ryan shook his head. "Can't. I deliver the *Dallas Morning News*."

Kristy was getting really steamed. "An afternoon nap, then."

"The Spooner paper comes out in the afternoon," Ry explained.

She was tearing her hair. "You deliver that, too?"

He shrugged. "I wanted to pick up a little extra money."

She snapped. "What are you — *General Motors*? Are you listed on the stock exchange? Sure you're not into any other little businesses? Like aerospace? Shipbuilding? Putting out oil well fires?"

Ry scratched his head. "Well — I make deliveries for Mr. Shaughnessy at the drugstore, I walk dogs, I water plants for people who are out of town, I caddy at the country club, cut lawns, and I sometimes baby-sit."

We all stared at him. No wonder he had fallen asleep in right field. I'm amazed he didn't *die* out there! None of us knew Ry Crisp that well, even though he went to school with us. He lived on a farm out of town, so we saw him in class but that was pretty much it. Now we knew why. The guy worked twenty-five hours a day!

"Why don't you stick a broom up your pants?" Kristy suggested. "That way you can sweep the street while you're doing all that stuff! I mean — you're a major corporation, man! How much do you make — the Gross National Product?"

Ryan looked hurt. "I like to do my bit to help out my family," he said with dignity.

It shut up even Kristy. It was easy to picture. A small farm, tough times, struggling parents, and their son — who was working night and day to pull his weight. Who could get mad at a guy like that?

We practiced for a while, but then Ry had to run off to deliver the afternoon paper. Kristy immediately called a meeting. "We've got to do something about Ryan."

"Oh yeah!" Tuba Dave said bitterly. "He's working to help his parents; he really needs crabgrass!"

"Lay off Ry," I told her. "He's got enough problems."

Kristy rolled her eyes at me. "Would those of us whose IQ's are *larger* than our shoe sizes please listen up," she said to the others. "Now — how are we going to help Ry?"

"Help him?" I repeated. "How can we make his dad's farm any better? We'd have to control the weather, and the price of corn, and stuff!"

"Paging Doctor Brain!" she sang out. "Look — Ry is the greatest guy in the world for what he's doing. When he was talking about helping out his folks, I had tears in my eyes!"

Luis was thunderstruck. "Cry? *You?*"

"New Yorkers are human, too, you know," said Kristy, insulted. "Just because we're twenty times cooler than everybody else doesn't mean we don't have emotions. So here's my plan."

"Let me guess," I snarled. "You're going to threaten that unless he grows twenty million bushels of corn this year, you'll develop The Picture."

"Oh, that," Kristy said airily. "I already developed it."

There was a gasp as all eight of us sucked in air.

"Well, I had to make room for the smoke bomb," she reasoned.

Ernie's eyes popped. "Not at the mall?"

"Chill out," she advised. "P.P. has a darkroom in the basement. It's a hype hobby, you know."

"You lied to us!" I stormed. "You said if Ernie passed that test—"

"Don't be wimps! Nobody's seen it yet." Her eyes gleamed. "Except me."

We were in agony. When The Picture was just film, it wasn't really a picture — it was the *possibility* of a picture. Now there was a real Picture in the world. It was like living with a ticking time bomb.

"What's it look like?" Tuba Dave barely whispered.

"Oh, very artistic. Brilliant camera angle. You want to hear the plan or not?"

Typical Kristy. Now that she had us over a barrel, she was going to tell us what we had to do. I steeled myself for the most outrageous scheme of all.

"We're going to pitch in and help Ry help his folks," she said with determination.

None of us could believe it. I almost felt guilty for my letter to Mr. Lopez. Here was a noncrazy idea from Kristy! No sneaking around, no hiding, no tree climbing, just plain honest work for a good cause. We help Ryan and his parents, and help the team, too. With a little less work, Ry wouldn't be falling asleep in right field anymore.

★★★

Ry was really grateful. "You guys are the best! I can't believe you'd do this for me!"

And there followed several days of the hardest work

we'd ever known. I don't know how Ry managed to do all this by himself, because it was far too much work for the eight of us, *and* Kristy, *and* the professor. Kristy had him making drugstore deliveries in his van.

The paper routes were the worst. With a hundred and fourteen addresses straight up the steepest hill in town, the *Morning News* could take until midnight to deliver! And on Sunday, forget it! The wagon weighed ten thousand pounds! Not to mention boring! When my Walkman batteries ran out, I cried!

"You're lucky," said Luis bitterly. "I baby-sat the Feliciano triplets. They got saxophones for their birthday!"

Ernie held out his hands, which were covered in Band-Aids. "Look at this!"

"Nice manicure!" Kristy guffawed. "What'd you use — a lawnmower?"

"It's paper cuts!" said Ernie indignantly. "I was stuffing envelopes until two o'clock in the morning! And the licking part! Yeccch!"

"I'll do that next," offered Tuba Dave.

"Oh, no you don't," put in Kristy. "The glue is peppermint flavor, and that means calories, big guy. You're on caddy duty. That's good exercise."

"Try not to get Father Flanagan," groaned Bobby Ray. "He drove our golf cart into the water hazard and left me there. How does Ryan stand it?"

"He's helping out his folks," Kristy reminded him. "He's a great kid."

"By the way, where *is* Ry?" I asked.

"At home," Kristy replied. "I gave him the day off so he could catch up on his sleep."

On Wednesday, I flipped out. I swallowed my pride, got down on my knees, and begged Kristy to take me off the paper route.

"Okay, but stop groveling," she ordered. "You're making me sick." She began manipulating game pieces on her handmade job board. "If I move Luis to papers" — she switched places between a toy soldier and a size "C" battery — "that bumps Caspar over to Sal's Diner—"

"Who's the raisin?" I asked.

"That's Kevin. He switches to envelope stuffing."

"Where am I?"

She pointed. "You're the dead cricket."

"Aw, come on!" I exploded. "Why do I have to be a bug? Can't you find a rock or something?"

"We've got a rock. It's Ernie."

I've had stupider conversations, but not many. "What's *your* symbol?" But I could already see it — a silver Statue of Liberty placed over a square marked Control Center. I guess the professor's game piece was a lepton, because I couldn't see it.

With her pen, Kristy pushed the dead cricket over past

the Feliciano triplets, across the dairy, round the caddy shack, and over to a red fire hydrant.

I looked at her questioningly. "Ryan's on the fire department, too?"

She laughed in my face. "You're a dog walker. Have a nice day."

★★★

Big Al was named after Al Capone, the Chicago gangster. I now know this is a terrible insult to Mr. Capone. Big Al was part St. Bernard, part elephant, and part warthog. He thought he was a person, but he wasn't even a dog. When we walked by, little kids burst into tears. One six-year-old looked at his mom accusingly and said, "You told me the mammoths all died like the dinosaurs!"

They crossed the street to walk on the other side.

Big Al smelled like a wet rug, except for his breath, which was in a category by itself. Squirrels and chipmunks scattered from half a block away. I practiced mouth-breathing.

Big Al weighed two hundred pounds; I weighed ninety. He was taking me for a drag down Main Street, smashing me off mailboxes and trees, when I spotted the professor's van. I called out a greeting: "HE-E-E-E-ELP!"

Kristy's grinning face poked out of the passenger window. "'Tsup? Hey, what a cute puppy!"

"*Sit!*" I pleaded. "Heel! Roll over! Play dead! Aw, come on, dog, *stop*!"

The professor parked, and Kristy leaned out the window and bellowed at the top of her lungs, "*Yo!*"

Big Al stopped in his tracks, which caused me to rear-end him. Then he trotted up to the car and presented his big ugly head to be patted.

"Who's the hypest, freshest canine dude?" Kristy crooned, stroking his fur — no two hairs pointed in the same direction!

Wouldn't you know it? Big Al, who hated everything and everybody, including his own tail, which he thought was following him, was a sucker for Kristy Pendergast. She played with his ridiculous ears, rubbed noses, shook hands, traded kisses, and treated him a heck of a lot better than she ever treated me.

Then the professor said, "Come along, Princess. We've got deliveries to make." He started the van and drove off.

It hit me a split second too late that Big Al might not want to lose the one thing he'd ever liked in his misera-ble, smelly life. His first lunge yanked the leash out of my hands; his second took him a block down the street. I ran like crazy, but in two minutes the van was out of sight, and ten seconds later, so was Big Al.

★★★

The police wouldn't take my report.

"I thought you said it was a dog!" exclaimed Officer Col-lins after I gave the description.

"It *is*!"

"Okay, let's start again. What color?"

"A sort of blackish, brownish, grayish, mustard—"

"Nothing looks like that," said the officer, ripping up the paper. "Get out of here."

I spent the next two-and-a-half hours on my bike, scouring Spooner for Big Al. All I found was Ry. He was just coming out of the movies. It kind of bugged me for a second. Here I was, busting my hump over *his* dog-walking job, while he had fun! Not that I didn't think it was great how he was earning money for his family. But we were supposed to be *helping*, not *doing* it for him!

I gave up and headed for Mr. Cacciatore's place. I was going to have to do the honorable thing, and tell the man I'd lost his beloved pet.

When I arrived, bathed in sweat and limp as a rag, I found Kristy there, playing in the yard with her dear friend Big Al.

"You're late, dude."

I put in my request to go back on the paper routes.

★★★

At practice the next day, Ry looked like a million dollars; *I* fell asleep in the outfield. Bobby Ray was allergic to the dishwashing soap at Sal's, so he was one big itch from head to toe. Luis was so stiff from sweeping the print shop that, when he went into his catcher's crouch, he couldn't straighten up again. Kevin had been cutting lawns all week, and was too exhausted to put any zip on his pitches. But that was okay. Except for Ryan, none of us had enough energy to swing at them. Poor Ernie missed the practice altogether. He'd been watering plants, and was now at the doctor's office, having three cactus needles removed from his behind. The professor/drugstore delivery boy was sacked out in the dugout.

When the practice was over, Ry left to go swimming, and I stormed Kristy. "Hey, wait a minute! Isn't he going to stay and help on *some* of his jobs?"

Kristy shrugged. "It's only been a few days. That's not enough time for a full recovery."

"He just blasted the longest home run ever hit in this park! He can *at least* do the afternoon papers!"

"Look," Kristy challenged, "who's running this team, you or me?"

"The *professor*!" I shot back.

As if on cue, a loud juicy snore rumbled out of the dugout.

"Okay, everybody," Kristy called out, "cough up the do-re-mi! Produce the juice! Fork over the *dinero*! Lay out the moola! Bank the bread! Lose the bucks! Pay up," she translated. She held open a Bloomingdale's bag, and we all stuffed in the money we'd made doing Ryan's work.

"I don't see why I should have to pay!" I said bitterly.

"I almost got killed walking Big Al!"

"That's nothing," said Tim feelingly. "I was on plant watering and the Venus flytrap closed on my hand! It was *gross*!"

Tuba Dave stared into the bag. "We've got a fortune here!"

"We could buy Ry a whole new farm!" Ernie added, breathless with wonder.

"Isn't it hype?" grinned Kristy. "It's going to be totally heartwarming to see the Crisps' faces when we hand them all this cash-ola!"

I think she was trying to make us believe she had a heart.

★★★

By Saturday, the bag was bursting at the seams with money, and the Feather-Soft Tigers were the best paper boys, dishwashers, envelope stuffers, sweepers, plant waterers, delivery boys, caddies, dog walkers, and baby-sitters in all of Little League, even if we still stank at baseball.

So the professor loaded us into his van for the ride out to the Crisp farm.

Kristy was rubbing her hands together with anticipation. "What a great surprise for Ry!"

"Now, Princess," said Professor Pendergast as we tooled along the highway through flat, open pasture land. "You know money doesn't solve everything."

"I know, Grandpa," said Kristy, "but it's a really good beginning."

"Beginning?!" Ernie was horrified. "You can't mean I have to go back to the Millers' cactus garden?" he asked from atop a stack of soft pillows on the seat.

"Of course not," she replied. "But now the Crisps have a nice little nest egg, and Ry can quit some of his jobs without feeling guilty."

"And since he's taking it easier," Tim added, "he won't be falling asleep in right field."

"It feels terrific to help someone," said Luis. "Right, Corey?"

"Right," I said absently, but I wasn't really paying attention. Where was Ryan's house? We'd passed the sign that said CRISP at least twenty minutes ago. On both sides of the road, there was grazing land as far as the eye could see, and about a zillion head of cattle, mostly longhorns and Brahmas.

"We must've missed it," Kristy decided.

"There haven't been any exits," the professor pointed out.

At that moment, a shiny white car marked RANCH SECURITY flagged us down, and a uniformed man in mirrored sunglasses got out.

"Can I help you folks?"

"We're looking for a small farm — the name is Crisp."

The man laughed as though the professor had just told the most hilarious joke in history. "Straight up the road on the right. You can't miss it."

It *was* straight up the road — thirty miles later — the biggest, most beautiful sprawling ranch house in the universe, dotted with skylights and cedar decks. We stopped on a rise just to look at it, spread out before us. It had a four-car garage, two swimming pools, tennis courts, and riding stables.

I think it hit all of us at the same time. We weren't *on our way* to the Crisp farm; we'd been *there* for the last hour. And all that land, all that cattle, and this Texas mansion belonged to Mr. and Mrs. Crisp, whose son Ry was "helping out" by doing a few odd jobs around Spooner!

"You know those ranches you hear about," said Ernie, "where it takes a day to drive from one end to the other? Well, I think this is one of the bigger ones."

"It's got everything!" breathed Tuba Dave.

"Where's the cemetery?" said Kristy between clenched teeth. "They're going to need one as soon as I get my hands on Ry! Can you believe him — maxin' and relaxin', livin' large on our hard labor?"

"Not The Picture?" gasped Ernie.

But Kristy was already herding us back into the van.

"Come on, Grandpa. I'm really looking forward to giving Ry what he's got coming to him."

We parked in the circular driveway, and the maid directed us out back to the hot tub. There, in solitary splendor, soaked our right fielder.

I was carrying the Bloomingdale's bag. "Are we really going to give this to him?" I whispered.

Kristy grabbed the bag from my hands, and dumped all the money out on Ryan's towel. "Here's the cash we earned so that you and your parents don't have to starve!"

Ryan was taken aback. "I never said we were starving; I just said I was helping them out."

"Well, you did a great job," said Kristy sarcastically. "I'll bet all this was a pile of dirt before you started delivering the *Dallas Morning News*! Well, keep your mitts off *this dinero*!" It's going straight to charity! Now, any last requests before I throw a toaster in there and fry you?"

Ryan shrugged. "I thought you knew about our ranch."

I had to speak up. "But all those jobs! Big Al! The paper routes! Why? What do you do with the money?"

In answer, Ryan got out of the water, and led us to a gleaming white structure that had once been a barn. He threw the doors wide.

We gawked. Six Flags didn't have that much stuff. There were pinball machines, arcade games, Skee-ball, juke boxes, Pokerino, Foosball, air hockey, Bowlerama, three holes of miniature golf, fortune-telling machines, prize wheels, Indy 500 — *everything*! Even one of those test-your-strength doohickeys where you hit the thingamajig with a hammer and try to ring the bell.

"I bought it all with my own money," said Ry proudly.

We were blown away, all except Kristy. She had this intense look on her face. I couldn't tell if she was going to strangle Ry, or go play Super Mario Brothers. She walked up to a midway game called Tank Command, and sat down at the tank turret. Then she swung it around and fired a tennis ball with deadly accuracy right at Ryan's chest.

A delighted grin split her face. "Batter up?"

CHAPTER 6

Third Base —
Caspar Howard

Here's a confession. I was really glad Mr. Lopez didn't show up that week. If he had, Kristy would have been gone, and we never would have discovered Tank Command. The game shot tennis balls at cardboard cutouts of helicopters and troop carriers, but it was *perfect* for batting practice. We hauled the gun part onto our diamond, and plunked it down in the middle of the outfield. Then we formed a wide circle around it, standing poised with our bats. Wearing Luis's catcher's mask, Kristy would sit at the gun and fire her way around the circle, pitching to us one at a time.

It was amazing! We could all practice at once; the air-powered gun never got a sore arm, and fired the tennis balls faster than any pitcher in the league; and was it ever accurate! Kristy could pitch them high, low, inside, outside — I'm amazed the pros never thought of this! With Tuba Dave looking slimmer every day, and Ry cutting his jobs down to just the print shop and the Felicianos, the Tigers were shaping up into a lean, mean baseball machine.

Except for Caspar Howard.

The professor noticed first. "That boy there — the one playing left base — I don't think he's having fun." I guess left base was lepton language for third, since it was to the left of the plate.

It was true. Caspar didn't look happy, and it had nothing to do with our 0–4 season. He was an okay third baseman, but he played like a zombie. And as a hitter — forget it. You could tell he was just swinging to get his at bat over with. I don't think he'd had a hit all season. Even during Tank Command batting practice, Caspar looked like he was reading the telephone book. If Little League was supposed to be a great experience, it sure wasn't working for Caspar Howard.

"P.P.'s right," said Kristy. "'Tsup with that guy?"

"It's none of our business," I said hastily.

Wrong. Everything in the known universe was Kristy's business. She pointed at Caspar's sad-sack face. "*That* is like chicken pox. It's contagious. If we don't stop it now, pretty soon the whole team's going to be moping around like a bunch of undertakers with that wack sourpuss frown. Remember, happy dudes hit more home runs."

"You sure made Tuba Dave happy," I said sarcastically.

If you don't agree with Kristy, she pretends you didn't speak at all. "Yo, Caspar!" she called. "Come on over here!" And when he came, she said, "Johnson here wants to have a talk with you, man to man." And she walked away!

"Uh — right," I managed. "So — what's new?"

"Nothing much," Caspar shrugged. "What did you want to talk about?"

I swear — if I could have thought of any other subject, I'd have done it! But you can't just pull a guy off third base and say, "Hey, how about those new doughnuts with the cream in the middle?" And I ended up doing what Kristy wanted. Again. "So, Caspar, what do you think of the Tigers?"

He looked unimpressed. "They're okay, I guess."

"You don't seem to be getting into it," I pointed out.

"Sure I am," he lied. "It's just that I'm not a real big baseball fan."

"Then why did you sign up for Little League?"

Caspar avoided my eyes. "My dad really wanted me to."

I thought back. Mr. Howard had been there for our first couple of games, but not since then. Who could blame him? For a true baseball fan, watching the Tigers would be almost painful. And, let's face it, Caspar *was* kind of the crummiest of the crummy.

"He played baseball in college," our third baseman explained. "He even had a tryout with San Diego. I—" He studied the grass. "I've got other interests."

"Such as?" I prompted. Talk about nosy! Kristy was turning me into a Junior New Yorker!

Caspar avoided my question. "You know, hobbies — personal stuff."

Fair enough. Caspar was doing his best for the Tigers, even though he was into other stuff.

"What other stuff?" Kristy asked after practice.

I shrugged. "He didn't want to talk about it."

She threw her hands up in disbelief. "Way to go, Johnson!" she blamed me. "Now we've got to deal with this problem, and we don't even know the tip!"

"The tip?"

"The scoop! The lowdown! The story! The info! The bottom line! The deal!"

I glared at her. "Sorry. I'll bet in New York Little League everyone can read minds!"

"They can ask a simple question! The reality sandwich makes you sharp, man! Now we have to find out Caspar's hobby."

"Count me out," I told her.

★★★

She counted me in. And, worse still, she did it at five o'clock in the morning, with the old rocks against the window trick. But this was Texas in July. The gravel got caught in my window fan. It sounded like a machine gun firing at a helicopter. I peeled myself off the ceiling in time to see my fan short out in a shower of sparks. In the silence that followed, a voice called, "Pssst, Johnson! 'Tsup?"

"If I have to come out there," I hissed, "you're going to regret it!"

"Get down here, Johnson!" she rasped. "P.D.Q.!"

"Go back to bed!" I snarled. "That's what I'm doing!"

And then the barrage of pebbles against the broken fan was so loud that I had to get dressed and go downstairs before she woke up my parents. I got out onto the lawn just in time to keep her from launching a hunk of concrete that would have gone through my window, clear down to the basement, and pushed our house halfway to the earth's core.

She grabbed my arm and began hauling me down the street. "Caspar's on the move!"

"It's five o'clock in the morning! Where would he be going?"

She cast me a look of disgust. "If you had *asked* him yesterday, we wouldn't have to be doing this!"

Oh, so this was *my* fault. That explained it. "How do you know he's up? Were you hiding in his closet?"

"Nah. My main man P.P.'s got this hype telescope. He looks at Jupiter, but it works for Caspar's place, too." She pointed. "There he is!"

We slipped into the shadow of a fence. There was Caspar, a gym bag over his shoulder, walking down the street. Believe me, a predawn stroll with my worst enemy wasn't what I had in mind. But as soon as I saw Caspar, curiosity got the better of me. We followed him past the baseball diamond, past downtown, to the Spooner Public Library and Community Center on Lamar Street. The library was closed, and so was the Community Center, but the ice rink — the only one in town — was open.

"Hockey?" I whispered.

Kristy shook her head. "No stick."

We slipped inside and hid behind the scoreboard. From there we could see the whole ice surface, but nobody could see us. The cold of the arena made me shiver after the muggy air outside.

Caspar laced on a pair of skates and stepped over the boards. In three long strides, he was up to speed. He was a figure skater, and he was great, executing spins, leaps, and unbelievable jumps. I don't know much about figure skating, but Caspar Howard looked as good as those guys from the Winter Olympics.

I waited for Kristy to fire away at our third baseman with both barrels. He was a wimp, and a sissy, and a ballerina, and a loser, and in a million years no guy from New York would behave like this. Instead, she said, "Do you realize what a great athlete you have to be to do what he's doing?"

On cue, Caspar executed a triple jump that blew me away. "He's fantastic!" I enthused. "Let's go congratulate him!"

She looked at me pityingly. "It's five A.M — do you know where your brain is? If we show up now, he'll see we've been spying on him, and he'll never trust us again. And then the Tigers lose all that energy that could be channeled toward baseball."

"Toward *baseball*?" I repeated. "I'm not putting down skating, but it's got nothing to do with baseball. Caspar doesn't even *like* baseball. He's only on the team to please his dad."

"An athlete is an athlete," lectured Kristy the great sports expert. "If he can do that" — she indicated the rink — "he can play baseball. He just has to *want* it."

"He'll say no." I told her.

"I'm not planning to *ask*."

★★★

Tuba Dave looked around the field. "No Tank Command?" It was practice the next day, and Ry's carnival game was nowhere in sight.

"Chill out, Babe Ruth," said Kristy. "We're working on our legs today."

"Legs?" repeated Ernie.

There was general grumbling. We all loved Tank Command.

"Legs," said Kristy. "You know — the two skinny things that hold up the rest of you. After all this batting practice, there's a slight chance some of you might get on base. And your base running is toiletsville. So we're putting you to work."

"Running?" asked Luis.

"Skating," she amended.

In the confused murmur that followed, I snuck a look at Caspar. For the first time all summer, he had come to life.

Kristy was annoying, but never let it be said that she wasn't prepared. When the guys all started complaining, she pulled out a diagram of the human leg. The lecture started: The Achilles tendon goes here, and the uvula tenses the muscles around the fibius and, if you don't skate, you may as well chop your legs off. Who could argue with that?

The professor loaded us into the van and took us over to the Community Center. While the others were renting skates, I snuck into the library and pounced on the dictionary. There is no such thing as a fibius, and the uvula is in your mouth. In other words, Kristy was doing it to us again.

Where was Mr. Lopez? It had been *weeks* since he'd

gotten my letter. How busy can a guy be? I felt a chill deep in my bones. Last year when I sent away for the "Great Pitchers" sticker album, it took two months to show up. If Mr. Lopez made us wait that long, the season would be over! We'd be insulted, and blackmailed, and pushed around by that obnoxious New Yorker *all summer*! I'd *never* get the chance to pitch!

"Yo, Johnson," came Kristy's voice. "Get your butt in here and score some skates."

In East Texas, if your behind isn't dragging on the ice, you're skating. Most of us had only tried it once or twice in our whole lives. We hated it; and we hated Caspar for being good at it. Even I, who knew in advance about Caspar, kept hoping that the giant Zamboni ice scraper would drive out and flatten him.

We fell down; we ran into each other; we skated on our ankles; when we finally did get going a little bit, the spiked part on the front of the blade would dig in, and we'd go flying. Then Kristy made us try skating backwards. It gave us a whole new side of our heads to smash on the ice when we went down. Caspar started doing jumps and spins. We wanted him dead.

"Come on, dudes!" cheered Kristy. "Exercise those uvulas!"

I grabbed a bunch of guys and we tripped/limped/crawled over to Kristy.

"All right, the joke's over!" I said, making for the gate. "If we hurry, we can still get in a half-practice."

She blocked my way. "Get back out there, Johnson."

I shook my fist, causing me to lose my balance and fall crashing to the ice. Tuba Dave and Tim hauled me up again. "Skating has nothing to do with baseball!" I rasped. "It's a waste of time and everybody hates it! We're leaving *now*!"

She was unimpressed. "Aren't you forgetting my new hobby, *photography*? My main man P.P. says I'm getting really good in that darkroom."

The others backed up and Luis slipped and conked his head, but I stood firm. "I'm not so sure. You said you developed The Picture more than a week ago. So where is it?"

"Don't worry," said Kristy. "It's safe and sound."

"How do we know there even *is* a Picture?" put in Tim.

"Maybe you were lying to us," added Tuba Dave.

In answer, Kristy reached into her pocket and produced an envelope. "It's right in here."

"Big deal, an envelope!" I snorted. "Come on, Kristy, is there a Picture or not?"

The problem with calling Kristy's bluff is that she's never bluffing. She opened the envelope, and pulled the contents out about a third of the way.

We stared. It was The Picture all right! Only the bottom

was showing, but we could still make out a row of bare feet on a concrete floor. Then Kristy snapped the envelope out of view. The other players panicked. They started skating at breakneck speed, falling all over each other.

I scrambled after them. "Come back! We can't let her spook us like this!"

They accelerated. "I'm not messing with her," yelled Tuba Dave. "That's The Picture! The *real* Picture!"

"'Attaway, dudes!" called Kristy.

At last, the professor stepped forward, bearing hot chocolate for everybody. Never mind that is was ninety-eight degrees outside. Actually, it was fantastic. It tasted like *no more skating.*

"Boy, that was fun!" Caspar enthused to total silence.

It took all nine of us to pick open the knots in Ernie's skate laces.

★★★

The next day, Kristy was ready for another vigorous workout. "Okay, guys, back to the rink."

A babble of protest exploded: "Not again!"

"I'm quitting the team!"

"My uvula's busted!"

"We want Tank Command!"

"Look," said Kristy, "we didn't master it yesterday—"

"I don't see how skating makes you a better baseball player," interrupted Tuba Dave.

So out came the leg, and we got the uvula lecture again. But this time no one was buying it.

"How can I be a base stealer if I've got two broken ankles?" demanded Ryan.

"And a fractured skull!" added Luis, who had an egg-size lump on his forehead.

I played my trump card. "Caspar's a great skater. Let's see him run the bases." It was brilliant. When Caspar couldn't run any faster than the rest of us, it would prove that skating meant nothing, and my uvulas would never have to touch that ice again.

Professor Pendergast didn't remember the steal signal, even though he'd invented it. So while Caspar limbered up on first, we coached the coach. Finally, the professor was ready. He rubbed his hands over his knees, and our third baseman took off like he'd been fired out of a cannon. Caspar slid into second in a cloud of dust.

"It works!" breathed Tim. "Skating works!"

"Look at the uvulas on that guy!" added Ernie.

Next we tried a game situation — Kevin on the mound, Luis behind the plate, Tuba Dave at second base. Caspar was the runner on first. They *knew* he was going to steal. They executed a perfect pitchout. But Caspar was so fast that he was practically into second before Luis could draw his arm back to throw. By the time Tuba Dave had the ball, Caspar was sliding into third.

Above our cheers and applause came the voice of Ernie MacIntosh. "Can we go to the rink now?"

Kristy jogged up to Caspar. "How come you never do that during a *game*?"

Caspar shrugged uncomfortably. "I've never been on base."

"Why not?"

"I strike out a lot."

So out came Tank Command, and Caspar showed us why he'd never been a base runner. He swung too early, he swung too late. And somehow you just knew by watching him that this was as good as he was ever going to get. The sheer waste ate me up alive. His leg muscles from figure skating made him the world's greatest speedster, but he'd never get to show it.

Kristy relinquished her Tank Command seat to Tuba Dave. "You guys practice on your own. I'm going to work with Caspar, one on one."

★★★

The morning of our fifth game, Kristy called up Mr. Howard to get him to take an early lunch so he wouldn't miss Caspar and the Tigers.

"'Tsup, sir. Kristy Pendergast from New York. Assistant coach of Feather-Soft . . ."

"I hate this girl," I said aloud to no one in particular as Kristy shmoozed. *Her* team was playing a big game, and

Caspar had been personally coached by *her*, and was a big part of *her* major strategy, blah, blah, blah.

Sure enough, Mr. Howard was the first guy in the bleachers that morning.

She had rearranged the entire batting order, demoting me to eighth spot. Get this — Caspar was now our leadoff man.

"Aw come on!" I whispered. "I know his dad's here, but the kid couldn't hit Ohio from downtown Cleveland! It's like starting with an automatic out!"

"Take a ride on the chill train," Kristy replied.

Our opponents were the Vic's Volvoville Wolf Pack, and they had just discovered the thirty-pound bag of sheep manure Kristy had unloaded in their dugout. Mr. Rudolph, the umpire, figured out a way to ensure that it would never happen again. He made us switch dugouts.

"Grandpa, why is Mr. Rudolph always being mean to us?" pouted the little princess.

"Just ignore it, dear," said the professor with dignity. "We'll show we're made of stronger stuff."

But there was no stuff stronger than what Kristy had dumped in the dugout. And before we could even run for a shovel, Mr. Rudolph hollered, "Play ball!"

We were down 1–0 when Caspar stepped up to the plate to open our half of the first. Suddenly, his whole body crumpled, and he looked like a little Japanese *bonsai* tree, all twisted and gnarled. He squatted low, and doubled over at the waist, with his left shoulder six inches above the knee. The other team laughed, all except their pitcher. He was squinting in off the mound, trying to figure out where was the strike zone on this pretzel?

In the stands, Mr. Howard sat forward in confusion.

"Why's he doing that?" asked Luis.

The answer came. The first pitch was over Caspar's head; the second was in the dirt.

I knew instantly. The bat that Caspar held up by his ear, and dangled down his back, was never going to move. He was going for a base on balls.

The pitcher settled down a little and threw what I considered to be a pretty good pitch. It was still a touch too high. Ball three.

"Time out!" The Wolf Pack coach ran up to the plate, red-faced. "He's just waiting to get walked! He's not going to swing!"

Mr. Rudolph shrugged. "No crime in that."

"What about an improper batting stance?" the coach demanded.

"No such thing," replied the umpire. "Play ball."

By now the pitcher was so spooked that the fourth ball was two feet behind Caspar. He trotted down to first base. In our smelly dugout, we celebrated like this walk had been a grand slam.

On the very first pitch, the speedy Caspar stole second. The infield was powerless to stop him. One pitch later he was zooming into third.

Ernie hit a pop fly to center field, and Caspar tagged up and came home. Tie score. Now Mr. Howard understood. He was on his feet, clapping and cheering.

All that Tank Command was starting to pay off, but our defense wasn't so terrific, and Kevin's pitching, as usual, was pretty bad. I ached to pitch. But that didn't seem possible unless Mr. Lopez magically appeared to save the day.

By the end of two-and-a-half innings, the Wolf Pack was ahead, 3–2.

Looking back on it, I think the turning point in the Tigers' whole season came right then. After three weeks of a grueling crabgrass diet, Tuba Dave Jablonski stepped up to the plate, blasted the ball into the outfield, and set out for first. He was still pretty slow, but he made it a split second before the throw.

Our bench cleared, and it had nothing to do with the sheep manure. We mobbed Tuba Dave, back-slapping and howling. Mr. Rudolph had to order us to settle down.

Predictably, Kristy took all the credit. "No biggie," she shrugged. "I said it would happen, and it happened."

Tuba Dave batted ninth, so the next man up was Caspar. He went back into that weird scrunched-up stance, and you could just tell the pitcher had been stewing about it since the first inning. He sizzled a pitch at just the right height. I thought it was a strike for sure. But Caspar's shoulder was sticking out so far that the ball grazed it. The Wolf Pack groaned. The speedster was aboard again.

Ernie came on and hit a booming drive down the first base line. Tuba Dave headed for third, his stubby legs pumping.

"Faster, Tuba! Faster!" screamed Kristy.

It was no use. Caspar bore down on Tuba Dave like an F-15 in a dogfight. He zoomed past, rounded third, and scored. Coming back to the bench, he looked at our agonized faces in confusion. "Aren't you going to clap?"

But it wasn't over yet. The throw from right field went wild, and Ernie decided to go for third. He slid in head first, and when he stood up and dusted himself off, there was Tuba Dave.

"What are you doing here?" Ernie demanded. "Why aren't you home?"

"I'm in the middle of a game!"

"Not that home! Home plate!"

"I'm on third!"

"*I'm* on third!"

Mr. Rudolph was totally stumped. He had to get out the rule book. And it couldn't have been easy to read with Kristy talking his ear off about how the rule book was full of beans. Caspar was out for passing a runner; Ernie was out for taking an occupied base; only Tuba Dave was safe. But he thought the inning was over, and started walking away. He was tagged out.

Kristy rallied the team. "Okay, guys, don't freak out just because we did the stupidest thing that's ever happened in a baseball game! Stay cool! We're still in this thing!"

Our secret weapon (besides the professor, who was shoveling out our dugout) was Caspar. The Wolf Pack just couldn't pitch to him. And once he was on base, there was no stopping the guy.

It kept us close. By the middle of the sixth, we were tied, 5–5.

"The game is ours to *win*!" I crowed excitedly. Then I went to the plate and promptly struck out.

Up went Tuba Dave, and he murdered the first pitch. It sailed away — right into the center fielder's glove.

Now there were two out, and we pinned all our hopes on Caspar Howard. Would the master come through yet again, maintain his sparkling .000 average, and get yet another walk?

Only — something happened that hadn't happened all game. The pitcher floated a slow, straight ball just above Caspar's knees.

"Strike one!" bawled Mr. Rudolph.

"Fluke!" screeched Kristy.

The fluke happened again, same pitch, same place.

"Strike two!"

Kristy sat down in disgust. "What a rip-off! We couldn't even get a whole game out of our miracle!"

The Wolf Pack pitcher lofted the identical throw and you could tell he had solved the Caspar mystery.

From the bleachers came Mr. Howard's cry. "*Swing!!*"

Caspar swung, a halfhearted little chop. But it connected. It was almost like a bunt, a weak dribbler out toward the mound. The pitcher and catcher both went for it, meeting with a resounding crunch. The pitcher's throw to first was high. And by the time the Wolf Pack got things under control, there stood Caspar in his usual spot, on third base.

Kristy sent Ernie up to the plate with a message — hit or die. All eyes focused on the plate. You could have heard a pin drop — that and the sound of Professor Pendergast's shovel scraping against the cement steps. Poor old guy. He was a top scientist, a renowned genius, working like a stable hand, without a word of complaint. He tossed his shovel aside and stepped out to the field where he stood, brushing off his pants.

It hit me in one instant of exquisite horror — *that was the steal sign*!

Caspar the human bullet fired himself down the third base line.

"No-o-o-o-o!" cried Kristy.

It unfolded like a nightmare. The pitcher threw. Ernie

swung and missed. There stood the Wolf Pack catcher, astride the plate, ball in hand, waiting to make the tag.

"I can't look!" howled Kevin.

Ten feet from home, our third baseman launched himself into the air in a spectacular leap. It was way too early for a slide, but figure skaters can do almost anything in midair. For a second he was up there, and the catcher was reaching out for the tag. But suddenly, Caspar dropped, diving headfirst between the defender's legs, in a shower of dirt. When the dust cleared, there lay the runner, his hand on home plate.

Final score, 6–5, Tigers.

CHAPTER 7

Center Field — Tim Laredo

When we told Professor Pendergast we'd won, he didn't believe us! So we showed him the scoreboard, but it said 6–5 for the home team, and we were in the visitors' dugout. For a minute there I questioned it myself. We were so great at losing — maybe I'd counted wrong.

But then Kristy remembered the big dugout switch, and we knew it was true. Victory. Very sweet.

The professor was so excited you'd have thought he'd seen another antilepton. He got an eighty-dollar speeding ticket taking us out to lunch.

I walked on air all day. I ate, drank, and breathed baseball. I talked nonstop about our first win. And when my folks couldn't stand me anymore, I watched baseball on TV. Then I rented *The Babe Ruth Story* and watched that. When that ended, there was no more baseball in the house except my dad's video of Little League from last year. So I popped it into the VCR, and feasted on me, Tim, and Tuba Dave on the Gunhold Auto Body Blue Jays. The Jays had won about half their games, but not one single "W" had meant as much as today.

"'Tsup?"

I was almost glad to see her — someone from the Tigers, a connection to our triumph.

She joined me in front of the TV. "Hey, that's you. You looked pretty geeky as a little kid. Check out those ears!"

"Shut up," I said in a friendly fashion. I was still mellow.

"Thought you were a pitcher," she commented.

I was playing third base on the video. "I started practicing over the winter. I figured I'd pitch this summer."

She nodded sympathetically. "I know what you mean. I always wanted to be a movie star. Reality sandwich."

I sighed. Suddenly I'd had enough baseball for one day.

But Kristy was really into the video. "Wow, look at that kid! What a fielder! Boffo arm! Wish the Tigers had him."

"We do," I replied. "It's Tim."

"In his dreams!" she sneered. "No way that's Tim."

I fast-forwarded to where we were at bat. Sure enough, good old number nine, Tim Laredo, belted a stand-up double.

Kristy was furious. "The nerve of that guy! Why can't he play like that for *us*?"

That was a good question. Tim was okay as a Tiger, but I guess I'd forgotten that he'd been one of the Jays' best players. Very good question.

"He isn't injured." I mused. "He isn't out of shape — he played sports all winter."

Kristy ejected the tape and headed up the stairs. "Come on, Johnson. We've got work to do."

I folded my arms. "I refuse to go over there and bug Tim."

"This is a social call," she insisted. "We'll say 'tsup, max and relax, talk about the game, the weather, how he went from all-star to insect in one short year—"

I had to go with her, just to protect Tim.

★★★

"Def crib, bro'," approved Kristy, looking with an appraiser's eye around the room Tim shared with his brother, Terence the Terrorist.

Tim looked bewildered. "Crib?"

"You know — place, pad, digs, spread. Room," she added. She pointed to a strip of masking tape that stretched from wall to wall, more or less down the middle of the floor. "Yo, man, what's with the stripe?"

Tim looked sheepish. "That's the dividing line. Terence likes to keep our parts of the room separate."

"I notice he took the bigger half," I couldn't resist pointing out.

Uncomfortably, Tim changed the subject. "I'm still shaking from the game! What an ending!"

"Speaking of baseball," Kristy eased into her topic with the subtlety of a rampaging hippo. "How come you used to be so great and now you stink?"

"Oh, come on!" I blurted.

"Well, he's bound to know," she reasoned. "He's the one doing the stinking." She waved the video in Tim's face. "You were awesome last year! I was impressed, and I'm from New York! This year you're not terrible, but you're — you know — no better than Johnson here. 'Tsupwitchoo?"

I took it personally. "Hey!"

Tim looked unhappy. "You're right. I'm trying as hard as last year, but it's just not working out. Maybe the league got better and I stayed the same."

Kristy frowned. "What's different from last year?"

In the kitchen, the refrigerator door slammed. "*Hey, butt-brain! Who ate the rest of the chicken?*"

Tim went white to the ears. "It's Terence the Terrorist! Quick! Hide!"

"I'm not afraid of him," said Kristy.

Tim jammed both of us under his bed, which was a good thing because I *was*! "He hits the roof when I bring people here!"

"We're on your half," Kristy pointed out.

But before he could answer, the door flew open and in roared Tim's sixteen-year-old brother, in a rage as usual.

"Did you eat my chicken?"

"Who said it was *your* chicken?" Tim argued feebly.

"Because everything is mine! And nothing is yours!"

"Here," offered Tim. "I've got a chocolate bar."

Terence snatched it out of his hand. "If I get a zit, you're dead!"

"Not a reasonable guy," whispered Kristy under the bed.

"Shhh," I cautioned. The mattress was sagging in my face.

"All right, who moved my paperweight?" Terence demanded.

"I didn't touch it," said Tim. "It's on the desk where it always is."

"It's supposed to be in the *middle*! It's way over to the *side*! How many times do I have to tell you? Quit messing with my stuff!"

There was a loud ripping sound, and then Tim exclaimed, "Aw, come on, Terence, not again!"

The Terrorist stormed off, slamming the door behind him.

We scrambled out of our hiding place.

"Are you okay?" I asked. "What did he do to you?"

"He deducted another six inches from my side of the room," said Tim mournfully.

We looked at the tape. It was now just a little closer to Tim's bed.

"Claustrophobia city, man," Kristy commented. "And as for baseball — it's pretty obvious. Your problem is your brother."

"That's stupid!" Tim exploded. "He's never even seen me play!"

"Psychology, bro'," Kristy explained. "He's always in your face, and you can't get away from him because you live together. So on the field you think you're giving a hundred percent, but you're really not because the Terrorist has got you spooked."

"That doesn't explain last season," I put in. "Terence was his brother then, too, and Tim played great."

"Johnson, you're not as stupid as you look," Kristy praised me. "Maybe the answer is not what's different about Tim, but what's different about Terence."

"Well," said our center fielder thoughtfully. "He has been a lot meaner since his girlfriend dumped him."

Kristy grinned broadly. "Then that's the focus of our attack."

"Attack?!" I squeaked. "Are you crazy? Don't you

remember what he did to me after I hit him with the baseball?"

"He's soft," she snorted. "There he was with a chain saw, and all he did was punch you. He's history."

★★★

The *Spooner Gazette* was our daily paper — not bad for a smaller town. Even though most people read the Dallas papers for real news, all of Spooner subscribed to *The Gazette* to find out who was born and who died. Next to the obits, the favorite column in town was "Grandma Lacey," who was our version of Ann Landers.

At practice on Tuesday, Caspar was showing us how to slide into a base under the tag, when Kristy ran up, waving *The Gazette*, hooting and snickering. She called Tim and me over to the dugout, and showed us today's "Grandma Lacey."

> Dear Grandma Lacey,
>
> I am a sixteen-year-old girl from a farm north of Spooner. The last time I was in town, I got a wax job at Lone Star Car Wash, and I was waited on by the most gorgeous guy. He was very tall with blond hair and a red muscle-shirt. I can't stop thinking about him. What should I do? He doesn't even know I'm alive!
>
> Signed: Smitten in Spooner

Dear S in S,

Your young man is Terence Laredo, who'll be a senior at Spooner High this fall.

Terence, if you're out there, there's someone who wants to meet you, tee-hee!

Lacey

Tim looked puzzled. "Who'd write a letter like that about Terence?"

"I wrote it, stupid!" exclaimed Kristy. "It's part of our plan!"

"Our plan is to give him even more of a swelled head than he already has?" I said in disbelief.

She turned to face the side of the dugout. "Hello, wall," she said to the cement. "Pay attention, dudes. The Terrorist got evil when his chick gave him the heave-ho. So we've got to convince the guy that women dig him again."

"But Terence doesn't read the paper," said Tim. "I don't think he's ever even finished a book unless somebody was forcing him."

"Don't worry," laughed Kristy. "A hick town like this is like living in a fishbowl. Someone'll tell him." She ran off and disappeared into the phone booth.

Tim looked nervous. "I hope she isn't going to try to mess with Terence like she does with us!"

"It won't work," I concluded. "Terence isn't in The Picture."

***

All afternoon Kristy hung around my house like a bad smell. And every time I tried to kick her out, she'd start up a conversation with my mother and act like my closest friend. I couldn't get rid of her.

". . . so stay tuned to Spooner's own KSPN, country ninety-one," came the voice over the radio. "This next song goes out to Terence, over at Lone Star Car Wash, from your secret admirer. Here's 'I've Got My Eye on You.'"

I groaned. "*Now* are you going to go home?"

"We're just getting started," she retorted. "What other towns have radio stations around here?"

I shrugged. "Athens, Tyler. Some people can even get Dallas."

"We'll call them all, just to be on the safe side."

And she did. "To Terence from Kiki in the red Corvette," "To the Hunk of the Car Wash," "To T. L. from the French exchange student," and so on.

Then she called up our afternoon phone-in show, *Spooner Talks*. In a perfect East Texas accent with not a "yo" or "'tsup" in sight, she pledged undying love for the hot wax guy at Lone Star Car Wash.

The host asked, "Not the same boy who was written up in today's 'Grandma Lacey'?"

Instantly, Kristy hung up. "We have liftoff."

***

Kristy was right. The news got through to Terence. According to Tim, the Terrorist was constantly up at his dresser, staring at himself in the mirror.

"Was he any nicer than usual?" asked Kristy.

"Nicer?" repeated Tim. "He was horrible. First he said that I'd never be popular like him. Then he blamed me for fogging up his mirror, and he slammed a dictionary shut on my nose and deducted a whole foot from my half of the room! I can hardly stand beside my bed!"

"Well, I guess that's that," I said hopefully. Of all Kristy's weird plans, this one seemed the most bizarre.

"This is going to work," she told us. "Trust me."

★★★

It probably wasn't a coincidence that there was a little something extra on the Lone Star Car Wash flyers that went out to every house in town:

LONE STAR CAR WASH

FEATURING

TERENCE ON WAX.

"How did you pull it off?" I asked as we gathered up the equipment after practice.

"Simple," she replied. "Ry sweeps up at the print shop at night. I got him to do it. He knows he got off easy on the ranch thing. Hang out."

She expected me to stand there while she carved Terence's initials into a telephone pole.

"Why won't you just admit this is stupid?" I challenged. "It's not going to work."

"Wanna bet?"

★★★

"Strangest thing I ever saw," said Mr. Hofstetler, owner of Lone Star Car Wash. He indicated a dozen freshly washed vehicles waiting in the wax line. "All the teenage girls in this town are bringing their fathers' cars in. Why today?"

Kristy shrugged. "It's drive-in season. Everybody wants to look hype."

Mr. Hofstetler was unconvinced. "They could have been out of here an hour ago. I've got waxers sitting around doing nothing. The customers are all asking for the Laredo boy."

I shuffled uncomfortably. "Maybe he's a good worker."

The owner shook his head. "A wax job is a wax job."

Kristy glanced over at Terence, who was hardly working at all. His polishing cloth barely moved as he flirted with the pretty blonde driver of a Dodge pickup. "He's box office," she explained.

"Box office!?" Mr. Hofstetler repeated. "He's a waxer, not a movie star!"

"We New Yorkers know these things," Kristy assured him. "See?" she added as the pickup driver slipped

Terence her phone number and drove off.

At that moment, a rusty old station wagon rattled up. "We have to have Terence," insisted the driver as three of her friends convulsed with giggles. "We'll wait."

Kristy shrugged. "It's not what he does; it's how he does it. He has *aura*, man!"

★★★

A pyramid of crumpled up notes and phone numbers rose from Terence's desk. The scent of aftershave was in the air. We could hear Mrs. Laredo on the telephone in the kitchen. "Sorry, Wendy, Terence is out for the evening . . ."

I wondered if he was with the pickup truck, the four-by-four, or the Buick convertible.

Kristy was stretched out on Terence's bed, reading his calendar, and chortling. "'Lunch with Carol,' 'Coffee break with Ashley,' 'Dinner with Kiki,' 'Movies with Wanda.'" She turned to Tim. "I guess *your* life must be getting a lot easier."

"No way!" Tim groaned. "He's worse than ever!"

Kristy frowned. "Where does he get the time?"

"He *makes* the time," said Tim bitterly. "He comes back from those dates so bigheaded that I'm nothing but dirt under his feet!"

I checked the dividing line. The masking tape now came out from the wall eighteen inches from Tim's bed. From there, it cut sharply in, forming a tiny box around the bed and desk. Tim had to cross his brother's territory just to get to the closet.

At practice, he was having even more problems than before. And it didn't help that Terence had an upcoming date with Ernie's older sister.

"Can I trust your brother?" Ernie bugged Tim during Tank Command. "What are his intentions?"

"Will you leave me alone?" Tim exploded. He got the next tennis ball right in his face.

"But he's taking out my sister!" Ernie explained.

Kristy threw her arms wide. "He's taking out *everybody's* sister!"

Lone Star Car Wash was the hottest ticket in Spooner. It was an hour wait for a wax job. The streets looked like Beverly Hills, each car gleaming brighter than the next. I saw a Chevy that must have been older than my dad — it was roaring along at five miles per hour, dragging a broken muffler. And it was shinier than a brand-new Rolls-Royce.

It was all Terence. Across town at Wash 'n Wax, business was practically zero.

"This is your fault!" I accused Kristy. "Mr. Hofstetler's getting rich, Wash 'n Wax is going out of business, and Tim can hardly catch a fly ball!"

Kristy nodded. "I guess it's time to put our plan into the final phase."

"Plan?" I repeated. "Surely you're not telling me you *planned* all this?"

She shrugged airily. "We New Yorkers are always ready to wing it."

Dear Grandma Lacey,

I've been a big fan of Terence Laredo, but I just found out that he's mean to his little brother. I think that, for a guy with as much going for him as Terence has, picking on a little kid is just plain sad, and I refuse to pay good money to get my car waxed by a slimeball.

Signed: No More Wax Jobs

Dear NMWJ,

If what you say is true, it certainly seems like our Terence has some growing up to do!

Lacey

Kristy did the whole thing in reverse. She called up all those radio stations again. I figured no one gets on the air to complain about a bully. Wrong. Terence was so famous that even the deejays knew about him. In a couple of hours, Kristy had a first-class scandal brewing.

There was resistance, especially from girls who still had dates coming up. So Kristy, ever the photographer, took a picture of the Laredo boys' room. She carefully diagrammed whose side was whose, showing how Tim was being squeezed out. This she brought to Grandma Lacey herself, and it was published in the next day's *Gazette*, under the headline: "TERENCE, YOU LET US DOWN."

There was a miniriot at the car wash. Terence was pelted with sponges, and called every name in the book.

"Take the rest of the day off, son," advised Mr. Hofstetler kindly.

So Terence went home to find out that things weren't any better there. The phone was ringing off the hook — date breakers and angry ex-fans who wanted to give Terence a piece of their minds. A few of them were even coming to the door, demanding to speak to their former hero. A sign mysteriously appeared on the lawn:

TERENCE LAREDO UNFAIR TO TIM

Mrs. Laredo tried calling the police to complain about the harassment. She got a lecture about the way she and her husband had let Terence run roughshod over his younger brother — which made pretty good sense to me, actually.

Terence was on the edge. "This can't be legal! We can sue Grandma Lacey!"

"I already spoke to my lawyer," said Mr. Laredo bitterly. "You know what he gave me? A message from his daughter. You and she are *off* for dinner Saturday night, Lover Boy!"

Kristy and I were hiding under Tim's bed.

"You hear that?" I hissed. "This is *nuts*! If Terence ever finds out who's behind it, Tim's dead!"

Kristy shrugged. "So long as the baseball season's over, that's Tim's problem."

Terence came stomping in, slamming the door, and cracking the frame. "Has the whole world gone crazy?" he howled. "They're screaming for my head out there! They want me to get the electric chair over a dumb piece of masking tape!"

Even Tim felt bad for his brother. "I'm sorry, Terence."

"Thanks, kid," quavered the Terrorist. "You're the only friend I've got left. And the worst part is — I don't know how any of this happened to me!"

Kristy scrambled out from under the bed. "I did it."

The Terrorist's eyes bulged. "You?"

I emerged just in time to see Kristy unfold a paper and present it to Terence. It was a photocopy of the original Grandma Lacey letter.

Tim was ashen. I guess he was afraid his brother would go berserk and slaughter us all. I figured Tim's half of the room would be reduced to three square inches in a corner of the closet.

But Terence was paralyzed with horror, looking from the copy to Kristy, and back to the copy again. "But — but how?" he managed finally.

She shrugged modestly. "People talk, rumors spread. I built you up, I took you down. No biggie."

"Why?"

"Baseball," said Kristy.

"*Baseball!?*" Terence was totally bewildered.

Kristy put a protective arm around Tim. "My center fielder was stinking the joint out because a certain big brother was in his face and on his case. So I solved the problem."

"By doing *this*?"

Kristy was impatient. "If we'd've come to you like *oh-please-big-brother*, you'd've laughed in our faces, right?"

Terence was beyond speech.

"Cheer up, bro'," Kristy grinned. "This is your lucky day. I'm gonna get you off the hook. But remember — I can do it all again in two seconds. One wrong move and you're dissed like dirt!"

Terence stared at her. "Dissed?"

"You know, up the creek, nailed, rocked, stabbed and slabbed, zonked, keel-hauled." He still looked confused. She said, "You'll figure it out," and left, dragging me with her.

Dear Grandma Lacey,

My name is Tim Laredo, and I'm the younger brother of Terence Laredo, who you write about so much. I just want to say that Terence is a great guy and not mean at all. As for the masking tape, our house is built over an underground river, and we like to mark the line of the riverbed. Thanks to you and to my friend Kristy (from New York) for helping to work all this out.

Signed: Tim Laredo

Dear Tim,

Thanks for setting the record straight. Terence, we never doubted you for a second!

Lacey

I looked up from the paper. "Do we have underground rivers in Texas?"

"Who cares?" She pointed to the outfield, where Tim was catching fly balls and firing them to second without a hop. "We've got our star center fielder."

In a way, she was right. But did the end justify the means? I couldn't get Terence's words out of my mind. According to Tim, right after we left, the fearsome Terrorist turned to him and said, "Some people curse you out, give you dirty looks, maybe even pick a fight. Her? She ruins your life!"

CHAPTER 8

Shortstop — Bobby Ray Devereaux

Tim came on like a house on fire. In our next game he was awesome — batting 3 for 4, and throwing two runners out on monster heaves from center field. With Caspar burning up the base paths, and Tuba Dave making it to first more and more often, we killed the Mr. Halibut Fish and Chips Minutemen 8–2.

"They're as bad as you guys *used* to be!" Kristy said, just in case we were considering being proud of ourselves.

Two runs was the fewest we'd allowed all season. Kevin wasn't getting any better. But Bobby Ray Devereaux, our shortstop, had the game of his life. You'd hear the crack of the bat — and out of nowhere, there was Bobby Ray! He'd nab it in the air, or turn it into a double play, or get the ball to Luis for a tag at the plate. He was a one-man infield!

And a total loss at bat. He struck out twice, grounded out, and to cap it off, bunted foul on the third strike. He was hopeless.

"'Tsupwitchoor bat, bro'?" challenged Kristy after the game. "Does it have bad breath, so all the baseballs won't go near it?"

Bobby Ray didn't get it. "I beg your pardon?"

"Your fielding is *fly*, but your batting is toiletsville!"

He shuffled uncomfortably. "I'm not much of a hitter."

"Sure you are!" I put in. "Just last game you went three for three!"

Our shortstop looked mystified. "I did?"

Ernie couldn't believe it. "Don't you remember? That's the day you made five errors."

"Oh, right," Bobby Ray agreed quickly. And he ran off.

"All right, Johnson. What's the tip on him?"

I shrugged. "You know what we know. He goes to school in Eaton, so we don't see him much."

"His dad runs the gas station on Route 17," put in Kevin. "He helps out sometimes."

Kristy was wary. "He isn't another Fortune 500 kind of helper?" She indicated Ryan.

"It's a small station," said Kevin. "He washes windshields and stuff."

"Let's get in his face," Kristy decided.

She wanted us to *phone* Bobby Ray — day and night — to bug him about his hitting, and lecture on team loyalty.

"Aw, come on!" I cried, but everybody else thought it was a great idea!

"I think we should trust her," said Caspar when she was gone. "I used to hate baseball, but, thanks to her, I'm really having fun."

I couldn't believe my ears. "What about all that stuff she pulled? What about *horta*?"

"I used to be batting zero," said Tuba Dave. "Now I'm already over .200."

"She's a blackmailing sleazeball!" I grimaced. "What about The Picture?"

"She only does that stuff because she likes us, and she loves the professor, and she wants the Tigers to have a good season," Ernie explained.

"Oh, I get it," I said sarcastically. "All that rottenness is really niceness in disguise."

"Yesterday she caught me eating a doughnut at the mall," put in Tuba Dave, "and she really helped me get back on the diet."

That I couldn't believe. "How?"

"She dumped a bottle of Hershey's syrup over my head, and then she made me eat four bowls of *horta* before she agreed not to make eight hundred copies of The Picture."

I threw my arms up in dismay. "You guys are losing touch with reality! You need Mr. Lopez to straighten all this out!"

"Who's Mr. Lopez?" queried Ernie.

"The league president!" I exploded. "The guy I complained to!"

Tuba Dave stared at me in horror. "You mean you didn't write back and cancel the complaint?"

"Of course not! The complaint counts now more than ever!"

"Well," said Tim hopefully, "maybe the letter got lost in the mail so Kristy can stay."

And no matter how hard I tried, I just couldn't convince those guys that Kristy wasn't their best friend. My only hope was that Mr. Lopez *would* come. Then, once we had our team back, they'd realize how much better it was without Kristy.

★★★

Little League rules state that a pitcher has to have three days' rest between starts. Our next game was only two days later, so Kevin wasn't eligible.

I worked on the professor night and day. I hung around his house; I even made friendly small talk with Kristy. And it paid off. The night before the game, our coach agreed that I was the logical choice. Best of all, he said it right in front of his little princess. It was a glorious moment.

But come game time, when the roster was handed to Mr. Rudolph, *Tim* was the pitcher.

I hit the ceiling. "*You* did this!" I roared at Kristy. "After the coach promised I'd get the start!"

She didn't even bother fighting with me. "Looks like rain," she commented, glancing up.

It was the worst insult of all.

We were at bat first. Caspar got his usual walk, but there was no chance to steal second. Bobby Ray smashed the first pitch for a two-run homer.

Kristy took all the credit. "See? You lean on the dude and he comes through for you."

Then we took our 2–0 lead to the field. We were better off with Kevin on the mound. Tim had a good arm, sure. But all he could throw were straight fastballs. The Wiley's Cafeteria and Fertilizer Supply Cardinals were hitting him all over the place. In no time the bases were loaded, with only one out.

"Do I pitch like that?" called Kevin from center field.

"Nah," I replied. "You *walk* the bases full!"

We got lucky. The batter hit a weak grounder to shortstop — the perfect double play ball, to our best infielder.

Bobby Ray reached down to scoop it up, and the dribbler rolled under his glove, between his legs, and out toward left field. But our shortstop must have thought he had it — he actually reached into his glove, pulled out nothing, and tried to throw it home. By this time, I was barreling *in* after the ball, and Bobby Ray was running *out* for it. We met with a *crunch!* and I saw stars. By the time they cleared away, we were behind 4–2, and Kristy was looking murderously down at me.

"Yo, Johnson! Give the kid some space. He's only the best shortstop in the league!"

But if Bobby Ray was such a great shortstop, why was he playing like a confused baboon? I stopped counting his errors when he hit double digits. He bobbled grounders. He missed line drives. He booted the ball all over the infield. When he did make a catch, he threw to the wrong base, or into the stands. He lobbed one into our dugout that had the professor diving for his life.

The really weird part was his hitting was amazing! He had two homers, a double, and a single. So both teams were running up huge scores! *Us* because Bobby Ray was such a monster at the plate. And *them* because of Tim's pitching, and our gigantic hole at shortstop. The lead flip-flopped all game, 5–4 us, 8–6 them, 10–9 us, 13–11 them, and so on. Who made the difference? The weather. Because the thunderstorm hit after five innings with the Tigers ahead 15–14. The Cardinals were so heartbroken they left! We, the victors, had to lay down the waterproof ground sheet to cover the pitcher's mound. We got drenched.

"I can't believe I was the winning pitcher!" Tim

exclaimed, rain beating off the visor of his cap. "I allowed fourteen runs!"

At least he got to pitch.

We got out of there just before the scoreboard got struck by lightning.

★★★

The next day, I woke up determined to earn the job of pitcher for the Toilet Paper Tigers. The problem was that *I* knew I was better than Kevin and Tuba Dave and Tim, but nobody else did. I finally figured out a way to show them. I'd pretend to be helping Luis with his catching. Then I'd throw him my best stuff — my fastball, my change-up, and maybe even the curve I'd been working on in the spring. Luis would tell the guys how good I was, and the professor would have to put me in, no matter what Kristy said.

Right after breakfast, I rapped smartly on Luis's door. His mom answered.

"Hi, Mrs. Bono. Is Luis around?"

"You just missed him, Corey," she told me. "He's on his way to Kristy's house."

Kristy's house? What would Luis be doing there? I frowned. She was up to something again.

As I headed over to the professor's place, I wondered if this had anything to do with The Picture. I quickened my pace to a jog.

The professor let me in. "Kristy will be right with you, Corey. She's on the phone with her mother." He showed me into the living room. There, polishing off a tall glass of milk, sat Luis.

"What's going on?" I whispered.

Luis looked perplexed. "Nothing. Why?"

"What'd she say to you?"

Luis raised an eyebrow.

"To get you to come here!" I persisted.

Luis shrugged. "I just figured since there's no game or practice, she might want to go swimming, or to the mall, or something."

The doorbell rang and, a moment later, our coach was ushering Ernie and Tuba Dave into the living room.

I stared at my three teammates. "You mean, you guys are all here — *on purpose*?"

Tuba Dave nodded. "Where's Kristy?"

At that moment, Kristy's voice swelled from the kitchen. "Just because you and Dad came home early doesn't mean I have to! I'm having a great time! I've got tons of friends down here!"

I threw my hands up in exasperation. "Can't you guys tell a snow job when you hear one? She's not talking to her parents! It's all an act for *us*! I'll bet there's no one on the other end. See?" I picked up an extension phone and listened for the dial tone.

Instead, Kristy's voice barked, "Put it down, or forfeit your arm!"

"See?" said Ernie. "She really *is* on the phone. And she likes it here."

"Sure," I said coldly. "That's why she calls us hicks and hayseeds."

"'Tsup, dudes?" Kristy rolled in from the kitchen.

"'Tsup?" chorused Ernie, Tuba Dave, and Luis. I rolled my eyes.

"Got any plans for your day off?" asked Tuba Dave.

"What day off?" scoffed Kristy. "We've got *mucho* biz today."

"Biz?" I repeated.

"Business," she explained. "Check it out. How could a guy be a Golden Glove hype shortstop and a useless hitter on Tuesday, and by Thursday, he's forgotten how to field, but he hits like Joe DiMaggio?"

"You mean Bobby Ray?" asked Ernie.

"Word," she nodded. "I've finally figured out his problem. He's got a mental disorder."

I was angry. "Are you sure you're not reading the file marked Kristy Pendergast?"

"That's cold, man," she pretended to be hurt. "Here I am trying to help the team and you're *dissing* me."

"Look who's talking!" I exploded. "You just said the kid has a mental disorder! He never did anything to you!"

"I don't mean it like an insult!" she exclaimed. "Haven't you ever heard of a split personality? Like one minute you're an accountant, the next you're a third grader?"

"Hey, yeah!" exclaimed Tuba Dave. "I once heard of this lady in Arkansas — sometimes she was a nun, sometimes she thought she was a race car driver! They caught her going fifty over the speed limit!"

"That's Bobby Ray," confirmed Kristy.

"But he's not old enough to drive," Ernie protested.

"Look, if you can be a nun *and* a race car driver, you can also be a great shortstop *and* a great hitter. Split personality."

"Why just two personalities?" I said sarcastically. "Maybe he's a hitter and a shortstop *and* a race car driver! And in his spare time, he's Elvis!"

But my teammates were already congratulating Kristy on her brilliant diagnosis.

"Boy, I sure never would've thought of that," said Luis.

"Poor Bobby Ray," added Ernie.

I had to admit that she sort of had a point. I thought back to when Bobby Ray couldn't even remember his performance from last game. And split personality *was* a real thing. "Let's say you're right. What do we do?"

"It's a delicate situation," Kristy lectured like she'd just graduated from psychology school. From a bookcase she pulled a well-thumbed paperback entitled *Disorders of the Mind*. "The hitter personality doesn't know about the shortstop part, and vice versa. Our job is to kind of *introduce* the two parts."

"How do we do that?" asked Ernie, wide-eyed.

"It's not in the book," Kristy admitted. "But I figure if we talk about different games we've played, he'll have to jump back and forth from personality to personality so fast that it'll all meld into one."

"And once he's cured," added Tuba Dave, "we'll have a hitter and a shortstop at the same time."

"He'll be *the real deal*," she promised.

★★★

Bobby Ray lived in a town called Steep Rock Lake, halfway between Spooner and Eaton. Actually, Steep Rock Lake was a gas station, but it was outside the city limits, so it got to be its own town. Mr. Devereaux ran the station, and he and Bobby Ray were the only people who lived there.

Luis had an extra bike for Kristy, so the five of us rode out after lunch.

There wasn't much traffic on Route 17 since they built the Interstate, so the Devereaux gas station was deserted when we got there. We sat on our bikes for a few minutes, waiting to be noticed.

"He must be in the grease pit," Kristy decided, indicating the auto shop beside the gas pump. "Wait here."

She disappeared, and we rode up to the pumps. All four

of us rolled over the black hose, but only Tuba Dave was heavy enough to ring the bell.

"Aw, c'mon!" he groaned. "Five weeks of crabgrass, and I'm still heavy as a car!"

The bell was the signal that there were customers. On cue, Bobby Ray emerged from the house.

I waved to our shortstop, shouting "I found him!" into the auto shop.

At first I thought it was an echo. Kristy hollered "I found him!" right along with me.

"*You* found him? He's right here!"

That was when Kristy stepped out into the sunlight — *with Bobby Ray*! I looked back to the house. There was Bobby Ray. There were two of him!

Ernie gasped in horror. "Clones!"

Kristy had it right away. "Twins, dummy!" She stepped back. "Right? One's the hitter, one's the shortstop."

The two Bobby Rays exchanged agonized glances. "I'm Billy Ray," the one by me said finally. "He's Bobby Joe. We kind of averaged our names."

Kristy nodded wisely. "And you switched games, pretending to be one dude."

"So it looked like a guy who never played the same way twice," added Luis.

That also explained why "Bobby Ray" could never remember the last game.

"We're sorry," said Bobby Joe, studying the tarmac.

"But why?" asked Kristy. "Why couldn't you both play?"

Billy Ray studied his shoelaces. "There's not much business on Route 17 anymore. Our dad just couldn't pay for both of us."

"We were wrong," said Billy Ray. "The Tigers could've gotten in big trouble because of us. We just both wanted to play so bad, and since we look alike—" He turned to his brother. "You can finish the season. At least you can hit."

Bobby Joe shrugged. "Let's let Kristy decide. She's the coach."

I let that one pass. I felt so bad for the twins — I knew how much playing baseball meant to me. I'd always taken the money part for granted.

The other guys felt the same way. "You haven't been caught all summer," shrugged Luis. "Why not just keep on switching games?"

"I've got a better idea," said Kristy. "We'll use you both *every* game. You can change halfway through."

"It's too bad we can't switch them every half inning," I put in, mostly just to see what she'd say. "That way we'd always have Billy Ray at short, and Bobby Joe at bat."

"No way," said Kristy sternly. "The great Tigers — with a *New Yorker* behind them — don't need to break any rules to kick everybody's butt down here in the boondocks."

I couldn't believe my ears! "Look who's Miss Fair Play all

of a sudden! Gee, you have a short memory! What about trying to hypnotize the ump? Or tripping a runner? Or putting sheep manure in the visitors' dugout?"

"Yo, bro', if you can show me where there's a Little League rule against sheep manure, I'll tear up The Picture and burn the negative." She was triumphant. "So we'll start Billy Ray, and play Bobby Joe as a tenth man — just so long as we don't put in the twin who's been taken out."

Billy Ray had a sensible comment. "It's still illegal. We only paid for one kid."

"And only one kid is playing," she replied with an expansive shrug. "One at a time, that is." She looked pleased. "How about that? We finally have a substitute."

★★★

She had no problem explaining it to the professor. She just said, "Look, Grandpa, Bobby Ray has a twin!" and our coach welcomed the newcomer and went back to not understanding the game.

"Hey!" I hissed. "I thought you were going to tell him the plan!"

"That info comes on a 'need-to-know' basis," replied Agent Kristy of the CIA. "How could he need to know something that's only going to get him all confused?"

The "hype tip" (her words, not mine) was to start Billy Ray, so his brilliant defense would keep us from falling too far behind.

". . . meanwhile, Bobby Joe's chilling in the washroom hut," Kristy explained. "Halfway through the game, when you gotta go, you gotta go! Billy Ray boogies to the can. They switch jerseys, and we've got Bobby Joe's bat to blow the other team away."

We went on a tear, smashing the competition. Even the professor was starting to get the hang of it. He still didn't know anything about baseball, but he sensed the excitement of the players. And a man of science sure couldn't miss the numbers we were putting on the scoreboard!

We even got crowds. Not huge crowds, but the word was spreading among our families that the Feather-Soft Tigers were actually *winning* a few games. We acquired fans from Ryan's ex-jobs, too, mostly the paper routes. But Mr. Cacciatore became a regular booster. He even brought Big Al to a game. (Mr. Featherstone had to buy the league a new ball after Big Al *ate* a foul tip — no kidding!)

It was amazing! Not only *didn't* we stink — we were *great*! The two Devereaux twins made up the best one player in the league. Caspar was easily the fastest. Tim was very good, and the new, improved, crabgrass-eating Tuba Dave was a powerhouse! With the rest of us working hard and improving, the Tigers won four in a row, extending our streak to seven.

It was neat to be the hottest team around. It didn't even bother me so much that I was stuck out in left field. Back in June, I'd have been amazed if someone had told me we'd win a single game. Now we were almost stars. The other teams knew us, looked up to us, dreamed of beating us.

I'm not trying to say "and they all lived happily ever after." It wasn't perfect. I still thought a lot about pitching. But when Kevin got a sore arm in the fifth inning, Ernie came in, not me. Another time it was a Devereaux — I forget which one. Even Caspar faced one batter. I stayed in left field.

Of course, the biggest frustration of all was that we were too far behind to make the playoffs. Only the four best records in the whole county advanced to postseason. Last year, even the third and fourth spots had gone to teams with only three losses all summer.

But it was *fun*. Our last game was like a big celebration. We scored twelve runs in a huge victory, and every guy crossed the plate at least once. Our families gave us a standing ovation.

Even Mr. Rudolph was impressed. He shook hands solemnly with the professor. "Pendergast, you turned these boys into a real team. I'm nominating you for Coach of the Year."

The professor beamed. "I enjoyed every single touchdown."

We laughed. Everything was funny. Everything was great.

Then there was a party at the professor's house. We gave "three cheers" for the professor, and then for Mr. Featherstone, our sponsor. And everyone was bragging about how, if we'd made the playoffs, we'd have killed the competition. It's easy to make promises you don't have to keep.

"'Tsup?" Kristy approached, working on a chocolate ice cream rootbeer float. "Hey, check out Tuba Dave. He's chowing down."

I laughed a little. "That's because he's off *horta* for the first time in months." I glanced at her. She was smiling, and joking, and friendly — she didn't seem to know that she and I had been fighting nonstop since Day One. Suddenly, I blurted, "Kristy, why do you hate me so much?"

"I don't hate anybody."

"Come on!" I scoffed. "You knew I wanted to pitch, and you made sure I never got near the mound! On purpose! Even when Kevin couldn't start, you went out of your way not to put me in! You were practically dragging relief pitchers in off the street! Why? What did I ever do to you?"

Wordlessly, she reached into her back pocket, pulled out a tattered piece of paper, and handed it to me. I unfolded it and gawked. It was a photocopy of my letter to Mr. Lopez.

"The league forwarded it to P.P." She shrugged. "I didn't want to bother him with details." She looked at me earnestly. "That was a lousy thing to do, Johnson. It really hurt."

"How — how do you know *I* wrote it?"

She laughed in my face. "Get real! 'Not letting people pitch!' Who else could it be?"

I felt pretty stupid. It had seemed so clever at the time!

"What was the crime in giving the sponsor's kid the first shot at pitching?" Kristy demanded. "You would've had your chance after a couple of games! But no! You went mental city — screaming at me, and even dissing my main man P.P. That's why you didn't pitch back *then*. But when you wrote that letter to Mr. Lopez, you could've gotten P.P. *fired*!"

I studied the carpet. I guess I never thought about making trouble for the professor — just Kristy!

She folded her arms in front of her. "It would've broken his heart! So I made up my mind — the seas would dry up, chickens would grow lips, and Mickey Mouse would get his face on Mount Rushmore before you got to pitch."

My guts were churning. An entire summer in left field! Two months of rage and frustration! And now I was supposed to believe it was all my own fault!

It was *so* unfair. Picture this: The neighbors' dog howls all night, you yell at him to shut up, and the police arrest *you* for disturbing the peace. That's how I felt. I made a legitimate complaint to try to help the team, and I got killed.

There was no justice — none except that the season was over, and I wouldn't have to think about this anymore.

Professor Pendergast was on the phone, a confused expression on his face. When he hung up, he was grave. "Attention everybody. I have some bad news. I just spoke to the umpire-in-chief. He says we aren't finished after all."

Mr. Featherstone regarded him in perplexity. "But the season's over."

"That's what I told him," replied the professor. "He said we have to play some more games."

"But there *aren't* any more games!" blurted Ernie.

The professor looked thoughtful. "It has something to do with a mumps epidemic. The Dodgers all have it. Which means we have to play these extra games — I forget what he called them."

"*Playoffs?*" I cried out.

Our coach snapped his fingers in recognition. "Right. The playoffs. I'm sorry," he added.

With a lightning motion, Kristy snapped the giant sandwich out of Tuba Dave's hands. "Hit the crabgrass, pal. This season's not over yet!"

CHAPTER 9

Pitcher —
Kevin Featherstone

Our most loyal fan was our sponsor, Mr. Featherstone. Here he was, a hardworking businessman, president of a company, but he always found the time to come out to the park and cheer us on.

Not that Feather-Soft Bathroom Tissue Inc. was like IBM, or some huge corporation like that. It was just a little factory in downtown Spooner. And they didn't make normal toilet paper; they made designer stuff — flowers, family crests, initials, and forest scenes. It really was as soft as feathers. I made my mom buy it, out of team loyalty. It falls apart in your hand! It's as useful as a moonbeam!

Mr. Featherstone always sat in the back row of the

bleachers, drenched with sweat from the climb, the heat, and the fact that he was wearing a three-piece suit.

"Come on pitch 'er in there right over the plate strike him out attaway he was out by a mile burn it in there baby watch the runner on second that was way foul easy does it ball three what're you blind ump no batter watch for the bunt way to go!"

No, that wasn't us. That was Mr. Featherstone, bellowing from the stands. Our sponsor provided jerseys, caps, equipment, and all the infield chatter you could stomach.

The best thing about Mr. Featherstone was that our team was *our team*. He never interfered. He never even made suggestions. He was just a fan and a dad.

That had been my first fight with Kristy. When she insisted Kevin had to be the pitcher because he was the sponsor's kid, I knew right then and there that she was trouble.

Kristy probably thought she could teach Kevin to pitch. After all, on the Tigers, stumblebums were turning into superstars overnight. Look at Tuba Dave, Caspar, and the twins. Somehow Kristy had figured out a way to make the most of their strengths and the least of their weaknesses.

It didn't work for Kevin. He was all weaknesses:

1. He couldn't find the plate with a map. The other teams called him the Travel Agent, because he sent so many players on trips around the bases.

2. He couldn't remember the signals.
3. He only had one pitch — the slow straight ball. If it was in your zip code, you could hit it.

Kristy nagged at him. "'Tsupwitchoor arm? 'Tsupwitchoor eye? 'Tsupwitchoor brain?" We even trekked back out to the Crisp ranch so Kevin could throw at carnival targets. He spent hours at it, and never improved one bit. As Kristy put it, "Squat — diddly — *nada* — the hole in the doughnut — zilcherooski!"

So he was bad. But so were the other guys. I was probably better, but I was banished from the mound, thanks to my brilliant letter to Mr. Lopez.

★★★

It explained our jitters going into the playoffs. We were a good team — *but*. Our pitching was weak, we were only there because of the mumps, and our coach thought this was all some kind of punishment handed down by the league. Plus we had to go to a field way on the other side of town. It was almost exactly like our own ballpark, right down to the parched, weedy outfield, and unpainted wooden bleachers. But to me it looked as alien as the surface of Mars.

For starters, we lost all our fans, except for the die-hard parents. We weren't supposed to be in this game, so nobody knew to come and watch us play. We barely figured it out ourselves. Three of the guys went to our own park, and Ernie somehow ended up at a dog racing track.

Mr. Rudolph was only the regular season umpire, so we were playing with a stranger behind the plate. Plus there was one extra ump who stood behind the pitcher to make the calls at the bases. He looked out of place, like some spectator who'd wandered out onto the field by mistake.

It got worse. Nobody told us there were *two* washroom huts. We tried the Devereaux switch early for Bobby Joe's extra hitting punch. But Billy Ray went to the wrong building. There he was, in the *east* washroom, wondering why he couldn't find his brother, who was waiting for him in the *west* washroom! And we'd gone from too many players to not enough! We had only eight guys!

The professor went to get our shortstop, but he came back with Billy Ray again. We were pretty far behind by the time Kristy stormed the right men's room, and straightened it all out.

It didn't help. With a record of 11 and 1, the Spooner Rotary Club Giants were the second winningest team in the league. And they were pretty good, sure — but their pitcher was a real ace. He was twenty times better than me, which made him at least forty times better than Kevin. Most guys our age can manage a little curveball; this guy had a bender. The ball would be there when you started to swing, and be gone when your bat arrived. But mostly he had heat. His fastball couldn't be hit because it couldn't be seen. I never got near the ball. Our top hitters, Tuba Dave and Bobby Joe, couldn't do anything better than a few foul balls. And Caspar was worthless. No matter how he crouched and crowded the plate, the Giants' star found the strike zone. After three innings, we trailed 4–zip, and that pitcher was working on a perfect game.

If you think we were frustrated, you should have seen Kristy. "Look at him!" she raged. "He's a nerd! His hat's too big! His socks are drooping! *He's not even from New York!*"

"Yeah, but did you see that fastball?" breathed Tim.

"No," said Tuba Dave honestly. "I haven't seen anything leave his hand all day."

"We're never going to hit that guy!" Ernie sighed. "It's impossible. This is our last game."

Kristy held up her hands for order. "Let's take a group chillathon. Mellow on the moaning. Lose the loser talk. *Get a grip!* Sure, he's a good pitcher. He's terrific. But we've got something even better."

"A bazooka?" asked Luis.

Kristy ignored him, and held up a glass bottle. The label read: MAGNIFICENT PICKLE COMPANY.

"Oh, wow," I said sarcastically. "An empty jar."

"It's not empty," she countered. "I took it over to the particle accelerator last night." Her voice dropped. "There's a lepton in here."

We all looked. I have no idea what we expected to see.

"There's nothing," said Ernie.

Tuba Dave elbowed him in the ribs. "Don't you know anything? You can't see a lepton!"

"Wow!" breathed Ernie. He looked puzzled. "What good is it?"

"Every great team has a lucky charm that makes them unbeatable," lectured Kristy. "Like homer hankies, or rally caps, or pyramid power. Hockey players stop shaving for the playoffs. Whole basketball teams put their shoes on left foot first. Did you know that the Chicago Bears are undefeated on odd-numbered days when the quarterback wears boxer shorts with a picture of Mount McKinley on them?"

"If it works for the pros, it can work for us!" cried Ernie.

"Aw, come on!" I protested. "It's nothing but superstition!"

"Yo, bro'," said Kristy. "Some of the greatest athletes in the world are superstitious. Now, all you have to do is focus the energy of the lepton into your bats."

I was next in the order, and I had to stand there while she held that empty pickle jar over my head, and then ran it along the end of the bat. The Giants were staring into our dugout. It was the most humiliating experience of my life.

"This jar stinks!" I complained. "I'll bet you found it in the garbage ten minutes ago!"

"Get out there, Johnson!" she ordered. "You're a lean, mean hitting machine."

I took my place at the plate. "I'm going to hit a home run," I informed the catcher bitterly. "I've got lepton power."

"Strike!" My lepton power didn't even see the first pitch.

"Strike two!"

I looked to our dugout. Every eye was upon me. Kristy was pointing that stupid pickle jar like a ray gun. Did she think we were all morons?

The pitcher wound up and the ball left his hand. I don't know what made me close my eyes. I just knew I could never time a pitch that fast, so I might as well swing blindly, and get it over with.

CRACK!

My shoulders jarred as the bat made contact. I opened my eyes to see the ball soaring away from me. There was no fence in this park, but that ball sailed high over the outfielders' heads, across the street, and straight down an open manhole.

When I trotted triumphantly back to the dugout, I found my teammates lined up, waiting for Kristy to hold that stupid pickle jar over their heads.

"Aw, come *on*!" I protested. "A lepton didn't hit that home run! *I* did!"

"Sure!" said Ernie. "Because you had lepton power!"

I didn't even get credit for my one home run. "We all know there's nothing in that jar," I said weakly. "And even if there was, how would it make you a better baseball player?" But my protests fell on deaf ears, especially when Kevin, our worst player, got a single. Then Caspar, at the top of the order, managed a walk.

Kristy grinned at me. "What do you say to that, bro'?"

I grasped at straws. "Maybe their pitcher's getting tired. Or rattled. Maybe he's starting to lose confidence."

"Or?" she prompted.

"Or maybe he's only good for three innings. Or maybe the catcher's calling the wrong signals."

"Or?" she persisted.

"Or maybe there's a lepton in that idiot pickle jar!" I howled in surrender. No, I didn't believe it. But neither did anybody else, *really*.

By the middle of the fourth, we had cut the lead to 4–3. I was almost happy when the Giants scored another run. At least it proved that pickle jar wasn't perfect!

Kevin threw down his glove. "I don't get it," he said. "Maybe I've been holding the jar wrong."

We whittled the lead down to 5–4, but with Billy Ray in the washroom hut, Bobby Joe was at short, so our defense was weak. It was a miracle that we only gave up one more run to trail 6–4.

"Stay loose," Kristy advised, rubbing the pickle jar on

Bobby Joe's bat. "Relax your muscles, and let the lepton do the rest."

I watched in disbelief as the lepton scored three runs. I couldn't explain it to save my life. Their pitcher was still great, but we were swinging at those super-fastballs with confidence and authority. And not just our big guns, either. Luis, Ryan, and Ernie all recorded hits against the ace of the league.

Then we went into the bottom of the sixth to protect our 7–6 lead. This was the worst part of being the visiting team. Since the Giants were up last, the game was really theirs to win. We couldn't get any more runs, but we could give some up. It was nail-biting time.

The leadoff man hit a triple. Two walks later, I was dying. With the bases loaded, the winning run was on second, and there were no outs yet!

Then Caspar pounced on a grounder, and fired it home for the force-out. Luis sizzled it to first to complete a tough double play. We still had the lead, with runners on second and third.

But with Kevin pitching, an empty base didn't stay that way for long. Four balls later, they were loaded again.

The Giants' captain came to bat. He took three balls, and it looked like Kevin was about to walk in the tying run. I'm sure the signal must have been for no swing, but Kevin served him a pitch *nobody* could pass up.

He crushed it. It flew so high that we lost it in the clouds.

When it reappeared, it was heading straight down the middle, and it was a home run for sure.

I cried out, "*Deep center!*" and Tim was sprinting backward, but this one was headed for Louisiana. The bases cleared as, one by one, four Giants crossed the plate.

Our season was over, and everybody knew it except Tim Laredo. From the curb at the edge of the field, he launched himself wildly upward. I thought he was a dead man, because he came down flat on his back into a moving convertible on the street. And the last thing I saw before Tim and the car disappeared down the road was this beautiful glint of white ball against brown mitt.

"You're out!" bellowed the field umpire.

And the Tigers were in the final!

The owner of the convertible charged Mr. Featherstone for the cleat marks on his bucket seats. Our sponsor was happy to pay up.

★★★

There never was such a Cinderella story. There we were, the rejects of the league, the leftovers the professor got because he forgot to go to the draft meeting. We didn't have a coach — not a real one, anyway; we had to put up with a crazy New Yorker who just wouldn't leave us alone; we lived with the constant threat of The Picture and public humiliation; we were misfits — a catcher who was afraid of the ball, an overeater, a summer school dropout, a workaholic, a figure skater, a victim, a guy who was really two guys, a pitcher who couldn't pitch, and me, stranded out in left field. And most of them ready to put all their faith in a subatomic particle in a pickle jar! In three days, *this* would be playing in the championship game!

During the wild victory celebration, I pulled the professor aside and asked him if it was possible to catch a lepton. He laughed like crazy, and said, "That's a good one. Now I've got a joke for you. How many quantum physicists does it take to screw in a lightbulb?"

I don't remember the answer.

★★★

The plan was to take Thursday off, with a final practice Friday, and the big game Saturday at one.

I *needed* that day off. The sheer excitement of who we were, and where we were going, was driving me nuts. I alternated between joy and misery, the thrill of victory and the deep-rooted feeling that it was all a mistake, and we didn't belong, and disaster was just around the corner.

Everything reminded me of baseball — the posters on my wall were all pitchers; my dad wore his Astros cap to cut the grass; our aluminum siding matched my favorite bat. I couldn't even escape it in Spooner Park. All the birds seemed to be orioles, cardinals, and blue jays — the baseball birds.

I sat in the tunnel part of the big jungle gym. It didn't help. Kristy tracked me down anyway.

“’Tsup? Hibernation City, man. C’mon. We’re late for the game.”

“What game?” I growled.

“The dodgeball game at the nursery school!” she shot back. “Get with the program, Johnson! The other semifinal! Wouldn’t it be nice to have an idea of who we’re playing on Saturday?”

I shrugged. “The coach is supposed to do that . . .” My voice trailed off. Okay. For the team, and *only* for the team, I would allow myself to be in the company of this rotten backstabber. But after Saturday’s game, she no longer counted as a life form!

We went to the same field as our own semifinal. But there seemed to be a lot more interest in this game. The bleachers were jam-packed. We squeezed into a back-row bench behind third base.

“Aren’t you going to take notes?” I muttered.

“No paper, bro’,” Kristy replied.

“So what’s in there?” I indicated the enormous shopping bag she’d lugged from home.

It was crammed full of food — sandwiches, chips, cake, popcorn, pretzels, candy, and a six-pack of Coke. She stretched out, elbowing the man next to her until he gave way and made room. And then she watched the game, munching, and swigging soda. I got a nibble in here and there, but as the innings progressed, my appetite left me.

It wasn't a game; it was a massacre. The Raiders were sponsored by East Texas Demolition, and there was a lot of that going on. They were big, they were mean, they were tough — half of them had mustaches! They hit like monsters, fielded like precision machines, and strutted around like they owned the world. They did. Most Little League teams attracted relatives and friends. The Raiders had *fans*! Real fans! Strangers! Hundreds of them! Baseball nuts who put their hearts and souls behind the best Little League team they'd ever seen!

The Raiders looked unbeatable. They had signals the CIA couldn't figure out! They had coaches at first and third! They had relief pitchers in the bullpen — not that the starting guy needed any help! It was already 8–0, and they were only in the third inning! Their opponents were pretty good, too — fourth best in the league. Nobody had to get the mumps for them to make the playoffs! Yet they were getting smashed. I thought of Saturday and went cold all over.

"I'm feeling kind of woozy," I told Kristy.

She held out a chicken leg. "Chow down."

"Aren't you watching?" I raved.

"Sure. Hype game. A little one-sided."

"*One-sided?!*" I howled. "We can't play those guys! They're *pros*!"

"We've got lepton power," she mumbled, mouth full.

"Could we trade it in for *nuclear* power?" I asked bitingly. "'Cause if we can't, you should be praying, not stuffing your face!"

The Raiders steamrolled on, ringing up runs like a cash register. By the time the bloodletting was over, it was 14–0. The crowd roared its approval, but I was very quiet.

On the way out, we ran into, of all people, the professor! What a great guy. Who would believe he was related to that miserable Kristy? Even though he knew nothing about baseball, he had come to do his job as coach and scout the game.

"What did you learn, Grandpa?"

The professor put on his reading glasses and flipped open his notebook. "They're not very strong," he reported. "They didn't get any runs today, while allowing a great many—"

Inside, I turned to stone. Our coach had scouted the wrong team!

"But, Grandpa," Kristy interrupted. "Those are the losers. They're eliminated. We need information on the other team."

"Ah, yes, the other team," he said thoughtfully, and fell silent as he searched his mind for his impressions. "Well — they had hats." He brightened. "*We* have hats! I predict an even contest!"

And you had to take it as gospel truth from a man who couldn't tell the winners from the losers in a 14–0 blowout.

CHAPTER 10

Left Field — Corey Johnson

The championship game was scheduled for one o'clock at Legion Field, a small park on the outskirts of Dallas. The professor was picking me up at ten. I was ready at 7:03.

I never thought of myself as a nervous person, but by eight-thirty, I was sitting on my gym bag in the driveway. I'd already phoned the coach three times, but I kept getting Kristy. Now I was following her advice. I was chilling. In East Texas in August, this is impossible.

They picked me up last. I was a wreck. The rest of the guys were pumped up, but kind of loose and relaxed. They passed around the lepton jar, rubbing it carefully.

“This isn’t the way to Dallas,” I pointed out as the professor took an unfamiliar turn.

“I’ve got a special treat,” our coach announced. “I know a shortcut; and it takes us right by the particle accelerator, so you can see where I work.”

“Maybe we can get another lepton!” exclaimed Ernie.

The professor laughed. “You boys are full of fun. We’re going to have a wonderful day.” And we all cheered as he turned onto County Road 5416.

“Johnson and I checked out the Raiders,” announced Kristy. “They’re *nothing*. Right, Johnson?”

I almost fell out of the van. “Oh — yeah, sure. Nothing.” Nothing short of invincible.

“I wonder how they made it to the final,” mused Billy Ray.

“It was a fluke,” Kristy snorted. Then she had the *nerve* to launch into a lecture about how, when playing a weaker team, you have to watch out for overconfidence. *Overconfidence* against the undefeated number-one team in the league!

I glared at Kristy. Through clenched teeth I whispered, “Don’t you think they’re going to notice when we’re down 40–zip?”

“Take a chill-pill.”

About twenty minutes later, we passed the particle accelerator. At least, the professor said we did. All I could see was a fifteen-foot electrified barbed-wire fence, with signs about attack dogs in eight different languages.

"What do you think, boys?" asked the professor proudly.

"They love it," Kristy answered for us. "Grab some Z's, dudes. Absolutely nothing can keep us from winning the championship!"

And with that, the van died. No rattle, no smoke, not so much as a cough. The professor didn't even have time to pull over to the side. We just passed out on County Road 5416, too far from home to walk back, too far from the Interstate to get help.

Our coach tried the key. There wasn't so much as a sputter. Get this: Professor Pendergast, Ph.D. in physics, needed help to find the hood release. Of course, once the hood was up, he stood there and stared at all that silent machinery.

"What's wrong with it, Grandpa?" asked Kristy.

"I have absolutely no idea," said the world-renowned genius.

"But I thought you knew all about science," said Tuba Dave.

"I only know about very, very small things," our coach explained. "This engine alone must be a billion billion times bigger than a lepton."

The Devereaux twins peered at the ailing engine.

"Uh-oh," said Billy Ray.

"Uh-oh," agreed Bobby Joe.

"What's the tip?" Kristy demanded.

"The distributor cap is split," said Billy Ray. "We're not going anywhere."

There was an uneasy murmur from the team.

Tim snapped his fingers. "Let's go get help at your office, Professor!"

"Oh, but my office is forty miles away," said our coach.

"I thought you worked at the particle accelerator," said Ernie.

"I do. But the particle accelerator is a big circle, a hundred and ten miles around."

No way! I always thought it was a *machine*, the size of a dishwasher, or something!

We were so shocked that it took a few seconds for us to realize we were totally out of touch. To our left, deserted range; to our right, a one-hundred-and-ten-mile-long electric fence.

Kevin was the first to panic. "If we can't get there by game time, we lose automatically!"

"Against a team we could beat *easy*!" added Bobby Joe.

"I ate all that crabgrass for nothing!" mourned Tuba Dave.

"What a bunch of hicks!" sighed Kristy in disgust. "A little engine trouble, and you're having a freakorama! P.P. and I'll flag down the next car, and ride back to Spooner for some wheels! So C — H — I double hockey sticks!"

Half an hour later, not one single car had come along in either direction.

"Where are our parents?" wailed Ernie. "They have to drive by us to get to the game!"

"Not if they take the Interstate!" growled Tuba Dave. "We're out by the particle accelerator!"

"Northeast sector," supplied the professor, playing tour guide. "Not far from where the antilepton was recorded."

Even Kristy was showing signs of stress. "What kind of a stupid, unchill, wack place *is* this?" she raved, her face a thundercloud. "Where are all the people? In New York, eight hundred taxis would have gone by! The van would be stripped naked! We'd all be arrested for loitering!"

Her voice was the only sound. It was eerie.

There we sat, cross-legged on the shoulder, stretched out in the grass, draped over the van. It was the worst moment of everybody's life. Even if a high-speed train pulled up to take us express to the ballpark, we'd still be cutting it close. It was almost noon!

We had come so far, only to lose by default in a ditch in the middle of nowhere. Suddenly, I understood those Olympic athletes who train for years only to finish dead last, and still say, "I'm happy just to be here!" Sure, we were probably going to lose anyway. But we had the right to *be there*, to play in a championship game!

Something in me must have snapped. I got up out of the

ditch, and marched into the van like a robot guided by remote control. Even then, part of me knew it was stupid. But I picked up that empty pickle jar, and I put it on my head.

"Okay, lepton, I'm not asking just for myself. We *need* to make that ballgame! Please! *Please! PLEASE!*" I peered out the windshield. Out of the heat shimmer at the vanishing point of the highway, a black shape appeared.

The others jumped up, eyes fixed on the horizon. I squinted at the approaching dust cloud until I could make out the form in front of it. My jaw dropped in horror. It was a black-jacketed motorcycle gang, coming up *fast*!

I watched, transfixed, as Kristy Pendergast stepped fearlessly out into the middle of the road. She stood there, directly in the path of all that hurtling, roaring machinery, raised her right arm, and bellowed, "*YO!*"

I don't buy all this New York stuff, but I've got to say that nobody in Spooner could have done that.

They didn't slow down.

Kristy never flinched.

At the last second, the leader braked hard. The others squealed into formation behind him in a cloud of burning rubber. They looked like cavemen on wheels, and they weren't too happy about leaving half their tire treads on the road. Their leather jackets said TIGERS OF TERROR. The leader growled; I think it was speech. The others just glared at Kristy, and revved their engines.

Kristy grinned broadly. "'Tsup?" she greeted. "How'd you like to help out some fellow Tigers?"

★★★

I rode on the back of a 2000 cc Harley, with a guy named Sawdust. It's not easy hanging on to a chopper doing ninety-five, while trying to balance a duffel bag full of baseball bats. But I would have done it standing on my head, juggling flaming swords. We were late, but we were on our way.

Kristy was riding up front with the gang leader, Shlomo. The professor was with Shlomo's girlfriend, Crusher, who thought he was kind of cute. And the rest of the team was portioned out among the fifty or so riders of the Tigers of Terror, East Texas Branch.

I don't know why they helped us. Kristy didn't have pictures of any of *them* in their jockstraps. It was probably the way she got everything done. She wouldn't shut up, and the only way to get on with your life was to do what she wanted. Plus they had to have respect for a twelve-year-old girl who could flag down a motorcycle gang like she was hailing a cab on Broadway.

So the Tigers of Terror brought the Tigers of Toilet Paper to our date with destiny. Thirty-nine minutes later, we roared onto the field, just in the nick of time.

Mr. Featherstone and Mrs. Jablonski were on their way to their cars to search for us. Luis's mom was at a pay phone, probably calling the State Police to put out an A.P.B. on a lost baseball team. All our parents looked pretty frazzled. It was a combination of relief that we showed up, and shock at who we showed up *with*.

The umpires were counting off minutes. Ninety seconds later would have meant a forfeit. You can't get much closer than that.

The Little League crowd wasn't thrilled with our method of transportation. Fifty-odd bikers made a pretty fearsome sight in a suburban neighborhood, especially when they didn't leave. The Tigers of Terror took over a section of bleachers, and settled in to watch the game.

We got no batting practice, and no warm-up. Instead, they gave us two minutes to change. We did it in one. The twins didn't even need a bathroom to hide in. In this park, each team had its own clubhouse in the back of the dugout.

On my way to left field, it hit me. We were sending Kevin — *Kevin* — to pitch to East Texas Demolition. 12 and 0, not including their semifinal blowout. The Tigers had maybe two dozen fans in the whole stadium. Everyone else was there to see the Raiders murder us.

My stomach was very tight as I watched the group of gorilla-size Little Leaguers in their dugout. There was a lot of confident backslapping and joking around. Finally, a gorilla with 33 on his uniform came out to lead off.

It took exactly one pitch. The CRACK! sounded like he broke the stadium. The ball sailed high over my head, and number 33 trotted around the bases.

Tim called to me from center, "I think that's the kid who won the Little League batting title."

The next two guys must have been the runners-up, because they added a single each. And just when it seemed that things couldn't get any worse, they did! I squinted into the dugout.

Kristy was flashing the signal for the old hidden ball trick. She always made us practice it, but I never thought she'd be stupid enough to try it in a game.

Luis called time, and the whole infield had a conference on the mound.

I waved my arms and tried to call her off. The old hidden ball trick hadn't worked in fifty years! Bad enough that the Raiders were going to kill us! Now Kristy was setting us up to look like clowns!

Even from left field, it was obvious. Kevin slipped the ball to Tuba Dave, and the infielders went back to their positions. Kevin tried to pretend that he was about to start pitching again. The idea of this tired old play was that, when the guy on second took his lead, Tuba Dave could pull out the hidden ball, and tag him off base.

Everybody knew. The runner on second was laughing.

In the Raiders' dugout, they were rolling on the floor. Spectators in the last row of bleachers were onto us. If the Goodyear blimp had been up there, the pilot would have looked down and said, "Oh, it's the old hidden ball trick."

Finally, we had to humiliate ourselves further. Tuba Dave waddled back to the mound and slipped Kevin the ball. Everybody saw that, too.

On our side, the only infielder who deserved to be on the same field as East Texas Demolition was Billy Ray. And the humiliation of the failed trick must have really smarted, because he stepped up his game with some brilliant diving stops. Even with his amazing play, we gave up another run. We were lucky to get out of the inning down only 2–0.

"We've got 'em on the ropes!" Kristy assured us as we dragged ourselves into the dugout and prepared for our at bat.

That was over all too quickly, because their pitcher made short work of our guys. The only Tiger to get a hit was Tuba Dave. With two outs, he got the brilliant idea to steal second. It got an even bigger laugh than the old hidden ball trick.

The Raiders were destroying us, but they always seemed to strand a lot of men on base. So we were only behind 3–0 when I first came to bat in the bottom of the second. Nobody was panicking yet as we rubbed our bats with the pickle jar.

Their pitcher wasn't as tough as the ace from our semi-final, but he was the only Little Leaguer I've ever seen who could throw knuckleballs. Hitting a knuckleball is like chasing a butterfly. You never know what it's going to do. I took a mighty cut and hit a screaming foul liner. It sliced right into our dugout. I could see the guys diving in all directions. And then . . .

Crash! Tinkle!

I ran over there to see if everyone was okay. Nobody was moving. They were scattered like tenpins, their faces white as chalk. I followed their staring eyes to the center of the bench. There sat a little pile of broken glass with a baseball in the middle of it. The lid was on the dugout floor — MAGNIFICENT PICKLE COMPANY.

Ernie was the first to react. "Our lepton!" he wailed, sifting through the pieces of shattered glass. Like he was going to find a lepton just sitting there in the dugout!

"It's gone!" said Tuba Dave mournfully.

Luis looked at me reproachfully. "You lost our lepton."

Professor Pendergast had just heard the one word that could bring him out of his usual baseball coma. "Lepton? What's all this about a lepton?"

"We had a lepton in the jar," Tim explained, "and Corey broke it, and now it got away."

The professor smiled indulgently. "Boys, boys, whoever told you that you could keep a lepton in a jar? A lepton is so tiny that it would slip right between the glass molecules. Besides, leptons only exist for a fraction of a second."

We all glared at Kristy. There was a long silence.

"All right, there wasn't any lepton," she admitted finally. "I found the jar in the garbage, like Johnson said. But don't you see what that means? That was *you* last game, not any power, or magic, or lucky charm! *You* beat those guys! *You* got seven runs off the best pitcher in Little League! We're here today because of *you*! You're my *posse*!"

"Posse?" queried Caspar.

"You know. My squad, my dudes, my boys, my homeys. My *team*!" she translated.

"What's the delay here?" came a voice from the field. A tall, dark man stood there, bending over to peer into our dugout.

"Yo, bub, this is a private team meeting!" snapped Kristy. "Buzz off!"

The man was taken aback. "Are you Kristy Pendergast?"

Kristy frowned. "Who wants to know?"

The man glared at her. "I happen to be Jack Lopez, president of this league." He turned to the professor sternly. "Pendergast, I forwarded you a complaint about this girl, but it's obvious she's still causing problems within the team. Why haven't you resolved the situation?"

The professor was speechless. He regarded Mr. Lopez, then his granddaughter, then Mr. Lopez again. "Uhhhhhh—"

The league president didn't wait for an answer. He turned to Kristy. "Young lady, I'm asking you to leave this dugout."

There was a gasp from our players.

It was the moment I'd waited for — prayed for — all season, and it was unfolding exactly the way I'd imagined it. Better, even. Not only did she have to leave us alone; she was being kicked out!

But all I could think of was . . .

"*No!*"

I blurted it right in the league president's face.

There was only one person in the world crazy enough to have faith in the Tigers when we were hopelessly outclassed. Suddenly, I couldn't face the rest of this game without Kristy.

"Sorry," Mr. Lopez told me, "but there's been a complaint. It's a serious matter."

"But *I* wrote the letter! And it was a mistake! I take it all back!"

"The letter was anonymous," said Mr. Lopez.

Ernie pointed at me. "That's him! *He's* anonymous!"

"He *un*-complains!" added Tuba Dave.

"I was wrong!" I babbled. "She *doesn't* push us around! I mean, she *does*, but it's all for the team! We wouldn't be here if it wasn't for her!"

Finally, the professor figured out enough to realize that his little princess was being badmouthed. He squared his shoulders and faced the league president.

"Sir, kindly return to your seat. We are in the middle of baseballing."

As Mr. Lopez left, Kristy put a friendly arm around my shoulders. "That was beautiful, Johnson. You're a true friend." She gave me a shove toward home plate. "Now get a hit, or never show your face around here again!"

She was obviously the sentimental type.

Back at the plate, I hit a weak grounder to third. It was an easy out, but I had to try — for the team, and even for Kristy. I put on the afterburners and blasted into first. Guess what? The throw was a little high, and the first baseman had to take his foot off the bag to catch it. Safe.

My teammates began moving me around the bases. It wasn't pretty, but it was baseball. Kevin sacrificed me to second. A knuckleball got away from the pitcher while he was searching for Caspar's tiny strike zone — I made it to third. Caspar struck out, but Tuba Dave's solid single brought me home. 3–1.

"We're *slamming*!" cheered Kristy, whatever that meant.

We had two outs on the Raiders in the top of the third when the leadoff man came up again. This time it took a whole three pitches, then POW! 4–1, East Texas Demolition.

We bounced back. Caspar finally got himself walked and proceeded to conduct a stolen base clinic. It took him two pitches to make it to third. He took huge leads, diving back to get a finger on the bag just before the throw. It bugged the Raiders' pitcher so much that he heaved the ball over the third baseman's head, trying to pick Caspar off. Caspar strolled home, and that was it for the starter. A relief pitcher came in to get the Raiders out of the inning, still ahead, 4–2.

For a team like us to stay with East Texas Demolition, we have to be perfect. And you just can't keep that up for a whole game. Fatigue made us sloppy. With only one out in the fourth, Billy Ray made an error on a routine ground ball. And it felt like, if a player *that good* could make a play *that bad* in a game *this big*, then surely none of the rest of us could do anything right. We fell apart. Ryan lost a fly ball in the sun, and then Luis let a pitch get away from him. And all of a sudden the bases were loaded. Kevin got spooked and walked in a run. And we all wanted to die.

From the dugout, Kristy fired a stream of New Yorkese about "being cooler than cool," but we were caving in.

Suddenly, a volley of cries from the stands reached us. "Come on Tigers! You can do it!"

"These guys can't hit! Pitch it in there!"

"Strike 'im out!"

It wasn't our parents. And everyone else in the park was

there to see the Raiders kick butt. I searched the crowd. Where did we get fans so far from home? And then I saw them — our motorcycle gang, the Tigers of Terror. Sawdust, Crusher, Shlomo, and the boys — they were on their feet, chanting, "*Here we go, Tigers. Here we go!*" (Stomp! Stomp!)

The Raiders' boosters were staring at them — fifty voices drowning out an entire stadium.

It sounded great and felt even better. It put the fires of hope back into Feather-Soft Bathroom Tissue Inc.

Billy Ray redeemed himself by scooping up a tricky grounder. The double play went shortstop to second to first. That got us back up to bat. We pulled the big Devereaux switch, adding Bobby Joe's offensive power to the order. The timing was perfect. The Raiders had already pegged Billy Ray as a lightweight, so the pitcher wasn't too careful with his lookalike. Bobby Joe smashed the first pitch into the gap in center field and went into third base standing up. Luis sacrificed him home. 5–3. The Tigers of Terror were dancing in the aisles.

We outfielders got a workout in the fifth. Everything Kevin threw was smashed back at us a country mile. Tim saved a sure triple by literally climbing the center field wall to pull in the ball. In right, Ryan had to sprint forward to make a diving catch for a short pop that was too far out for Tuba Dave. The next blast came to me. At the last second,

I realized I'd misjudged the hit. Desperately, I threw my bare hand up, and felt the ball smack into my palm. The force carried me into the wall, but I held on, giddy with exultation — three up, three down.

Our big hitters were finally starting to click. In the bottom of the fifth, Tim and Tuba Dave both came through with singles, and the Raiders' coaches yanked the pitcher and put in their closer to face Bobby Joe.

This kid threw sidearm, with his release a foot off the ground, sending a projectile that looked like it was coming at you from an underground launcher. The first pitch sizzled in at waist level. Bobby Joe swung mightily. But by the time the bat got there, the ball was up at his shoulders. Strike one. The next came screaming in two inches off the ground, so our big hitter didn't swing. But suddenly, the ball rose sharply to cross the plate just above the knees. Strike two.

In the dugout, Kristy turned to me. "He's gonna hit a dinger."

I frowned. "What's a dinger?"

The third pitch was a wobbler nowhere near the plate. But Bobby Joe was sick of this game, and he reached for it. He made solid contact right at the end of the bat, pulling to the left to keep it fair. Nobody jumped for this one. It was over the moon.

Kristy turned to me. "*That's* a dinger."

I hardly heard her. We were screaming ourselves hoarse as Tim, Tuba Dave, and finally Bobby Joe crossed the plate. Our motorcycle gang was going berserk. Sawdust and Shlomo had climbed down the back of the bleachers, and were involved in a footrace for the home run souvenir. Most important of all, the Feather-Soft Tigers had our first lead of the game, 6–5. We were three outs away from the championship. Everything rested on . . .

". . . on Kevin," Kristy was saying.

Our celebration died abruptly. Kevin looked sick.

"If you shut them down here, there won't *be* a bottom of the sixth," she reminded him. "So don't choke."

He choked. He hit the first batter on the leg, then gave up a double that put runners on second and third. Four balls later, the bases were loaded, with nobody out. A pop fly would bring in the tying run; a single would put us behind again; a (gulp) home run would give the Raiders a 9–6 lead. We'd never come back from that!

I squinted in from left field, and almost wept. The guy up there, swinging a bat that looked like a telephone pole, was none other than number 33, the Little League batting champion!

★★★

Kristy was out talking with Kevin and Luis. They seemed to agree on something, and suddenly they were beckoning me in. Why me? Who calls in the left fielder for a conference on the mound? Did they think I'd have some super strategy that would get us out of this no-win situation?

I jogged in and joined them. "What's going on?"

In answer, Kristy pressed the ball into my hand, and started back to the dugout. Luis headed for the plate, and Kevin was on his way to left field!

I nearly choked. She was expecting me to pitch! *Now!* When we had *no chance*! She didn't want a pitcher; she wanted a goat! It was her final revenge for my letter to Mr. Lopez! I was going to be the guy who threw the pitch that sank the Tigers!

"*How can you do this to me?*" I howled.

She wheeled to face me, eyes flashing. "Isn't that just like a rural dude! All season you've been sweating me about how you're this hype pitcher."

"Yeah, but—"

"But nothing! This is your *dream*, Johnson! How many of us ever get the chance to spit back the reality sandwich?" She pointed a casual thumb in the direction of big number 33. "Throw this guy curveballs."

I was in a daze. "What?"

"Curveballs," she repeated. "You *do* have a curveball?"

"Of course I do!" I said indignantly.

Shakily, I threw a few warm-ups. They'd give me as much time as I needed, coming in cold like that. But how could it make up for an entire season of not pitching? My legs were shaking. The eighty cents in my pocket jingled — everybody was looking for the ice cream man. I now understood why the big leaguers shuffle and twitch and fiddle so much. They're really putting off the pitch to the last second. If I could have delayed until next summer, it would have suited me fine.

Finally, I went into my stretch and threw a curveball. It didn't curve.

POW!

It sailed up, up, and away, and cleared the right field fence about three inches foul. The spectators let out a collective "Ooooh!"

I waited till my heartbeat returned to normal. I calmed myself — so what if it was three inches away from being a monster grand slam? It was just a strike. A very loud strike.

Breathing a silent prayer, I tried again.

POW!

This time it rocketed for left field, going, going — foul, by only *two* inches. He was getting closer.

Kristy called time, and trotted out toward me, gathering the infield for a conference on the mound. I steeled myself for the lecture. She just said, "You told me you had a curveball."

"It was about to curve," I declared defiantly, "but some guy's bat was in the way!"

"Hilarious, Johnson. Now, listen up, everybody. It's a perfect time for the old hidden ball trick."

The other guys all nodded their agreement.

I stared at her. "You're kidding."

"Chill out," she said mildly. "It's going to work."

"It *never* works!"

She shrugged. "This time there's a New York twist."

I looked to the plate. Number 33 was already laughing. The umpires were looking at their watches impatiently. In the murmur from the crowd, I only heard the words *hidden ball trick* about fifty times! Can you blame them for thinking we were idiots? Roars of laughter passed like a wave through the stadium. When we returned to our positions, we got a standing ovation.

The runners stayed on base. But wait a minute — Ernie didn't have the ball; Tuba Dave's glove was empty; and at third, Caspar was showing he had nothing. All eyes turned to Bobby Joe, but our shortstop didn't have it either. The crowd moaned its disappointment. It wasn't the hidden ball trick after all.

I pretended to go into my stance, and the runners took their leads. Suddenly, Luis rose from his crouch, pulled the ball from his mitt, and fired it down to first. The runner was watching for a throw from me, not the plate. His dive was late. Ernie tagged him out.

While this was going on, the man on third made a sprint for home. Ernie threw a perfect strike back to Luis. Our catcher caught the runner in mid-slide. It was going to be close!

"*You're out!*" bawled the plate umpire.

Unbelievable! Surely we were in the record book for turning the first ever old hidden ball trick double play! With a New York twist.

Number 33 wasn't laughing anymore. But he hadn't disappeared, either. And with a man on second, his big bat could put the Raiders into a tie, or even give them the lead.

Then it hit me — why not walk the guy? This kid was the Little League batting champion. With a huge foul to right and an even bigger one to left, the next ball was going dead center for sure!

I flashed a walk sign to the dugout.

No signal came back, but Kristy called out, "In your dreams, Johnson! Pitch!"

Oh, how I hated Kristy Pendergast! She'd brought us to the brink of victory, then set it up so that, if we lost it'd be *my* fault! Well, not this time! I'd pitch, all right, but first—

I turned to the infield. "You heard it! The little princess said pitch!"

The crowd was on its feet, stiff with tension. The Tigers of Terror were standing on their seats. The Raiders were all on the top step of their dugout, willing their star to hit. Our guys stood like statues at their positions, silent and scared. Kristy reclined on the bench, munching an apple, like she didn't know there was a game on.

I looked at number 33. Sure, I had two strikes on him. But how was I ever going to finish him off? Kristy wanted a curveball, but my curve wasn't curving. Maybe I should give him my fastball — or something off-speed. No, I decided. We were here because of Kristy. She'd even gotten us a ride to the game when there was no chance on earth of us getting there. If I live to be a thousand, I'll never forget her stepping out into the road in the path of all those speeding motorcycles.

I gripped the ball by the wide seams, the way I always do for a curve. I stepped on the rubber, reared back, and let fly.

When I think back to that pitch, it all seems hazy. I see the ball in slow motion, going straight as an arrow down the alley. I hear my own voice: "Curve! *Curve!*" And I have a clear impression of what will happen if it *doesn't* curve — of number 33 blasting it into the fourth dimension. The bat comes around! The ball's still straight! And then — and then — at the last possible second, the ball makes a tiny curve, sneaks past the swinging bat, and lands with a THUMP in Luis's mitt.

"Strike three!" bellowed the umpire. "You're—!"

You couldn't hear the last word, because a motorcycle gang was storming the field in full battle cry.

Still frozen in the release position on the mound, I felt the greatest happiness of my life. The Feather-Soft Tigers came charging in from the field. I braced myself for an onslaught of joyous congratulation, but they ran straight past me. They roared into the dugout, and emerged with

Kristy Pendergast on their shoulders. Not me, the hero, but Kristy! *Kristy!*

She looked down at us, her posse. "Why's everybody freaking? I told you this was going to happen." Her eyes met mine, and she grinned. "Yo, Johnson — you really *can* throw a curveball."

They presented the professor with the championship trophy. Our coach looked at the gleaming silver cup, read the words *League Champions* and, in that moment, it all came to him — a whole season of achievements that he'd missed along the way. He burst into tears. He didn't know a bat from a base, but we wouldn't have traded him for five World Series managers.

We all gathered round into a giant team bear hug, and the Tigers of Terror joined in. They offered to drive us all the way back to Spooner. We didn't even change. We just grabbed our trophy and our stuff, hopped on the motorcycles, and began the triumphant procession home. We forgot our folks. We forgot everything but the need to stay together, and go out the way we'd come in — as a team.

★★★

I beat my parents home, so I was alone when the call came in. It was from the pay phone in the locker room at Legion Field — collect from Billy Ray.

"Is it safe to come out yet? Who won?"

EPILOGUE

The big blowout victory celebration was like New Year's Eve. I didn't get to sleep until 2 A.M. Guess who rang our doorbell at quarter to six!

Red-eyed, dazed, and exhausted, I hardly recognized Kristy. All her New York funky clothes were gone. Now she wore a DEEP IN THE ♥ OF TEXAS T-shirt, real cowboy boots, and a ten-gallon hat. Around her neck was a bolo tie with a wagon wheel on it. Her belt buckle was a lethal pair of steer horns, and her knapsack proclaimed, REMEMBER THE ALAMO, PARDNER.

"Howdy," she greeted me.

"'Tsup?" I said, disgusted.

"Man, you look terrible. You need to sleep more."

I stood fuming in my pajamas. "What do you want?" I barked.

She shrugged. "To say good-bye, Johnson. I'm going home today."

Good-bye? Going home? It felt like Kristy had been in Spooner for a thousand years, and she'd be here for a thousand more. I guess I'd forgotten she was just visiting.

I invited her into the kitchen for some farewell cereal. "You must be pretty happy to be getting back to New York." I couldn't resist adding, "You know — the Apple, N.Y.C., Gotham, the Big Smoke, New Jack City—"

She looked at me like she'd never heard of the place. "I've got a present for you." She handed me a small envelope marked:

I was sort of embarrassed. "Gee, I didn't get you anything."

"Don't sweat it. The guys gave me tons of stuff." She indicated her all-Texas outfit.

I studied my Raisin Bran. "Sorry."

She shrugged. "You gave me something."

Team spirit? Support? "What?"

"A curveball when I really needed one."

I tore open the envelope, and gasped. Her good-bye gift was The Picture! The real McCoy! With the negative stapled to the corner!

There it was — the row of bare feet that she'd shown us

on skating day. And above that — an extreme close-up of Kristy's finger!

I couldn't believe it! I thought back to the panic — the *terror*! — we all felt over this photograph! The ridiculous stunts we pulled to try to get the film! And Kristy had gotten her finger in front of the lens! You couldn't even see our faces! It looked like a big pink blimp with eighteen legs! She'd bamboozled us with *nothing*!

I felt my face flame. "You're really *something*—" I began angrily.

She took it as a compliment. "Thanks, Johnson. Check out the other side."

I flipped the photograph. On the back she had neatly printed:

Ms. K. Pendergast
Box 43
Bedrock Dam, NY 16902
Don't forget to write.

I frowned. "Bedrock Dam is in New York City?"

Kristy was tight-lipped. "Not exactly."

I pulled out the atlas. Bedrock Dam was nowhere near New York City! It wasn't even a town! It was a village up near the Canadian border! A tiny dot in the snow! *Half* the size of Spooner!

I looked daggers at her. "I don't know how you have the nerve to show your face in this town! You called us hicks, hayseeds, rural dudes! You made fun of Spooner and never shut up about how much better it was in New York! And all that time, *you* were the real hick!"

She took it all good-naturedly, and even laughed at my barb about what a comedown it was going to be for her to leave the bright lights of big city Spooner.

"It was my sixth-grade field trip," she explained slowly, her eyes distant. "We went to the Statue of Liberty, and the Empire State Building. And I just *knew* New York was the place for me. The energy on the street, the pulse of the city — I was *meant* to be a New Yorker. So when I came down here where nobody knew me, and found out I'd be coaching nine dudes on a Little League team, I figured this was my big chance."

"You lied to us!" I seethed.

She shook her head. "The *real* New York's not a place, Johnson. It's an *attitude*. It doesn't matter if you're in Bedrock Dam, or Spooner, Texas, or the planet Mars. If you've got the attitude you're a New Yorker." She stood up. "I'm outta here, bro'. P.P.'s waiting to take me to the airport."

I walked her to the door, still shaking with rage. "Some New Yorker!" I seethed. "When I tell the guys—!"

"Lighten up," she laughed in my face. "You got to pitch, didn't you?"

"Oh, sure! Three pitches!"

"But in the whole season, they were the three best," she pointed out. "Later, dude."

I looked at her. "Later?"

"You know — *ciao, au revoir*, stay loose, toodle-oo, peace, *hasta la vista.* Good-bye," she translated, and was gone.

And suddenly, I was running after her, calling, "See you next summer?"

She flashed me thumbs-up and a big New York grin.

Gordon Korman is the #1 *New York Times* bestselling author of more than ninety-five books for kids and young adults. His writing career began at the age of twelve when his grade seven English assignment became his first novel, *This Can't Be Happening at Macdonald Hall.* Now, decades later, he has more than seventeen million copies of his novels in print and his books have been translated into fourteen languages. Favorite titles include *Linked*, *Unplugged*, *Notorious*, *The Unteachables*, *Restart*, *Slacker*, *Ungifted*, *Supergifted,* and the Macdonald Hall series. Gordon grew up in Thornhill, Ontario, and now lives with his family in New York.